NO HIDING FROM YESTERDAY

by

Wilfrid N Fox

Published by CompletelyNovel

First published in Great Britain in 2014
by CompletelyNovel
www.completelynovel.com
ISBN - 9781849145855
Printed in Great Britain by
Anthony Rowe CPI
Edited by Caroline Insall and Nicola Ruggier
Front cover by Nicola Ruggier
Photos ©123RF

This is a work of fiction. Names, characters, places, and
incidents are either the products of the author's
imagination or are used fictitiously. The author would
also like to beg the reader's indulgence with some aspects
of the physics involved in the story!

No Hiding From Yesterday

Acknowledgments:

I would like to thank my cousin, Peter Wagstaffe,
for proofreading and punctuation, and my daughters Nicola
and Caroline for finally making me a published author!

This book is dedicated with love to my wife Janet, children Nicola,
Caroline and Tony, and grandchildren Jake, Harry, Molly, Dylan,
Jack, Georgia and Abi. Not forgetting Tati and Petal too!

No Hiding From Yesterday

NO HIDING FROM YESTERDAY

by

Wilfrid N Fox

Characters in order of appearance:

Dr. Harry Aldborough: Our protagonist; a young, ambitious petroleum engineer and entrepreneur.

Frank Taylor / Frank Schneider: German spy. Lands in Dorset during WW2 and takes the place of the murdered Lord Egliston.

Henry [Major McLean] Lord Egliston: Not what he seems: see above. He runs the Egliston Corporation. It has legitimate and illegal interests internationally within the oil and energy industries. Takes over Summerfield Tools and Bakuoil. He has a son, Nicolas who looks after Egliston's interests in the Caspian region.

Nicole Taylor: Housekeeper for the Lords Egliston; also mother of Peter Taylor.

Julie McLean: Bright, 30 years old; works in the city, in banking. Object of Aldborough's desires, and daughter of Charles McClean.

Charles McLean: Lord Egliston's younger brother. Retired government Scientist from the Radar Research Establishment in Malvern. His is the theory about the possibility of visible flashbacks as a phenomenon of the activity of gravity waves.

Professor Hans Reise: Physics fellow at Oxford University and Harry Aldborough's tutor. Helps Harry find funding for his commercial oil industry ideas.

Colonel Rushton: MI5 officer

Charlie Tizzard: Harry's lab assistant.

Terry Colliston: British trade attaché at the Consulate in Baku.

Farouk al Tehrani: Harry's guide in Baku

Ivan Klanski: MD of Bakuoil

Anna Kaplinska: Polish industrial spy working in Azerbaijan for the Russian Embassy.

Environs of Poole Harbour and the
Isle of Purbeck

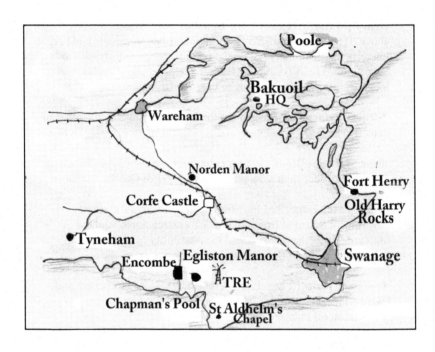

Chapter 1. The return of the traitor- 1940

St Aldhelm's Head

St Aldhelm's Headland, magnificent and brooding, towers over a hundred metres above the waves of the English Channel, on the Purbeck coast of Southern England. It isn't a place to visit from the sea in rough weather, especially in the early hours of the morning. Even on a fine day it can fill me with a feeling of darkness and menace, especially after the events of the past three years.

Black oily rocks beneath the crumbling cliff, which have been the agents of death to many an unfortunate seafarer, unlucky or imprudent enough to venture too closely to the shore, skirt the headland crowned by the stone chapel of St Aldhelm built some eight hundred years ago. In years gone by, the small cove nestling beneath the Head was the landing place of choice for smugglers of the area owing to the difficulties the Excise men had in policing it and the ease with which men and contraband could melt into the hinterland. Back in the year 1940, Britain's World War 2 defences against attack added to the natural hazards faced by seaborne intruders.

Just inland from the rocky coast at that time was the important Air Ministry Telecommunications Research Establishment where no effort was being spared to provide the country with radar warning of attack from across the English Channel. Today there is very little that remains of the site, but to me the ghosts of that time linger on both in memory and in their present day impact.

I must introduce myself. I'm Harry Aldborough. Let me tell you what happened to me in the Purbeck Hills and the discovery that changed my life. This is my story. It started over seventy years ago, long before I was born.

****

The captain of a U-boat lurking five hundred metres offshore at midnight on 1st August 1940 was well aware of all the hazards that the Dorset coast presented but had strict and confidential orders to disembark a passenger regardless of the submarine's safety. His surface approach under the cover of torrential rain and gale force winds had been uneventful and the boat had been turned head-to-wind while the dinghy and its passenger were launched. This had not gone well. The fierceness of the wind and the sheets of rain had resulted in the loss of one of the crew overboard, together with the dinghy. The crew member disappeared without trace although the dinghy was saved, but the passenger failed to get into the dinghy and was thrown into the boiling sea.

It was at that time their luck really ran out. Despite the poor visibility the U-boat had been seen against a backdrop of sheet lightning by a gun-crew on the nearby brow of the highest point of the coast, Swyre Head, and shells homed in on the submarine after the first ranging shots. One struck the conning tower, killing two crewmen and delaying the dive. The gunners struck twice more as the crash dive started: the sea rushed in the gaping hatch and it was then all over for the mariners save for their suffering. The boat shuddered in its death throes and rapidly disappeared beneath the waves, drifting down with its doomed crew to join the debris of centuries past in the ships' graveyard fifty metres below. Its mission had been accomplished at a lethal cost.

The black clad passenger who had fallen overboard a minute before the first shell struck, dwelt briefly on the fate of the crew he barely knew, aware he could soon follow them if his own luck failed. His peril was made even worse by the rapid loss of his rubber dinghy in the turmoil. Frank Taylor, the man for whom the crew were at that moment drowning, was now in mortal danger. The spray, the darkness and his disorientation meant he was in danger of missing his planned landing place in the cove known as Chapman's Pool, below the Head. He knew this stretch of coast well, having lived in the Purbeck Hills of Dorset from his birth until his departure for Germany three years previously. The smell of oil from the bituminous rocks in the cliffs, mingling with that of the sea, hit him, bringing back memories of childhood days, but he pushed them from his mind, concentrating on the task of staying alive.

Another gun crew on St Aldhelm's headland now had a searchlight in action sweeping backwards and forwards across the spume-topped waves that served both to hide and to endanger him. A heavy machine gun opened up, tracer shells arcing towards the dinghy, now floating freely, caught in the beam fifty metres away from Taylor. A freak wave several metres high reflected off the rocks and amplified by the tidal race off the headland spun him round under a mountain of water. After holding his breath for what seemed an eternity he was able briefly to snatch some air before being engulfed again.

His training over the last two years had given him the physical strength and mental will to survive and with a superhuman effort he swam on. He was smashed against a submerged rock, the limpets covering it tearing his rubber suit, while the impact drove out precious air from his lungs and he was pushed out to sea again. He could feel the rip tide pulling him further out to sea and this released last reserves of adrenaline. He struggled on and regained his sighting along a line of prominent on-shore rocks when the waves briefly abated. Suddenly he was scrambling over the slippery boulders on to the shingle. He tensed, constantly expecting a bullet from the onshore watchers, but none came.

A break in the clouds allowed the moon briefly to silhouette the outline of Swyre Head in the distance, with its ancient burial mound and gun battery, helping him to regain his bearings. The pillboxes, observation posts and radar of Britain's defensive network were located back from the shore on the higher ground and by keeping among the rocks and moving slowly, he knew he would not be seen. Hopefully the gun crew, celebrating their success in hitting the U-boat and the dinghy, would assume there were no survivors, but he could take no chances.

The photographs of the coast he had taken from a fishing boat, as a youth, before leaving for Germany had served him well in making his preparations. He also knew from an agent's reports the positions of barbed wire barriers across the valley and the best route to take. He preferred to find a gap rather than to cut his way through and thereby leave evidence of his landing. His main problem was avoiding the landmines he knew had been laid to the seaward side of the barbed wire. Once he was above the high-water mark he crawled along on his knees in the pouring rain looking for the telltale signs of mine emplacement, patiently moving along the line of the wire. He was sweating profusely now but his mind was racing with the surge of adrenaline.

The atmosphere was unreal, he felt detached from reality and he recalled a long forgotten memory when as a small boy he had seen a ghostly detachment of Roman soldiers marching along the base of these cliffs in the early morning mist before it faded away. He had returned many times over the years to the same spot but had not seen them again and had put it down to childhood imagination. He came out of his reverie and the present flooded over him. Real flesh-and-blood soldiers occupied his mind at that moment.

After an eternity of patient progress he found a gap in the barbed wire and worked his way through. The roar of the surf was now muffled in the dense foliage into which he ran. Slipping on the mud he threaded his way silently up through a valley the locals called a gwyle, covered with a wood of stunted trees, towards the large old manor house and its farm he had once known so well but had hated so much. It and other ancient manors along the coast had seen intrigue and high treason over the centuries and Taylor in his private mind had worked out equally seditious plans for this one in the future. The estate had been requisitioned by the military for the duration of the war, but his agent had reported that it was not yet occupied. It could be a safe temporary haven where he could hide until the furore faded away.

Rounding a corner, Taylor's heart jumped violently at the unexpected sight, only twenty metres away, of a glowing cigarette that faintly illuminated the face of a guard with a rifle over his shoulder sheltering in a doorway of the farmhouse. Fortunately Taylor had not been detected and he melted back into the shadows, his movements masked by the noise of the rain downpour.

Taylor wondered what to do at this unexpected development. He could have killed the man without a second thought but that would have stirred up a hornets' nest of activity. The sound of an approaching vehicle solved his problem. The guard was galvanised into action, throwing down his unfinished cigarette in the mud and grinding it out of sight with his boot before shouting for his sergeant to come out of the farmhouse.

The vehicle was a lorry, full of waterproof-clad soldiers who poured out and stood unenthusiastically in the rain stamping their feet whilst waiting for orders. The sergeant had clearly been expecting their arrival, rapidly dispersing the men in a cordon across the valley. It was clear to Taylor from the sergeant's words that he had not been seen during his recent ordeal in the sea and that the deployment was only a precaution.

To Taylor's dismay, however, they had two German Shepherd dogs that would limit his chances of getting away, although the rain might well destroy his scent trail. He clearly couldn't hide at the manor or farmhouse as he had planned, and to go up through the wooded valley to the high coastal plateau a kilometre away would risk his detection.

There was, however, a third way.

Taylor, unlike most of his pursuers, who were conscripts from other parts of Britain and based in a barracks in nearby Poole town, was on well-known territory. After thinking for a few minutes he smiled inwardly, his self-assurance returning. The estate, its hiding places and secrets were etched in his memory from his childhood. It would not be necessary to take his chances slipping through the cordon; there was a possible alternative.

He carefully made his way beyond the farm where other soldiers were obviously billeted, around the weed-choked lake with its dormant fountain fronting the elegant ashlar stone-fronted main building with its large black staring windows, and pushed open the door of a stone structure adjacent to the lake. This was his escape route.

He felt his way down slippery steps to the increasing sound of rushing water. He flicked on his waterproof torch when he knew it would not be seen from outside. His surroundings were as he remembered. Long ago, a previous owner of the manor in conjunction with the owner of the Encombe Manor in the next valley had built kilometre long stone-lined tunnels through the hill. They were made to high masonry standards to bring water from a reservoir high above the valley to the lake and estate. They were large enough to walk through while stooping and Taylor set off in the manner of a miner with his hands clasped behind his back and head down striding up the gentle gradient, being careful not to slip on the slimy stone slabs.

He paused occasionally to listen for sounds of pursuit, his heart now beating a steady rhythm. Twenty minutes later he reached the top and stopped again to listen. To his annoyance he could hear movements outside. Had the soldiers anticipated the use of the tunnel? He froze, drew his gun and waited.

After a few minutes he was relieved to hear only the bleating and shuffling of sheep as they sheltered from the wind and rain in the lee of the building. He pushed open the trapdoor in the roof and was met by the full blast of the gale. He was through the cordon! He was a little disorientated in the total darkness and crouched there waiting for the moon to show briefly. When it came, he was shocked to find he was close to buildings and radar masts. When he was here in 1937 it had been open farmland surrounding the bleak Renscombe Farm. The installation must be the radar research site he had been briefed about.

There would be more guards. He sank to the ground to rethink his position. He would have to move under cover of the darkness, it was no use waiting for daylight. There would be the farm nearby. If he could find that he would be better able to find his way. He started off but was startled by a dog barking. Someone could be with the animal, a guard or a farmer. Fortunately for Taylor at that minute a car approached with dim slatted headlights, missing him closely as he jumped off the track. It stopped some fifty metres away at what was obviously a gate to the radar compound. The voices carried across.

"You've not seen any signs of anyone on the way here? We've been told to keep a look out for any spies who might have landed from a sub that has been sunk off the headland. There's a rumour a body's been washed ashore at Chapman's Pool."

"You're joking, it's impossible to see the road in front let alone a man," came the reply. The gate was opened and the sound of the car's engine receded.

His weariness and the bruising from the fight against wind, tide and rocks were now forgotten. The bleeding from the wounds caused by the sharp limpets that had ripped his suit and cut into his thigh had ceased. Fear for his life had not been one of the emotions he had experienced, just the fear of failure, and now that had gone as well. He had his bearings. He had to go in the direction from which the car had come, through the village of Worth Matravers and across the heath.

Before him was a four kilometre walk to his destination, Norden Manor House, on the edge of Corfe. With rising optimism he set off, keeping to the hedges and walls fringing the road that eventually snaked down a steep escarpment from Kingston village to the coastal plateau before reaching the undulating moorland stretching towards Poole harbour. He dare not go far from the road. There were many deep bogs in which he could come to grief in the darkness. In the daylight he would have known the route. Occasionally he had to dive into the ditch at the roadside as military vehicles sped past heading towards the coast and the futile search for survivors from the submarine.

Soon he saw in the distance, for the storm was now abating, the jagged outline of the ruined keep of the medieval Corfe Castle thrown into a ghostly silhouette by the continuing lightning flashes. In times gone by it had been a centre for rebellion and bloodshed starting with the murder of a King Edward in the year 978. It had been the centre of local power over the succeeding seven hundred years but eventually the government under Oliver Cromwell ordered its destruction at the end of the Civil War. Even then it resisted the attempts of the engineers of the Roundhead army who tried to raze it to the ground but who had had to leave giant columns of stone pointing to the sky.

On top of the prominent hill sitting between two chalk escarpments it still dominated the surrounding countryside casting a shadow of the past across the area. He had to skirt round the village of Corfe, itself built largely from stone taken from the ruin, a process far more effective in destroying the castle than that of Cromwell's army. He decided to cross over the main road, taking the route of the single-track railway line and soon saw his destination, an ivy-clad Elizabethan manor house. Scurrying in the darkness across the gardens of nearby cottages, hoping there were no dogs loose, he pressed against the rear wall of the manor.

He had to be very careful now. It was vital he made contact with the housekeeper at the manor, none other than his mother, Nicole, who had lived all her married life in the area and was accepted by the locals as English. She had been born German but had married an English soldier after the First World War, returning to his Dorset home within the semi-feudal Egliston estate that employed him as a gamekeeper. Within ten years, however, he was dead, killed in an unfortunate accident during a game shoot.

The Lord of the Manor was culpable of negligence but in a travesty of justice and exercise of privilege typical of the time, was absolved of all blame at the inquest. She nursed a hidden hatred of all things English thereafter. She had passed on her feelings to her son and it was she who had pressed him, seeing the gathering power of the German State in the 1930's, to throw in his lot with the Hitler Youth. With the certainty of war she had conceived the idea of his return as an undercover agent.

Taylor was naturally dominant. His height at six feet two inches and his weight of 240lbs were themselves intimidating, but he had also deliberately cultivated an attitude that overwhelmed weaker men. As a child his intelligence and physical prowess had been repressed by the semi-feudal nature of life on the estate. His time in Germany had allowed him to develop his natural strengths, now devoted to the service of his Fatherland.

Despite his self-centred nature he felt a tug at his emotions at the prospect of reunion with his mother and crept forward pressing against the wall until he reached the porch and slid inside. He knew she would be watching for his arrival in the porch at the rear of the manor.

The door opened and she was hugging him, pulling him into the darkened kitchen. His mission was under way. Nothing would stop him now.

Chapter 2. Ghosts of the Purbeck Hills – 2002

Sandbanks Ferry 1930's

My story starts with a flickering blue flash of lightning which sent a bright cascade of light through the stone framed leaded glass window and across the room, bringing out the carving on the oak panelled walls of the darkened study in stark relief. An almost simultaneous crash of thunder tore me out of my after-dinner dream as I relaxed in a comfortably worn armchair.

The room switched from a warm haven to an alien place. The historical atmosphere of this Elizabethan Norborough manor house had percolated into my system over the last few days. Despite this I found it difficult to recall for a moment where I was.

My confused brain saw, through half closed eyes, a flickering and blurred image of a man in British Army uniform seated at a table some six feet away from my armchair. As I watched in disbelief, rooted to my chair, he rose with a gun in his hand and walked towards me. Almost immediately the whole scene faded and I was left in the gloom and silence of the now sombre empty room with the occasional, more distant rumble of thunder in the distance.

The whole thing cannot have taken more than ten seconds and I was left in the ensuing silence with that feeling one has after waking from a nightmare. As the hair in the nape of my neck subsided after this ghostly appearance the door behind me creaked and opened, making me jump violently.

"I wondered where you'd hidden yourself Harry. Why the devil are you sitting in the dark all by yourself," said Julie, "Why don't you join Dad and me for coffee in the lounge?"

Julie is the cute, bright thirty-year-old daughter of Charles MacLean the owner of this house. She span round, her long auburn hair trailing behind her and she left without waiting for a reply. I sat there for a moment wondering whether I'd had a dream brought on by the food, drink and atmosphere of this house or whether I'd really had an encounter with a ghost. It was, I told myself, probably the wine - the ghost idea was all Charles's fault. He has a way-out hobby of trying to understand what prehistoric monuments were built for and their relation to astronomical sightings. He also thinks that many reported ghostly appearances have a scientific explanation and had spent a lot of time telling me about his ideas. I'll come back to that later.

Anyway, let me introduce myself. I'm thirty-two years old, six feet one inch tall in my stocking feet, good looking with a lot of fair wavy hair, good at sports, and a physicist by training, working in the oil industry. I think I'm rather modest too, as you'll have guessed, and I've a modicum of ambition. My name's Harry Aldborough and Julie and I had at that time a great but unconsummated personal relationship. The large old house that we were in would appear, after experiencing the thunderstorm that evening, to have a ghost in residence if my dream was not indeed a dream. It, the manor not the ghost, belongs to her father who, before he retired some years ago, was a government scientist at the Royal Radar Establishment in Malvern. That's why he likes to hear about the latest gossip in the world of scientific research.

I'd only known him for a short time but I had the impression that he's genuinely slightly eccentric. He is demonstrably very comfortably off because his home is this desirable Elizabethan manor house. Government scientists usually aren't the best paid of civil servants and I was somewhat surprised by his apparent affluence. However, it wouldn't be long before all was revealed.

My life had been relatively well ordered until about two months previously. I'd trained as a research scientist at Oxford University, England, and then at MIT in Cambridge, Massachusetts, returning to work with the British Petroleum oil company to give me the chance to travel and to gain some oilfield operational experience. That period was great and I had some good postings in relatively civilised parts of the world. However when I was moved to work in Alaska on the North Slope oilfield my enthusiasm cooled.

After six months on the Slope with nothing but caribou and the occasional bear to break the monotony, I decided I didn't appreciate the corporate life and decided to throw it in and take up a research fellowship at Oxford University where I could work at some ideas I had for making my fame and fortune.

All I needed was funding to carry out research to prove my ideas, of which I had plenty, and to get them to market. This was a simple process in theory but not so easy in practice. Luckily, one of the college fellows at the university, Professor Hans Reise, who was a veteran member of quasi-autonomous non-governmental organisations - 'quangos' and committees came to the rescue. He suggested I investigated one of the government schemes that were designed to encourage innovation.

If you, as a small-to-medium sized company, could persuade an oil or service company to put up half the money, Her Majesty's government might fund the rest provided it could be seen to be of ultimate benefit to UK Ltd. All you needed was a good idea, the stamina to survive the bureaucracy of government committees and an inside track.

With Reise's contacts and advice I was, a year later, granted a quarter of a million pounds in total to spend, with more administrative strings than a puppet attached of course. The British company Bakuoil, having been persuaded by the government department that awards production and exploration licenses in the UK, stumped up half the industry money jointly with a subsidiary British commercial company, Summerfield Tools, that makes and uses tools for use in oil wells. I also set up a small company with some venture capital from a major bank to carry out the work and to exploit any inventions coming out of the research.

That's how I met Julie. She was a high-flying financial analyst working for the venture capital arm of the bank, and was responsible for keeping tabs on its technology investments. She was assigned as part of her portfolio to monitor my company and its research, but it wasn't long before a non-platonic close relationship promised to complement our professional one. She's bright, and she looks fantastic. I've mentioned her auburn hair, but this is combined with a shapely five foot four high figure and good looks, including a cute retrousse nose. She is sharp intellectually and a great companion. I had not known her long enough to work out what made her tick but we seemed to have a mutual chemistry that made it unnecessary to ask her things; she seemed to work it out before I'd spoken. Enough of that for now!

An arrangement that seemed to satisfy both aspects of our relationship evolved, largely through her suggestions. First she introduced me to the government-owned Research Establishment in the Isle of Purbeck, known as the Winfrith Technology Centre, as an ideal base for my research work. It would be secure from prying eyes; it was near to the large oil field, Wytch Farm, in which Bakuoil had a major stake and the Centre had a good in-house supporting technology. The financial terms offered were attractive and I signed up.

Julie had a further excellent idea and suggested that I might find lodging at the Elizabethan manor owned by her father in Corfe Castle village. The place was really too large for him, she said, and he would welcome the company. She would also be able to visit whenever her job allowed. I signed up for that as well!

The Isle of Purbeck isn't an island at all but a corner of Dorsetshire, full of natural beauty and with a long history. The tourism industry knows it —encouraged by the success of a film on dinosaurs - as the Jurassic Coast, because the rocks exposed on its cliffs span 200 million years of time from one end to the other. Fossils can be found everywhere on the beaches and cliffs and the white Portland stone has been used in buildings far and wide, including St Paul's Cathedral in London. Earth movements and erosion have created cliffs and valleys of stunning beauty. The rock strata that outcrop along the coast have also, under Poole Harbour, produced the largest on-shore oil field in the country. The rolling heath land and villages are well known from the novels of Thomas Hardy.

Over its history, blood has been spilt in large volumes. The suppression of the indigenous peoples by the invading Romans, the murder of kings, the bloody assizes of Judge Jeffries, are all part of that history.

George Washington's ancestors had lived here long before one of its scions emigrated to the new world. The Isle had captivated me years ago when I visited it during a sailing trip. Going on to the rumbling chain ferry from Poole across the narrow entrance to the harbour into the unspoilt moorland from which rise the Purbeck Hills, you were suddenly in a completely different world and age. Life moved at a slower pace.

The night of the storm was my first in residence at the manor as a paying guest. Until then I had suffered the rigours of a clean, functional but characterless hotel tolerated by commercial travellers, in the town of Poole across the harbour.

Anyway, back to that evening. I pulled myself out of the comfortable leather armchair in the room from which I'd just seen my ghost and made my way past the impressive curved staircase to the lounge opposite. Julie and Charles were installed in front of a roaring wood fire with a percolator of coffee emitting an aromatic welcome, sitting on the hearth. She was staying for the weekend, being based in London during the week, and we planned to go walking along the coast the next day taking in one or two country pubs on the way.

I collapsed in another of the large leather clad chairs that filled the place and balanced the cup of coffee Julie gave me on my knee. Charles looked at me quizzically over his half-moon spectacles, his shock of greying hair sticking up like Albert Einstein's and, overall, appearing as the eccentric ex-boffin he was. (I think of myself as a budding entrepreneur, rather than a boffin). He had an aristocratic air about him, however, and his probing questions made me take him seriously. Julie had warned me about his latest interest, that of trying to put forward a scientific basis for ghost sightings. I think it was that story that had made me imagine I saw a ghost.

"That was a meal to remember. I've heard of roast Dorset lamb but never tasted it," I said, hoping to get the conversation going in a direction different from the supernatural. A homely lady called Gladys from the village called in several times a day to look after Charles. She was clearly an accomplished cook and I promised myself that whenever I could I'd join him for his evening meal.

My attempt to get the conversation moving away from his pet subject failed immediately. He leaned over to a side table, and my heart sank as he handed me a book manuscript. It was indeed a 'manuscript': Charles clearly had no time for computers or even typewriters.

"I'd be grateful if you'd read this, Harry. During dinner I regaled you with my collection of Dorset ghost stories. I'm sure Julie's warned you about my obsession with this topic, but I'm convinced that there's a scientific explanation for the wealth of reported ghostly sightings in this area. I've lived around here for a long time and seen several in this house. This is the evidence. It's not convincing, but I've a gut feeling that I'm right". I accepted the manuscript with a heavy heart. The last thing I wanted was a collection of semi-scientific theories. Julie read my thoughts and mischievously volunteered that I would love to read it.

The atmosphere of the Purbecks, it must be said, cried out for ghost stories. The history, the profusion of old castles and manors and the shipwrecks along the coast were fertile grounds for old wives' tales (I'm sexist as well, you'll notice). I could see that even a sceptic like me would be overwhelmed in the course of time.

"Change the subject, Dad, you're embarrassing Harry – and me," Julie chipped in taking pity on me.

"Actually I've got an open mind on the subject," I said tactfully and described my after-dinner experience.

"Come on Harry you're making it up to please Dad," exclaimed Julie scornfully.

Charles's face lit up like a beacon. "There you are Julie, I know I'm supposed to be eccentric and a silly old sod, but both Gladys and I have had sightings in this house over the years, and now you Harry," he said jubilantly. "I'm convinced there really are flashbacks of times past. In this house I believe I've seen the two old aunts of mine who lived here eighty years ago. I must admit your sighting is a new one to me, Harry. It's also very disturbing for reasons I'm not going to talk about. I've no doubt Julie will enlighten you in the fullness of time".

"I'm not saying all sightings are genuine. Some are undoubtedly figments of the imagination of the locals seen after indulging at the 'Bankes Arms' pub. The 'lady in grey' who's alleged to haunt the valley at the edge of the village might be a mixture of genuine and imagined sightings. There are some stories, however, where there's corroboration from several people." Julie was behind him pulling a face and trying to make me laugh. However she took pity and came and sat close to me.

He was getting into his stride now and both Julie and I resigned ourselves to a lecture. We refilled our coffee cups, snuggled together on the high-backed settee and listened. I determined not to fall asleep again.

"I've made a study of reported sightings over several years and in that manuscript you've got in your hands I've tried to describe in detail the environment in which they took place, such as weather, surroundings, time and history. I noticed for what it's worth that two factors are common to the more believable sightings, for example they occur near to or in old buildings that haven't been renovated, or rocky environments that haven't been disturbed for years.

Secondly, simultaneously with the sighting, there's been some natural disturbance like a thunderstorm or in one case the firing on the artillery ranges over in Lulworth. Some parts of this house qualify like the lounge you were in. This thunderstorm tonight might have been a trigger for the appearance."

He went on for a full half-hour and by that time Julie was asleep. I was quite proud I hadn't also succumbed.

"My sighting was of a soldier," I reminded him. "To my inexperienced eye he had a uniform of 1940's vintage. If we are seeing flashbacks in time then who would that be?"

Charles suddenly became colder. "Clearly Julie hasn't been telling you about our family history," he muttered. "It's something I don't really want to talk about. I'm sorry, but it's a sensitive issue. It concerns my brother, and he certainly can't be a ghost, he's very much alive. He did live here for a time in the 1940's and I suppose it is possible you saw a flashback of that time." I decided to drop the subject - he was quite upset.

Over the next hour he went through a whole catalogue of his investigations and I must admit I began to think that there might be something in what he was saying. Unfortunately my concentration was waning. I promised to read his manuscript as soon as I could. Julie and I slipped away when he eventually dozed off in his chair. I'd hoped she'd share my four-poster bed but all I got was a chaste kiss.

Chapter 3. Stroll into forbidden territory

Chapman's Pool

The next day was perfect for a long walk, the dawn breaking across a misty panorama, with the distant hills blue and indistinct.

Later, the early spring sunshine would burn off the lingering haze to give us uninterrupted views of sea, rolling downs and steep cliffs, ranging from the Needles rocks off the Isle of Wight in the east, to the stark outline of the Isle of Portland, thirty miles to the west.

Julie and I, fortified by a robust breakfast provided by Gladys, set off across the heath keeping a close look out for poisonous adders, Dartford Warblers and other allegedly rare species lurking in the heather, as well as the odd bog. The wild life was hiding but the boggy ground made itself felt and I sank into mud to my knees while my attention was focussed on Julie. She found it amusing.

After clambering up a steep escarpment we reached the small village of Kingston that visually seemed to be unchanged from the times when it was beholden to and owned by the local aristocracy.

The pub, the Scott Arms, still bears its patronymic on its sign. We passed the ornate church, the construction of which had indirectly bankrupted the local quarrying industry for decades after it was built because all their other, neglected customers went elsewhere for their stone.

We joined the path leading towards the sea and the hills that fronted it and scrambled down the steep path towards the shore at the cove called Chapman's Pool, the sombre appearance of which I've mentioned before. Julie reminded me of one of her father's stories.

With a perfectly straight face she said,

"There are local tales of Roman soldiers having been seen down here even in daylight, and on more than one occasion. It could be a story that's improved with the telling, but Dad says that the detail of their uniforms described was impressive and he for one thinks it genuine. He says that this area is over a major geological fault cutting across the Purbecks, and minor earthquakes could be responsible for triggering the sightings by some unknown phenomenon."

On this sunny morning it seemed a most unlikely site for haunting but I could see that in a mist or fading light it would be spooky.

"Do you really think there might be anything in what he's saying, Harry?" she asked.

"Normally I'd say not a chance, but after last night he sowed a seed of doubt in my mind. The mind's a funny thing and I'm sure 99.9% of sightings are just figments of the imagination. Anyway it makes a good story. Your father is quite persuasive," I replied.

"I think you're just humouring me, Harry Aldborough," she said, giving me a kiss.

We paused for breath at the top of the first 100m climb along the cliff path. I thought the time ripe to probe more into the history of Julie's family hinted at by Charles the previous evening.

"Julie, your father clammed up when I asked him about the ghostly soldier I thought I saw in the lounge last night. What is it about his brother that's so sensitive?" I ventured.

Julie looked out to sea, which was dotted with dozens of yachts and pleasure boats, for a minute before she replied. "The events happened long before I was born, of course, so I only know what Dad's told me. This is all kept quiet and nobody talks about it. His brother Henry is the present Lord Egliston who lives in Egliston Hall just along the coast from here. The ghost you allege you saw could be him, except that he is still alive and well. He's the owner of a large industrial conglomerate as well as having his fingers in local and government pies"

The name struck a chord with me but I couldn't remember where I'd heard it before.

Julie went on "I don't suppose that he knows or even cares whether I exist or not. He certainly doesn't have anything to do with Dad. Henry's two years older than he is and joined the British army after leaving university in the mid-thirties. He had studied for a year in Germany and was reasonably fluent in the language. There was a military tradition in the family and he probably would have enlisted anyway but the impending war tipped the balance. He also hoped that his knowledge of German would be useful in any conflict with Germany. By all accounts he isn't a very pleasant individual; he was arrogant and self-centred, although Dad as a younger brother looked up to him."

Julie warmed up to her theme and I was happy to listen. Apparently Henry was in the ill-fated British Expeditionary Force in 1940 and won the Military Medal but was captured in Belgium after being injured. He was interned in what is now East Germany. The Germans had found out he was the heir to the Egliston title and presumably thought he might be useful for a future prisoner or spy exchange. His poor physical and mental condition resulting from the injury must have lulled his captors into complacency, because in April 1940 he escaped, managing to reach Switzerland and eventually home. He was still suffering from shell shock and was put on long-term sick leave.

He came to live here in the Norden manor where Charles lives today. Charles was at school in Scotland during the war. Henry and Charles's father, the old Lord Egliston, had died as a result of a fall from the cliffs on St Aldhelm's Head whilst Henry was still in captivity. It was probably suicide but the circumstances were hushed up. Henry inherited the title. The army had taken over Egliston Hall as a billet because of its nearness to the coast. That's why Henry was living at the Norden manor under the care of the old Lord Egliston's housekeeper Nicole rather than at the Egliston manor itself.

Julie paused before going on.

"Henry was by all accounts even more arrogant and unsociable at that time than he had been in earlier life and it took some time before he entered public activities as befitted a Lord of the Realm. His father was away from all this and wasn't allowed to meet him even after the war ended. In 1945 the army handed the family estate back except for some land at Tyneham, a few miles up the coast, and Henry set up in the family home at Egliston Hall, spending vast sums of money renovating it. His solicitors wrote to dad's guardian in Scotland giving him a sizeable chunk of the family money as well as the Norden manor. There weren't any other close members of the family with a possible claim.

There was a stipulation in the transfer documents that he would make no claim on the estate and would make no attempt ever again to meet Henry. Henry has a son, Nicolas, but I don't know anything about him except that he is as vile as Henry, if not more so. Dad was advised that the settlement was legally valid and there would be little point in contesting it.

Dad and I assumed that shell shock had caused Henry some permanent mental damage. Since that time there had been no contact. Dad is still very bitter about being cut off from his and his family's past but he doesn't usually show it. It has made him very introspective. He is a stereotype boffin, interested in things rather than people. He married my mother in the early 1950's. She was an extrovert and they had little in common apart from me. She left him when I went to university, but died shortly afterwards"

Julie hazarded that the trauma Henry had suffered might well have affected him mentally but clearly it hadn't affected his long-term business acumen because, as she said, he'd built up a massive clutch of businesses.

"That's it in a nutshell. Now can we get on with our walk?" she said. "I want to get to Lulworth for lunch."

We pressed on up to the top of the highest part of the coastal path. From there they say that the Cotentin peninsula of France can be seen, sixty miles away. That day it couldn't. From the decaying concrete base of an old, long-gone gun emplacement, we again took in the stunning scenery. At a point where the offshore wind hit the escarpment, causing an up-draught, hang-gliding enthusiasts in company with seagulls could be seen being lifted into the air current and flying down to the coast and back again. Nearer to us in a verdant valley with woods and lakes lay a large mansion and buildings that were clearly part of a large estate. The sound of a gun periodically echoed round the valley, presumably a gamekeeper going his rounds.

"I hate to bring up our murky family history again but that's Lord Henry Egliston's spread." said Julie. "The Dorset Coast Path takes us past the property. You can't go up into the estate proper because it's well fenced off and guarded by dogs. The family always did discourage visitors but Henry's been particularly paranoid about it."

The mystery of the place got to me and as we skirted the bottom part of the estate I saw that the gate was open.

"Julie," I said, "I'd love to have a closer look at the place. After what you've said I'm intrigued. We can always plead ignorance as ramblers if we're seen now that the gate has been left open. We might even see this mysterious relative of yours and you won't be recognised if he hasn't seen you in years."

"You won't get far," said Julie, "there are security cameras and another more secure gate further up the path. When I was still at school I went in with some of my friends and we were firmly escorted out: the security wasn't as tight in those days."

My curiosity was raised even more and I challenged her. "Where's your spirit of adventure then? We can always say we're ramblers."

Reluctantly she followed me. It seemed like entering another world. The trees hung over our heads and the thick foliage of shrubs made the road like a green cave and the coolness on leaving the sunlit coastal path was forbidding. A track snaked ahead. The sound of our steps in the crunchy gravel echoed and made me very aware of our trespassing.

After walking for five minutes we saw a farmhouse ahead but before we could reach it a dog started barking as two men came round the corner of the house. I pulled Julie into the wood as an involuntary reaction as they came down the track. One, exuding authority, was quite old, the other who appeared to be a gamekeeper, presumably the one whose gun we had heard, was feeling the lash of his tongue.

"That's him," whispered Julie.

Egliston had thick white hair, a florid face, the main features of which were bushy black eyebrows and a large moustache. He appeared to be about my height with a barrel of a chest and a trim stomach. As a young man he must have been a formidable sight and even now was impressive. He appeared to have no family resemblance to Charles.

"You bloody fool!" the old man was saying. "You left that gate open. I saw it myself on the security screen. I told you to keep it shut until Hassan had arrived with the delivery. Run down there damn quick and lock it before any fool ramblers decide to come in. You know very well that I don't want any prying eyes. Get going."

The gamekeeper with a shotgun crooked across his arm strode past muttering under his breath with the dog at his heels. The animal must have been aware of our presence and strained at his leash but the man's attention was clearly elsewhere and he swore at the dog and pulled him along.

Egliston turned and went back to the farmhouse. We heard the clang of the steel gate in the distance and shortly afterwards the gamekeeper returned up the path to the house.

All this time we had been crouching behind the trees not making a sound.

"That was a little close for comfort," I breathed. "Maybe we'd better get out. I guess the old boy wasn't in a mood to receive visitors. I've quite got over the idea of introducing ourselves."

Returning, this time making as little noise as we could, we came to the gate. It was unfortunately about seven feet tall with sharp spikes along the top, a fact I'd not noticed when we passed through it earlier. I hadn't seen the CCTV camera either but this time we kept well away from its field of view.

"A fine mess you've got us into!" complained Julie. "How do you propose we get out? I don't feel like climbing that gate. Anyway it's locked and probably alarmed, we know it's got CCTV and it might be electrified. Mr Clever Guy, tell me how to get out?"

I didn't feel too enthusiastic about it either. Just then we heard a vehicle outside coming up the gravel track I'd noticed earlier and which led to the small jetty at Chapman's Pool. We retreated into the wood just as the gamekeeper character came back without the dog and stood waiting.   A pick-up truck driven by a man of Middle Eastern appearance drew up and the gamekeeper let it in. The truck's contents were covered with a tarpaulin.

"Did anyone see you load up the truck from the boat, Hassan? The old man's paranoiac about these shipments being seen," said the gamekeeper.

"Relax, even if someone did see us they'd be fooled as to what it was," replied Hassan. After securing the gate the gamekeeper jumped in the front seat and they drove away.

"I'm going to see more of this; it smells of smuggling to me. Are you coming?" I whispered.

"I don't like this one little bit," Julie replied. "We're getting too deeply involved."

Anyway, she joined me as we followed the truck whilst keeping in the fringe of the wood. As we approached the farm we saw the truck was parked outside a modern farm building. Lord Egliston was there standing with folded arms and glaring at the truck. Two men came out of the building and stripped off the sheet stretched over the contents of the truck, which appeared to be a wooden box the size of a tea chest. Hassan then opened the box, revealing a white painted metal container about a foot high and nine inches diameter.

"That, unless I'm very much mistaken, is a radioactive source flask the oil industry uses," I whispered to Julie.

The flask was carried inside. We could see that the interior of the building was white and pristine like a laboratory. All the men entered and the door shut behind them.

"Come on, let's get out of here. If those guys are up to no good we might come to serious harm and at the very least Dad would go through the roof if he knew we had been in here," she said. "Because you've no bright ideas on how we can get out it looks as though I'm going to have to make use of my trespassing experience from girlhood years. There used to be a tunnel, a sort of culvert, which takes the stream down to the sea. It's probably overgrown now, but it was well-built then and we might still be able to get through."

I'd had enough of spying for the day as well and we scuttled into the thick of the wood following the sound of running water. It was as she had said: brambles and bushes had overgrown the path of the stream. Of the culvert there was no sign. As we neared the fence the sound of dogs came to our ears. They must have been released to guard the property and had presumably picked up our scent.

I pushed through the undergrowth and waded along the stream hoping it might put the dogs off our scent for a while, and was very relieved to find the culvert entrance as she had described. I was less pleased to see it covered by a steel grille. With the frightening sound of the dogs getting nearer I struggled trying to lift the grille but it was rusted in place.

"For God's sake move it!" shouted Julie, panicking.

I started hitting it with a rock from the stream and the fixing bolts came away on one side. With a heave I managed to make space for Julie to crawl through before getting into the culvert myself, pulling the grille behind me.

The first Alsatian hit the grille as it closed and clawed at it, barking furiously. We squeezed through about twenty metres of narrow stone-clad culvert about a yard in diameter. There was then a three metre high drop with the water sluicing on to the rocks below. I was able to climb up above the lip of the culvert exit and pull Julie up behind me. The dogs were still barking but were unable to follow.

We were wet and scratched but, importantly, out of the estate.

Julie hugged me. "Never do anything like that again," she said. "I was a fool to let you persuade me. Anyway I suppose you redeemed yourself by getting that grille off."

We clambered back up on to the path and resumed our legitimate role as ramblers.

"A radio-active container in such an unlikely setting doesn't make sense. I'd like to know more about this Lord Egliston. It comes back to me now. He's got an interest in the Wytch Farm oilfield, though no direct interest in the company that funds some of my work. Hans Reise, my old tutor who helped me get the funding might know him. I must ask him to fill in the background," I recalled.

We sat for five minutes getting our wind back.

"I forgive you for nearly getting me killed," she said with one of those looks designed to melt your soul.

What else could I do but kiss her with a passion born of being scared stiff ten minutes earlier.

At the top of Swyre Head, one of the highest points for miles round, we looked back at Egliston Hall nestling in its valley, appearing far more inviting in the distance than it had done at close range. The division of the Isle of Purbeck into manors centuries ago is still noticeable even today with the Encombe estate in the next valley rivalling that of Egliston's. Further on was the Tyneham village and estate that is still mainly in the hands of the army some fifty years after the end of World War 2.

The sight of a small Hughes helicopter coming up behind us startled us.

"My God, they are still after us!" said Julie. We threw ourselves to the ground as it missed us by only twenty yards coming to a hover. The man, Hassan, who we had seen with the truck leaned out and photographed us. The chopper then swept away, returning to the estate.

"Bloody cheek!" Julie shouted as our alarm subsided. "That man thinks he owns Dorset."

Some considerable time later, we passed the Clavell Tower folly on the coast at Kimmeridge Bay where the crystal clear water attracts scuba divers in search of corals and boat wrecks. Then went past the 'nodding donkey' oil well, which I knew from my days with BP, produced a few hundred barrels of oil each day and had done so long after the oil field reservoir should have been exhausted. The army had control of the next coastal strip as far as Lulworth, the planned end of our walk and we were fortunate that the path was open as the army firing ranges were quiet that day. Normally tank shells are lobbed from a site in Lulworth village at targets on these hills and the area was strewn with shrapnel and shell casings. There were notices warning against wandering on to MOD land.

"You don't feel like exploring that?" said Julie with irony.

We finally arrived at Lulworth Cove, a picturesque scene with fishing boats and tourists. In the rustic Castle Inn we had pints of best bitter and ploughman's lunches in front of us in double-quick time.

The events of our trespassing venture earlier on were still uppermost in my mind and I wanted to know more.

"Your side of the MacLean family seems much more human than that of the aristocratic Lord Egliston," I dared to comment. "I've no desire to meet him in either business or social circumstances but I might have to now that Bakuoil is bankrolling my research and he has a stake in the oil field. I can see why your father keeps well away from him. There's something strange going on in that Egliston estate. I have to work with radioactive materials in my research and you don't handle them in the haphazard way we saw back there."

"We'd better forget about the whole thing," she said. "It's unlikely you'll come into contact with Egliston during your work. In the financial negotiations I went through when the bank was negotiating your contract, he certainly was not involved. As far as your suspicions about importing radioactive materials I don't think he would be involved in petty smuggling. His reputation would suffer too much if it came to light. If he is involved in any illegal activity at all it will be big. Unless it affects your research or the bank, forget it." She then leaned forward and gave me a peck on the cheek.

"If you try to lead me astray like you did back there again I might change my mind about you."

I began to think that the four-poster bed might yet come into its own in the not too distant future.

"Now, let's get on with this walk. We'll go back on the inland path on the plateau on the way back so you aren't tempted again. If you're good I'll show you the nearest thing you'll get to real ghosts – fossil dinosaur footprints in the stone quarries. There shouldn't be any family skeletons up there either."

Chapter 4. Purbeck's past

Charles had left to go on his weekly outing to an orchestral concert by the Bournemouth Symphony Orchestra in the Poole Arts Centre by the time we returned in the early evening from our walk along the coast, footsore and hungry. We were able to enjoy a cosy evening together with a bottle of wine. Julie, as is the way with women I've been close to, was intent on finding out more about me, what makes me tick, my ambitions, hopes and fears.

I must admit that at that moment my intentions were more driven by testosterone than platonic thoughts but the exertions of walking all day and the wine made me receptive to talk. Before long with her hair draped across my shoulders and her green eyes gazing at me I was telling her my life story.

I admitted that I was a bit of a loner, having no brothers or sisters. My father had been too engrossed in his job in my early years to spend much time with me, and my mother was not very domesticated, preferring the social round. I tended to read a lot and found school the centre of my social life. That's how I got involved in sports, one of them being judo, and became very competitive. It stopped the bullying, which I'd experienced at first because as an only child I'd not developed many social skills. The competitiveness gained in sport also helped me get to the top academically.

When I got to university I realised there was more to life than rugby, squash and work and became very attached to a German girl in my digs. After that, as well as being encouraged to learn German, I never looked back.

I continued extolling my virtues as Julie was obviously fascinated by my monologue. I told her that I had an excellent memory and managed to keep the studies going without great mental exertion. My parents were killed in a car crash just after finals and I decided to make a complete break, going to the USA to do research at MIT. My tutor there said I had great mental stamina, a nice way of saying I was stubborn in argument and didn't know when to give up, and I threw myself into research single-mindedly, becoming quite good, if I say it myself.

Eventually I realised my life was getting very academic and to offset this I joined the BP oil company to see the world. Whilst with them I found that I increasingly disliked being told what to do and became interested in being an entrepreneur.

Julie had listened to all this in silence, no doubt forming a psychological profile and how best to handle me. I was about to suggest that we continue the discussion in a more comfortable location when her mobile rang. These bankers seem to be on 24-hour call.

"It's my boss," she mouthed silently. "I've got to prepare a presentation," she said when the call was over. "One of my projects looks as though it's going down the tubes. The boss wants me in London tomorrow afternoon to make a report to the board. Sorry, Harry, I'm going to have to spend half the night writing. I was getting quite romantic as well. Perhaps we can take up where we left off next weekend."

The four-poster bed was going to have another quiet time that night.

After an early breakfast she was away in her BMW sports car, kissing her father on the bald patch in the centre of his bushy tonsure of grey hair, and blowing me a kiss. I was left with Charles, the Sunday papers and the rest of the day. There was also the option of getting stuck into some report writing myself. Charles rose to the occasion.

"Why don't I take you a tour of Purbeck? I'm very proud of the area. So you don't forget my offbeat ideas, I might even show you a few of the places where I think it might be possible to see flashbacks in time." I'd re-read the manuscript he'd shown me and mentally consigned his ideas to the pigeonhole in my mind labelled 'interesting but far-fetched'. However, I did want to see the locality and Charles was an entertaining host with many anecdotes and historical facts at his fingertips.

"I'd appreciate that," I said.

"We'll start with Corfe Castle itself," he enthused.

The castle was the one item that made the village stand out for miles around. From the moors on the coastal ridge one could look back and see in a cleft in the main ridge of the hills a break - and in that break, the ruins of the castle. Two rocky fingers of the central keep pointed to the sky and the whole castle was silhouetted against the blue mists over Poole harbour. Closer up one could see the damage Cromwell's men had inflicted. Whole segments of the castle had slid down the hill on which it was built, by several metres, but the outline was still there. At night it was sinister and ghost-like.

He told me to put on walking boots, as we were going over some rugged ground. We walked first to the castle entrance in the village itself, paid our National Trust entrance fee just like dozens of tourists milling around and staggered up to the debris of the once proud buildings, parts of which towered above us. Oliver Cromwell had ordered the destruction around us four hundred years ago in order to snuff out opposition from

Royalists. It was nevertheless still an impressive sight and from the top one could see miles in every direction.

"If this is where you'd expect to see ghosts I think you would be mistaken," said Charles waving his arms about enthusiastically.

"The rocks under the castle and its masonry, according to my theory, have their past history imprinted on them in some unknown way. However, because they are now jumbled following the seventeenth century destruction and subsequent restoration work, any flashbacks you might otherwise see would be too confused, like a scattered jigsaw, to make a coherent picture. In fact it's interesting to note there are very few stories of ghost sightings here. Down there near that stone bridge where the road leaves the village it's a different matter. There have been sightings of the 'lady in grey' over many years. The stonework of the bridge is essentially the same as that of a hundred years ago and any according to my ideas; images from the past are embedded in the rock. By the way, there are rumours that there is a lost hidden passage between here and my house. You can have a look for it if you find yourself with nothing to do"

I took that with a pinch of salt because the castle had fallen into disuse even in Elizabethan times.

The next place he introduced me to was the village of Worth Matravers and its picturesque pub – the Square and Compass – then to the bleak windswept plateau of St Aldhelm's Head, where we parked at Renscombe farm and walked out along a gravel path to the small stone chapel standing out on the broad plateau like a pea on a drum.

"Now here's a likely candidate for my theories," enthused Charles. "It was built in the eleventh century and hasn't been changed much since. Unfortunately I've not heard of any sightings, but there again, who's likely to spend time here in this godforsaken place after dark?"

I was enjoying the guided tour but found Charles's attitude to his theories most unscientific. He was finding excuses to explain failures of his theory rather than trying to disprove it. It was fascinating to see graffiti from earlier centuries as well as the more recent 'Fred loves Marilyn' stuff carved in the rock of the chapel. Beyond the chapel we peered over the cliff to the rocky outcrops a hundred metres below.

"Don't go too near the edge, Harry. My father, the then Lord Egliston, was killed by a fall near here during the last war," he warned. "There was fog coming in from the sea at the time and he must have become disorientated. It was just after he had heard that my older brother had been taken prisoner in Belgium." I recall Julie saying he had probably committed suicide, but said nothing.

Charles carried on his guide duties as we returned to the car. "You might be interested in a bit of more recent history. Just a few hundred yards away is Renscombe farm. From 1940 to 1942 Britain's major research site for radar was built right there. In fact as a small boy, the excitement of tales of the research probably determined my career. As you know I worked on radar research myself. The site was known as AMRE or TRE. At its peak there were over 800 scientists and engineers up here"

We walked on in silence until he stopped and pointed. "Over there just beyond the farm there were four large aerial masts. On the cliffs behind us you can just see the remains of one of the radar posts. That building over there, used today for Outward Bound courses, is the only one left"

We stopped for a while to appreciate the green fields rolling away into the distance before Charles spoke. "Because Churchill became worried about possible German commando raids he had the whole set-up moved lock, stock and barrel up to Malvern where its successor the Royal Radar Establishment was built. Some facilities remained here until just after the war but only routine stuff. I've expected to hear reports of ghostly occurrences up here, you know, the odd German plane or two, but there've been none so far. There have been sightings of World War 2 planes near Fylingdales in Yorkshire, by the way. I think that those appearances are caused in a similar way to the appearances I'm interested in. Don't be so sceptical, Harry!"

He carried on through the day with a running commentary whilst he regaled me with the history of Purbeck. We called at the pub at Lulworth, that Julie and I had visited the previous day, for lunch while he went on with his stories. Apparently, some servants from the old castle nearby had perished in a fire in the nineteenth century. Their ghosts had allegedly been seen on the cliffs round the cove on several occasions since. I hadn't realised how saturated the area was in ghost reports. Charles himself didn't give much credence to most of them but was adamant that some had a scientific explanation.

He showed me the sad deserted village of Tyneham, which the army had occupied in 1943, promising to give it back to the inhabitants at the end of the war. They never did, of course, and it is still, as I had found out yesterday with Julie, a firing range for the tanks, with the public let in occasionally. Charles's family used to own part of the land and he was quite bitter that it would never be returned. The old Tyneham manor house that had housed service personnel had been destroyed by practice firing and only the church and school remained intact. I didn't realise then what trauma lay ahead for me in this spot.

He finally took me down to the village of Studland for a civilised cup of tea. When we had finished the cream muffins that appeared with the tea he led me outside. "You must see this," he said as we walked to the end of the garden of the Studland Manor. We walked round a large concrete relic of the war.

"This is Fort Henry, built by Canadian servicemen. It was named after a fort in Canada. It was not used as a machine gun post, as so many of these things were intended. It was built specially to let top brass officers view mock landings in preparation for the Normandy landings. An audacious attempt was made here on the lives of General Montgomery and the top brass just before D-Day. Thank goodness the saboteurs didn't succeed. Henry, my brother, achieved fame and gratitude by shooting the terrorist who made the attempt."

When we got back to the manor, Charles put me on the spot.

"The other night you saw in your room what I think was a real flashback to a previous time. I know you think it was a trick of the mind during that thunderstorm. All I ask is that you keep an open mind."

It certainly gave me food for thought and I was beginning to think there was something in what he was saying though my instincts were saying "what a load of codswallop"

Chapter 5. Professor Hans Reise

Professor Hans Reise, who was my tutor at Oxford University when I was an undergraduate, had invited me, in one of his occasional letters, to join him for formal dinner at his college. I'd made a point of staying in touch.

He was now in his eighties but was still as sharp as a knife intellectually. Over the years he had worked in a variety of areas starting with radar during the Second World War, after which he made a lot of money capitalising on his experience. He returned to academia in the sixties and made a name for himself in theoretical physics. He did some highly original work in particle physics at the Rutherford laboratory near Oxford and was in line for a Nobel Prize but for some reason he never actually made it.

Rumour had it that he had been blackballed in the vindictive atmosphere of university politics. We had stayed in contact ever since I left university and he had helped me with his networking skills to get funding for my current research project. In fact, networking was why he had asked me to dine, I suppose.

His college, Stirling, was one of the wealthiest in the university as a result of bequests from benefactors in centuries gone by and this showed in its ability to attract world-class fellows. The college had a reputation for the excellence of its food and invitations to dine were eagerly sought by dons from other colleges with a lesser culinary reputation. He made full use of the Senior Common Room and the college top-table to keep in touch both with his past students and the business contacts of which he still had plenty. He was also an emeritus professor of physics at the University of Heidelberg, where he had a home. His reason for inviting me was ostensibly to hear about my research on oil recovery engineering.

I arrived in time for sherry in the Senior Common Room before dinner, having by some miracle found a parking place in the warren of streets round the area. Checking in through the porters' lodge I was greeted by Bill Edmunds, the head scout, who was reputed to recognise all past students from the thirty years he had been there. Walking across the hallowed turf of the quadrangle, as I was entitled to do as a holder of a MA degree, I stepped through a wisteria-crowned doorway up a spiral staircase to Reise's rooms. I wondered how at his age he could climb up the worn stone steps, recalling how I had once fallen headlong down them as a drunken twenty-year-old student. He was just putting on his academic robe and hood as I knocked on the door.

"Welcome dear boy," he enthused, peering over the top of his horn-rimmed glasses,

"You're just in time." He was quite short but his vitality and personality made him appear taller. His aquiline features and head of wavy grey hair gave him a distinguished appearance and his eyes sparkled behind his glasses. He spoke with a slight Teutonic accent despite all his years in Britain and he used his hands all the time to complement his speech.

"I've a little surprise for you, in fact it is one reason I invited you. The Principal has invited two guests, one or both of whom you ought to meet. Lord Egliston is one because he has recently endowed a fellowship with the college. The other is the Minister of State, Clive Rowbury, responsible for oil matters at the Department of Energy and climate". My heart missed a beat at this news.

"I've known Egliston, who has a mansion down in Dorset near where you are, for a long time. It might be useful to meet him in case your paths cross. Rowbury, you have probably met before, when you got your contract with the Department. You'd better make a good impression; they are both useful men to know. Right, come on, we don't want to be late." With that he disappeared through the doorway.

I was quite ready to sing for my supper so to speak but was somewhat apprehensive about meeting Lord Egliston, especially after what I'd seen during my walk with Julie a few days ago. I hoped that he hadn't seen the photograph taken from the helicopter, in case he recognised me. Before I'd had chance to say anything about it we were down the staircase and walking towards the Senior Common Room. I didn't even have time, because of Reise's continuous chatter, before the meal to tell him I was staying with Egliston's brother and that there might be some embarrassment if it emerged in conversation.

Dining in such college surroundings can be intimidating, with the portraits of severe-faced past principals, robed clerics and benefactors looking down from the gold-framed paintings on the heavy dark oak panelling. High Table, where the dons and their visitors sat, was on a dais a foot above the undergraduate's tables.

The college servants in white jackets scurried to and fro between the Hall and the kitchens below. Most of the diners were in academic robes and there was a highly formal atmosphere. The company round the table was a bit off-putting as well. There appeared to be a certain amount of waspish interchange between the fellows and it was easy to visualise the academic backstabbing that occurs and about which one reads.

Hans gave me a big build up in introducing me and I said my piece, trying to impress with my scientific and political acumen. The government minister, Clive Rowbury, was witty and suave and gave the impression he was fascinated by what I had to say although probably completely disinterested – a typical politician who was going places. He said he would look forward to hearing more when the results started to come in.

Lord Egliston, who was even more domineering than he had seemed back in Dorset a few days ago, clearly wasn't happy unless he was dominating the conversation. It was the first time I'd seen him close to. Despite his age he was fit and sharp. His eyes were a clear steely blue and held you with an unblinking gaze. His eyebrows were more than ample and were black in contrast to his steely hair. He had the air of an aristocrat and had cultivated an approach designed to make you think you were something the cat had brought in.

"You scientists have it too easy, with the government willing to lavish taxpayers' money on research. Not content with that, industry is persuaded to throw their money in knowing that its applications for licensing might by viewed more sympathetically. You should have to convince private industry that what you want to do is commercially viable without pressure from our political masters."

He glared at Rowbury and me, daring us to take the bait. I decided to jump in.

"I cannot speak for the government but I can speak for myself. I know that the companies that have contributed to my research did so because they could see the benefit. Indeed I've put myself in the firing line by raising venture money with a bank. However, there are always plenty of projects to choose from, as I know. There are far too many British companies spending too little on R and D when compared to the USA. With respect, I'm sure that is not the case with Egliston Industries."

"Bravo!" said Hans. "Lord Egliston is of course a supporter of good research as I know from my own dealings with him, but he is a hard taskmaster."

"You are as bad as the rest. You will be asking for support next with those crackpot ideas of yours on space travel," Egliston threw at Hans.

That took the heat off me and he turned to the Government Minister.

"We pay far too much in tax from oil. When are you going to help developments by bringing the tax regime up to date?"

Rowbury then delivered a smooth, logical and coherent statement of how and why there was a need for regulation that took even more pressure off me. I could see that others round the table were not happy with Egliston's attitude.

Fortunately the conversation moved on. Egliston didn't appear interested in continuing discussion on oil matters, appearing to view me as a boffin who could be ignored. He obviously knew Hans well but was offhand with him also. He obviously relished his position of power and his arrogant air clearly ruffled the feathers of some of the dons present and verbal innuendoes flew during the rest of the meal.

I wasn't able to talk in depth with Hans at that time. After the port wine had been ritually circulated round the table and the Master of the college had solemnly closed the proceedings in the succinct Latin grace 'Benedictus benedictat', Hans and I adjourned to the Senior Common Room and sank into comfortable chairs.

Hans congratulated me on my standing up to Egliston. "I think you made an impression on him and the politician seemed to think you had done well. You might not want to get to know Egliston better but believe me; his tentacles stretch a long way."

Now was the time to tell Hans about my Dorset acquaintances.

"I didn't have time to tell you before the meal that I had heard of Egliston," I confessed. "In fact I am lodging with his younger brother at the Manor House in Norden. Egliston's reputation there is not good."

Hans was visibly shaken.

"Does that old house still belong to Lord Egliston?" he said "Thank God you didn't mention that over the meal"

I was surprised he knew about it. I explained that Egliston's brother Charles now owned it and briefly described how he had been completely shut out of Lord Egliston's life since WW2.

Hans went on, "You probably gathered from his attitude to me over dinner that we are not on the best of terms. I hoped I'd not cross paths with him much in the future and to tell the truth I'm unhappy about the college dealing with him. I voted against acceptance of his college donation but I was in a minority. Perhaps I shouldn't have exposed you to him. I knew him very well during the war – too well. I know Dorset and I visited him several times at the Norden manor where he lived, and be assured, it has no happy memories for me."

"Since the war I've kept well out of his way socially, although we do have extensive business contacts. I'm not going into personal details except to say that he's utterly ruthless. I do know that he had a vendetta against his brother, and it doesn't surprise me in the least to hear it's still going on. Don't mention where you're staying if you ever meet his lordship again."

I asked him how he came to be in Dorset during the war. It appeared that he had worked at the St Aldhelm's Head research station TRE that Charles had told me about a few days ago, before moving on to Malvern. I expressed surprise that as a German, he was allowed anywhere near such a sensitive area during the war. He settled back in his chair and seemed to forget I was there as he reminisced.

"I was a student at Heidelberg University before the war and came to England in 1937. The Clarendon laboratory in Oxford had been a home for refugee German physicists since the 1930s. I was briefly interned at the outbreak of war – like many refugee German Jews. Very soon I'd established to the authorities that I was a genuine refugee and was released. In fact during the war several Germans with excellent scientific and anti-Nazi credentials had gathered under Professor Lindemann, himself a refugee, to carry out work on microwave technology."

"It was a joke that as one entered the building a notice was prominently displayed saying 'Hier spricht man Deutsch'. When the Air Ministry moved its research on radar to that windswept headland in Dorset I was drafted there. It was fascinating. There was a galaxy of talent and some of the top men became famous after the war, some of them getting Nobel prizes, but not me," said he said wryly. "Egliston was assigned to the place as a military liaison officer with the local authorities. He seemed at first to cultivate my friendship as he spoke excellent German and said he wanted to keep in practice."

"When the time came for us to move to Malvern he asked me to stay in touch and keep him up to date with our progress. I refused on security grounds but he completely lost his temper and he said he would get me into trouble with security. He must have thought better of it because I didn't hear the threat from him again until after the war."

After a time Hans decided he'd dominated the conversation for long enough and asked me what I'd been doing since I got the go-ahead for my research. He had continued to sip port wine but because I had to drive back to Dorset I'd moved to tonic water. I told him that progress had been good and I would soon be ready for field trials of my oil recovery methods.

After I'd brought him up to date and he had given me a few ideas on which to work, I thought I would tell him about Charles's ideas, as a light-hearted contribution to the evening. He was becoming more and more mellow. I wanted to see what his reaction to Charles MacLean's theory on time flashbacks might be. Reise had written articles on interstellar space travel for the popular press and this hadn't endeared him to the more conservative members of the college so that I knew he would take it constructively. His comments might be instructive and might help me in my attempts to distance myself from Charles's enthusiasm.

Much has been written in science fiction about time travel and its logical impossibility and the subject is still being argued about by postulating all sorts of far-fetched ideas. Sightings of past events on the other hand didn't involve any logical impossibility and there could well be a perfectly respectable scientific explanation for my experience in the Manor and for Charles's theories.

I jumped in with both feet.

"Hans, I read your articles on time and intergalactic travel some years ago when I was a student. Some of the mathematics was beyond me. When Egliston threw in that gratuitous comment about your papers during the meal he was, by the way, completely out of order. I'm interested in the subject and decided I would bring up with you this evening a related topic that came up a month ago."

"No problem Harry – water off a duck's back as they say. I still read anything that is published on the topic including science fiction. There are others I know who are equally dismissive. What did happen to you a month ago?" he asked with a smile.

I felt sufficiently encouraged to go on.

"I had what I believe was a brief flashback of a scene in time to the 1940's. It came as a blurred image spreading about throughout a room in the Manor House at Norden during a lightning storm. I would have thought no more about it as being a figment of my imagination but Charles jumped on the idea when I mentioned it in passing. He had, he said, seen similar things. Indeed they started him off on a hobby of investigating ghosts in Dorset."

"You know Charles and his wild Einstein-like appearance. He has a hypothesis that flashbacks in time could be initiated by seismic or other violent events. I didn't take it seriously but from your studies, is there a possibility of seeing past events? Time-travel itself is unlikely I know."

Hans stretched his legs and to my relief smiled.

"I've an open mind on the subject, although I've yet to see any evidence. In principle, there is no theoretical reason why such flashbacks could not occur. A phenomenon being studied by cosmologists is called quantum entanglement, which appears to allow a measurement of position or momentum on one particle or photon instantaneously to change onto another particle even though the two are a substantial distance or time apart. This, on the face of it, challenges Einstein's theory that says that nothing can travel faster than light. It seems likely that photons at a past point in time can be 'entangled' under certain conditions with those of the present time. The next problem is how to link and control photons in a particular time in the past. My guess is that gravity waves might be used".

I had heard about these waves. As far as I knew nobody had yet detected them – they were still hypothetical. The problem was that if they exist they would be very, very weak. Two spheres of a heavy material such as lead or uranium ten centimetres in diameter a metre apart would have a gravitational attraction to each other of only 0.00000001 of the weight of a grain of salt. Gravity waves would be of that magnitude. They would be very difficult to measure.

Sensing my thoughts, Hans said,

"Of course only massive movements like earthquakes would produce a measurable effect, but if you could work out how to amplify the effect it might be possible to produce the time flashbacks you think you saw"

I hung on to two ideas – a visual snapshot of all previous times is embedded at the quantum level in our physical surroundings - gravity waves of the right frequency and strength might bring an image from the past to life

He wouldn't say any more on my Dorset experiences except to warn me to beware of Egliston, but we spent another two hours chatting about this and that before I left to return to Dorset.

As I drove the two-hour journey I thought about what he'd said but made no more progress. Overnight, under the joint influence of a bedtime whisky and a re-reading of Charles's manuscript, I dreamed I'd invented a time machine that had materialised in the middle of the demolition operations on Corfe Castle instigated by the old Roundheads. The vibrations from the machine got more and more intense and I woke in a cold sweat to the sound of my bedside alarm.

Chapter 6. Entrepreneur

Poole Harbour

The morning after I had dined with Hans dawned with frost on the trees, the beauty of which passed me by. I was somewhat bleary-eyed having stayed up re-reading Charles's manuscript book on Dorset ghosts or 'time flashbacks' as he called them. I was dreading telling him what I thought of it − mainly negative, despite my discussions with Hans - and had avoided having breakfast with him. It had some interesting theories on how supposed apparitions might appear but there was little scientific meat there − no reproducible results and no attempts to disprove the theories. I'd have to be careful what I said to him.

I threw my laptop and briefcase into the back seat of one love in my life, my red 1965 Mustang open-top - Julie to be, I hoped, the other love - and lost in thought, drove to the Winfrith Research Centre, arriving with no recollection of my journey or any speed limits I'd possibly broken on the way. I'd brought the car back from my time in America two years ago despite the high cost of importation. Its deep throated growl and sexy lines made it all worthwhile. The tax I paid on the gas alone must have kept the Chancellor of the Exchequer very happy.

I slowed down in recognition of the bored policeman toting a Colt 45 revolver at the gate of the Technology Centre. Although I'd got used to seeing side-arms carried by security guards and cops in the USA it seemed incongruous in this rural setting. He scanned my pass in a short-sighted sort of way; heaven knows what mayhem he would cause if he decided to use his gun. He peered in a slightly less bored way at the car and waved me on.

The site, a mile across, was a long way from the nearest town and was part of the Egdon Heath, made famous in the novels of the writer Thomas Hardy. My destination was a large building that housed my equipment. The whole set-up used to be a nuclear research laboratory and indeed I believe there's a small amount of such work going on still, which is a bit of a nuisance as far as I was concerned. It meant I had to carry a radiation monitor and be checked out regularly to see if I glowed.

The building had been converted, when nuclear power went out of favour, to a laboratory where commercial research could be carried out with full security back up. Here, in deepest Dorset it was well away from that band of oil industry 'scouts' in Aberdeen and London who nose around for information to sell to competitors. Tight security was the order of the day for my research into oil production. The Bovington army camp was nearby if real security were needed.

Charlie Tizzard, my ageing laboratory assistant, met me as I went in. His broad Dorset speech to an outsider like me needed some getting used to, especially when he was excited. If you wanted anything, from genuine farmhouse Blue Vinney cheese that had been declared illegal by the EEC in Brussels, to venison steaks from protected deer that had allegedly committed suicide on a local road, Charlie Tizzard was your man. If you wanted anything fixed, he would do it through his local network of contacts. My biggest worry was that in the local Red Lion pub he would hold forth to his cronies on what he perceived I was doing. It would be tantamount to publishing it in the local paper.

"Hey Doc, they big ultrathings were dropped off in the stores last night," he volunteered. "They weighs a ton or two."

He meant the high power ultrasonic generators I needed for my test apparatus. They were designed to produce vibrations at frequencies very much higher than audible sound and at kilowatt power levels. They'd been imported from Germany having been supplied by my sponsor, Bakuoil, and had been cleared through customs the previous week. I planned to get them installed in the reinforced concrete cell that years ago had once housed a small research nuclear reactor, but which was now a convenient place for my work.

I told him emphatically not to try switching the generators on until I had checked them out. The power levels were such that not only would they remove the wax from your ears and fillings from your teeth, they were potentially lethal. I retired to my office to check up on my e-mail and make a few phone calls.

Three hours later having got bogged down in telephone calls to Summerfield Tools I was surprised to find that the crane and Charlie Tizzard had been working flat out. The concrete blocks, each weighing six tons, forming the roof of the cell, had been removed; the equipment had been put in position, the blocks replaced and the whole set up made ready for wiring-in and commissioning. Charlie Tizzard was standing by expectantly having already delivered farm-eggs to his customers and caught up on the local gossip.

To give a flavour of what these oil companies were paying me good money for, let me explain the background. In oilfields, the crude oil is contained between the grains of rock, mixed in with a liberal amount of salty water. Normally, only between three-quarters to a half of the oil is easily produced, the rest is stuck by capillary forces and is left behind. If means can be found of cheaply getting at this oil it could be very profitable.

Many workers had tried and failed to produce an economic method. This is where I came in. I was researching how high power, very high frequency ultrasonic energy in tools lowered down well bores might emulsify the oil and make it moveable towards the well bore.

What I had found at Oxford Engineering laboratory was that using pulsed high power sound of various frequencies in certain ways so that it penetrated a distance from the oil well I could in fact get an economic enhanced flow of oil. I could assist the effect by having a high power microwave generator installed in the block - a bit like a microwave cooker.

The kit, 'they ultra things' to quote Charlie Tizzard, was designed to use realistic power levels and to demonstrate its potential. I couldn't wait to get it started. The general idea was that if these tests looked promising Bakuoil would try it out in the nearby Wytch Farm oil field.

This sounds a bit over the top, but at great expense for my laboratory research I'd acquired a thirty-ton block of porous sandstone. This had been soaked in crude oil and water to mock up a volume of an oil-bearing formation normally found thousands of feet below the surface. There it was, with its own six-inch diameter 'mini' oil well drilled in its centre, and bristling with instruments inside the concrete cell. The idea was to make it as realistic a test as possible but avoiding digging a hole a mile deep at well pressures above two thousand psi.

By the end of the afternoon we'd got it all ready for the first tests. We cleared the general workers out of the cell and switched on the vibrations at low power and raised the pressure on the oil to simulate field conditions and watched whether the oil coming into the mock oil well increased. As expected the effect was there but small. What we had to do was slowly vary all the parameters to optimise the effect. This was going to take some time. I sent Charlie Tizzard off home as it was past 6.00pm, to engage in his nefarious activities and I settled down to run the new kit through its paces by myself.

Two hours and a lot of measurements later my stomach was telling me it was time for food and, whilst anticipating dinner at the Manor, my mind drifted back to Charles's theories about ghostly sightings. Hans had mentioned the words 'gravity waves' as a key to linking past events with the present. I had read about such waves. They were produced when massive objects such as stars were subject to explosions or collapse. As far as I knew nobody had yet been able to produce and detect them because they were so weak.

Even if one were able to vibrate a hundred-ton mass the varying gravitational effect on another mass a short distance away would be difficult to measure. There were reports of some research done at the physics laboratory a century ago where gravitation attraction between suspended masses had been detected.

I had had an idea however. If one could get a mass to resonate at the atomic level by using a strong oscillating electrical field in synchronism with the ultrasonic field, high frequency gravity waves might build up like light waves do in a Laser. Anyway I thought I'd turn up the power of my ultrasonic generator, turn up the oscillating electric field and see if I could get the whole block of stone resonating like an ultrasonic bell. There might possibly be the faintest chance I might see a flashback. Not very scientific I'm afraid.

I turned on the CCTV inside the darkened cell and wound up the power slowly. I got it up to maximum, but as I had thought there was nothing. The next step was to vary the frequency of the vibrations. The vibrations were well above the hearing threshold but I could sense the power being generated. Suddenly there was a crash, plainly audible through the metre thick concrete, and the power trips were released. I turned on the interior lights and saw nothing but dust clouds. Eventually they settled and the damage was evident. A large section of stone had disintegrated taking several of my monitors with it. What a fool I'd been. Just on the off chance of seeing a far-fetched time flashback.

Anyway, it was too late to do anything at that time and I decided to pack up and clear up tomorrow. I rewound the CCTV tape and went home with mixed feelings. I remembered I'd have to tell Charles what I thought of his manuscript. Julie would not be there. It would not be a happy evening.

****

The oil services industry is highly competitive. The large companies such as Schlumberger and Halliburton with turnovers of billions of dollars a year carry out their own research in their own laboratories or buy up other companies that have a technology they need. Smaller companies like Summerfield Tools have to concentrate on niche technologies too small for the big boys.

My invention fitted their requirements very well and I had worked hard to get them, partially to fund my research in return for an exclusive licence, were it to be successful. The government had funded the rest. I had made good progress in the preliminary research culminating in the experiment at Winfrith and had reached the stage where Summerfield engineers were designing an actual prototype. My work at the technology centre was supposed to provide optimisation data. I would now have to go to them and explain that the apparatus had failed and there would be a delay. I wouldn't be telling them how it broke. It was also the opportunity to see their prototype construction unit near Oxford for the first time.

Summerfield's representative engineer was Joe King who met me at the unit's reception centre. He could keep talking for hours, and frequently did, about his experiences as a rig engineer in far-flung parts of the world dodging bullets, guerrillas and unfriendly wildlife. I'd got to know Joe quite well over the last few months and it was largely due to his efforts that we had got where we were. He'd worked in the industry for twenty-five years and what he didn't know about down-hole tools wasn't worth knowing. He was a droll Yorkshireman who didn't hesitate to let anyone know what he thought. He considered all scientists to be head-in-the cloud boffins who had to be taken firmly in hand. When I told him I'd had a fairly serious mechanical breakdown at the laboratory he wasn't at all pleased.

"Just what I'd expect from a scientist, no bloody sense at all" was his comment. He let the matter drop but I knew he would expect me to get things moving very quickly or I'd never hear the end of it.

"What are you going to call the tool?" he asked, but then went on: "You couldn't do better than EROS – extra recovery oil service," he declared, glaring at me daring me to contradict him. . As the cliché goes you can tell a Yorkshireman anywhere but you can't tell him much.

"Why not, at least it's pronounceable, I love it," I said thinking that there wasn't much in common with the tool and the eponymous statue of love in Piccadilly Circus in London. Most tools are given apparently meaningless names – DST, RFT, Density tool, why should we make an exception now?"

He took me into the workshop where the device, about twenty feet long and four inches diameter, cased in shiny stainless steel lay on the floor in a support structure. To me it was beautiful, the result of months of work and possibly my ticket to business success.

"We're keeping it under tight security," he said. "In fact, most of the stuff here is of new development status. As you know we've arranged to test the tool in the Wytch Farm oil field in Dorset, next door to your laboratory so to speak. Bakuoil is the operator there and they think that the tool might be of use in their Azerbeijan Caspian Sea field. We've an engineering base on one of the islands in Poole Harbour, where it'll be made ready for use and stored. I'm proposing to have it taken there next week. I'm sure you'll have the data for me by then or there'll be bloody trouble. I'll have to get you security passes and arrange clearance."

We spent the next few hours going over the latest design data and a possible schedule for the oil field programme before going back to a hotel in Oxford for dinner and more anecdotes of his past.

As good as his word, a week later, Joe sent the tool by boat to the base in Poole Harbour. The harbour is said to be the second largest natural harbour in the world and has five main islands. Most people know the area as one of recreation – nature reserves and water sports, and are surprised when they learn that the UK's largest oil field lies underneath the harbour and Poole Bay. Up to three oil reservoirs are up to two kilometres below the harbour itself and the islands are ideally located for wells drilled from them to reach the oil. These wells and the production facilities were well hidden and most visitors to the area would not realise they were there. An ex-oil man who was willing to lease it to Bakuoil had owned one of the islands, Long Island. The island had been leased for the lifetime of the field to provide a secure storage place and also a drilling platform.

I drove into Poole where I met Joe at the quayside and we were shipped to the island. Security guards met us at the jetty, checking ID's very carefully before escorting us to the offices in the large house that had been the residence of the island's owner. There we met the local manager for Summerfield, Bahir Farouk. Farouk was a severe-looking Iraqi who didn't waste time before getting down to business.

"I want to establish a few ground rules first," was his opening remark. "First, you will report directly to me when you are working on these field tests. Have you experience of field work?" He seemed mollified when he learned that I had been a petroleum engineer with BP. He went on.

"Secondly, we have some hazardous materials such as radioactive sources here on the island. Also, because much of our work is commercially sensitive you must be accompanied at all times by one of my staff. That means Joe here. Is that clear?"

"As long as Joe and I can work on the EROS tool without unnecessary restrictions I'll be happy," I replied.

Ignoring me he went on, "Keep to the compound where we're setting the tool up. When you go to the wellhead for the tests you will be part of our team, which operates as a unit under the Bakuoil operational manager. The main concern is safety. Any infringement and you'll be off this island like a bat out of hell."

After leaving his office Joe said, "He really needs a course on charm doesn't he? Don't worry; he'll warm up when he gets to know you. Let me show you the EROS tool set up."

The wellhead being used for our tests was on the island itself. The oil was extracted through wellheads in groups round the edge of the harbour as well as on this island. Deviated wells had been drilled down to the oil, some of them stretching several kilometres under the sea. All the production wellheads were on the mainland and the company was very loath to shut these down for our use alone.

Our main purpose was to test the tool at the high temperature and pressure of the oil reservoir and incidentally to see whether any extra oil came out with the water when the ultrasonics generator was turned on. We were allocated one of the wells on the island, which would otherwise be used to inject seawater to maintain the oil pressure underground.

We were admitted to a locked compound by one of the security guards and I saw my technological baby being fitted out and undergoing its final tests.

"There's not much we can do until the fitters have finished, let me show you round the compound. We've other experimental tools here under test," said Joe.

From my earlier employment with an oil company I recognised some of them but was fascinated by the progress that was being made. Clearly, Summerfield was in the forefront of research and despite my worry about Farouk I felt the tests were in good hands. As we were going back to the boat, Farouk called us into his office. He seemed even more miserable than when we had arrived.

"I've just had some bad news for you and for us I'm afraid," he said throwing a fax on to the desk in front of us. "It's all there. The Egliston Corporation has bought out Summerfield, lock, stock and barrel. It doesn't say anything about Bakuoil but I've heard rumours Egliston is going after a controlling interest in them as well. I didn't think it would happen because Egliston's are new to the oil business. It's effective as from today. I've been told that for the time being we are to carry on as normal."

Turning to me he said, "I can't guarantee that we will continue with your development. It all depends on whether Egliston has bought the company as an asset stripping job or indeed what their agenda is. I hope I'm here to see you next time you're here."

Joe and I stared at Farouk in disbelief. All our work over the last few months might be wasted. Joe wasn't showing his disappointment.

"What a bloody bombshell" he burst out "Who are these buggers Egliston? They know damn all about oil!"

With that he left to do battle with his management. At least this would give me some time at WTC to double-check my data. It might however be the last work I would do on this contract.

Chapter 7. The Egliston Take-Over

The UK Financial Times had an article on the Egliston take-over the next day. Summerfield's had been a private company whose owners had accepted a cash and shares deal. The outright purchase of Bakuoil was Egliston's corporation's first full entry into the oil exploration and production business and was seen as a logical extension of his growing business empire in the old Soviet Union.

The City was still in the dark as to what strategy the new management would adopt. The analysts expected him to extend his grip on the area by still more acquisitions. The whole exercise had been carried out in secrecy.

The next day I had several telephone conversations with Joe who was really depressed. He felt that the new management would not have the commitment to R& D that had kept Summerfield in its leading position. After my encounter with Egliston and knowing his background I was hardly jumping with joy either.

All we could do was to continue working, waiting to see what the new management would decide. I was worried as well about the government attitude to the take-over. Would they cancel their contribution to my project? I spoke to the Head of Petroleum R & D and licensing in the Energy Ministry who assured me he saw no reason to worry.

"Egliston is regarded here in government as a shining example of entrepreneurial British industry, old boy. He is always giving MPs freebie trips to foreign parts. Besides, if they want to keep us sweet for any more licenses in the UK they won't do anything precipitately," was his comment. Finally I wondered what Julie's attitude would be. When I rang she seemed less bothered than I had anticipated.

"Egliston won't be concerned with a relatively small contract like yours. He heads up a large organisation and probably won't even hear about it. Don't worry, his organisation has more resources than the previous owners and it might even mean a better opportunity."

To my surprise I was invited the next week to go with the senior Summerfield technical staff to Egliston's head office near Trafalgar Square for a briefing. Joe and Farouk with about twenty others were there already when I arrived. We were kept waiting for an hour before being ushered into a conference room overlooking the River Thames.

There was plenty of time to admire the view before a tall thickset individual strode in. It was obviously not going to be a round table discussion. We were all seated in rows in front of a lectern where he placed himself. He scanned his audience for thirty seconds before pushing his notes aside.

"I know that guy," whispered Joe. "He left Halliburton's, the previous company I was in, under a cloud but nobody knew why. His name's Giles Campbell."

He had no time to say any more. Campbell, in a broad Glaswegian accent, introduced himself.

"Some of you will know who I am - I recognise a few faces here. I'm Giles Campbell and I am now MD of Summerfield. This meeting is going to be fairly brief and is intended to give you a broad-brush view of our strategy. I must tell you, gentlemen, that Summerfield will be run in the future concentrating on the requirements of Bakuoil alone and specifically on our investments in the Caspian area. We shall specifically be cutting back on the R&D unless it is aimed directly at our immediate needs. Some of the long term and speculative work will stop immediately unless there are contractual reasons why not.

We in Egliston's intend to expand our oil holdings in the old Soviet Union and there will be specific problems to be addressed pertinent to those oil and gas reservoirs. There will therefore be a large change of emphasis. We intend to bring in staff with direct experience of that region and we shall have to let some of you go."

He went on for some time detailing the plans for the developments. Finally, he threw the meeting open to questions. These were hostile in general from staff that could clearly see their time was numbered. Campbell scribbled in his little black book but gave little away. Joe asked about our Wytch Farm EROS operation and was told that it had yet to be decided.

Campbell terminated the meeting after half an hour. A general air of despondency had settled on our group. Joe himself said that he would be searching for another job, adding that he had already approached Schlumberger, the largest oil services company in the business.

As we were about to enter the lift on our way out a secretary came up to me and asked if I was Dr Aldborough.

"Please will you follow me," she said. Joe looked at me quizzically and I shrugged my shoulders.

We went up several storeys to the penthouse suite. I was shown into a small but well fitted-out room and asked to wait. Coffee was offered and I browsed through various company glossies spread across the coffee table. The secretary had said simply that one of the senior executives wished to see me.

After ten minutes the door opened and none other than Egliston himself stood there. He was even more intimidating on his home ground than on our previous encounter.

"Good day, Dr Aldborough, we have met before at Reise's college dinner. Follow me."

His office also overlooked the river, in fact it looked down on the Houses of Parliament as well, a symbolism that I'm sure must have occurred to Egliston. His secretary poured me another cup of coffee. He signed some documents while I sat waiting to see what I had done to deserve this special treatment. His secretary then glided away.

"I was impressed by your performance at that college dinner. It was just right for that audience, the right mixture of academic content but with an awareness of commerce. I was particularly interested because I was in fact at that time in the late stages of planning the purchase of Bakuoil and Summerfield Services."

His voice was as I remembered it when Julie and I had wandered undetected into his estate. It was a voice that assumed there would be no dissent to what he was saying. His chiselled face exuded authority. His blue eyes had a mesmeric quality and I had some difficulty clearing my thoughts. Those eyes were focused on me and I felt them staring into my skull. I started to thank him for his comments but he cut in quickly as though I hadn't started to speak.

"I was taken by your enthusiasm for a project which could be very profitable according to my technical men. It could make you a lot of money. It could give our operations a commercial edge over the competition. I had the same feeling about the commercial potential of a radar project when I first met your tame Professor Reise over sixty years ago. There's another thing. I'm a good judge of character and I believe that your slight reticence hides ruthless ambition for financial success. I believe you are prepared to cast your net a lot wider than science and engineering. You could do that with me and make a lot more money. Tell me again what you want out of this collaboration with my companies."

I wasn't sure what hidden depths he was referring to but he had struck a note. I was an only child who was somewhat introspective and who had been bullied. I didn't form relationships easily. I enjoyed success and the fame it brought. I didn't like being told what to do and valued the acclaim of my peers. Yes, I liked power and people looking up to me. I did try to hide these feelings but this fellow had noticed it. What did he want me to say?

I decided to go in aggressively, pointing out the advantages to the Egliston Corporation and my wish to build up my business into a world-class service company. I saw Egliston as a company with its wide spread of business interests as an excellent partner for me. I even impressed myself and was afraid I might have gone over the top.

After five minutes he cut in and said,

"Thank you Dr Aldborough. I have already decided to continue funding your project and plan to use it if testing goes well in one of Bakuoil's Azerbaijan offshore fields. I trust you are happy with that. It will be necessary however to have your co-operation across other areas that I am not at liberty to talk about today. My company's development plans must be safeguarded."

"I shall be offering you a generous retainer in addition to the research funding for various technical services that are of a sensitive nature. In return I shall expect complete confidentiality and involvement. I cannot elaborate further except to say that if you make a success of this I anticipate a rosy future for you within my organisation or indeed as CEO of a separate company. I shall send you a confidentiality agreement and contract in the next day or so."

He stood up, terminating my audience and assuming that I would agree said

"Give my secretary your address and mobile number. Good day, Dr Aldborough". His handshake was vice-like and was a foretaste of his way of operating. I had the presence of mind to leave my WTC address rather than the Manor address.

****

I rang Julie at her London bank on the off chance she could meet me for lunch. I had to talk over this development with somebody, particularly Julie. She was fortunately free from a meeting at that time and we met in a pub filled with City traders and other city workers near to the imposing edifice of her bank in the City. It was hardly a cosy atmosphere, noisy and brash. I would have liked to work up to what I wanted to say in quieter surroundings. We only had half an hour before her next appointment and I dived straight in with Egliston's proposals.

It was a mistake. Her face became steadily grimmer as I progressed particularly talking about the 'other unspecified confidential commitments' referred to by Egliston.

"You've a bit of a problem haven't you?" was her first comment. "You know enough about Egliston already to know he's a first class shit. Hans doesn't like him, Dad doesn't like him and neither do I. We say he is unscrupulous and power mad. I can see that you need to keep the EROS project going, but to get into bed with his company and become part of the evil empire is a different thing altogether."

"Why are you so enthusiastic about it? If you had stuck up for an independent role as an exploiter of your EROS tool you might have lost control of it, but what the hell! Why didn't you press for continuation of the present setup where you exploit things with your own company? The bank would have supported you. Maybe you should know more about those other mysterious assignments he talked about before you enter this Faustian contract."

" Anyway, the decision is yours. I begin to wonder though whether I like this side of Harry Aldborough I'm seeing. I'm due in the conference room in ten minutes. Let me know what you decide," She rushed off before I could reply to the diatribe.

I decided to stay and have another drink or two. Life is difficult. After all the strife I'd been through to get the project underway I didn't want to see it die. I knew Egliston's invitation sounded a bit like a Faustian contract as she said: selling my soul to the devil. I knew my relationship with Julie could suffer.

To tell the truth, however, I was sorely tempted. There would be of a lot of money to be made and he had appealed to my basic money and power instincts. Julie appealed to my basic sexual instincts as well as being a friend. What the hell should I do?

I thought I'd better make a few other calls. Egliston hadn't mentioned the other funder of my research, the Oil Ministry. I phoned the Department to speak to the Under-Secretary running the Offshore Supply Office. He knew, of course, about the take-over by Egliston but was surprised at the speed at which things had gone. He had anticipated that my project would be cancelled despite his earlier bullish remarks. As I expected, he didn't give me a straight answer, saying that his Department would be talking to Bakuoil anyway in respect of tax and regulatory matters. He did say, however, that I was to carry on assuming that his funding would continue, but surmised that if Egliston wanted the project he might be happy to see the back of what he considered to be government interference in his affairs and supply all the funding.

Back in Dorset, I decided to tell Charles right away. He is the type of person with whom one can deal directly without beating about the bush.

"I know what Julie will have said, and my attitude is much the same," he said sadly. "I, on the other hand won't hold it against you if you decide to join Egliston's empire. It is clearly in your long-term interests provided he doesn't get you involved in anything illegal. It might be prudent for your sake, however, to leave here and find other lodgings. It wouldn't do you any good if Egliston were to find out you live in the Manor. I know I shouldn't say this, but I enjoy your company and you have been very tolerant about my time flashback theories. I know Julie thinks a lot of you despite her 'I'm an independent businesswoman attitude'. However, she is mulish and don't be surprised if you don't see much of her if you go ahead with the contract."

I decided not to ring Julie. I would leave her to stew for a day or two.

Life was getting complicated enough without emotional tangles. I drove to Winfrith where I felt a little more in control.

Chapter 8. Emotional Conflict

I decided to bury myself emotionally in the laboratory by repairing the damage to the equipment I'd caused trying to get a time flashback. I would make a decision about the Egliston job after a day or two and after I'd seen the draft contract. Charlie Tizzard at the laboratory had done a good job repairing the instrumentation and generally clearing up. The damage to the block of stone in particular wasn't as serious as I had thought and I figured that it would still provide the right environment for my tests. Charlie Tizzard was relishing the thought that I had made a complete cock-up of the apparatus and would no doubt be holding forth to his mates how that high-flying scientist couldn't be trusted to run things without Charlie Tizzard's guidance.

"Oi don' know what you was doin' t'other night, but you did a rare old job of It." he commented. "I been lookin' at the video tape from the camera inside t'cell. Reckon that you turned the wick up on that ultra thing a bit too much. Strange thing, I bin looking at the CCTV tape and in the flash of the explosion oi could swear as there's a man there. Faint he be, but unless oi knew differently oi'd think that you'd locked someone in there. If there was I don't know what you did with the body." He grinned stupidly and went away.

Amid the chaos of that evening I hadn't scanned the tape and went straight to it. Charlie Tizzard was right. There did seem to be an outline of a man fleetingly as the rupture of the rock occurred. Could the tape still have had some signal from a previous recording? It was there for only a second but there was the remote possibility that I had excited a flashback. Could it be a quarry worker from fifty years ago when the virgin block of rock was still in the quarry?

I resolved to have another attempt but this time I'd be more careful. I put this thought and that of Egliston and his offer in the back in my mind for the rest of the day whilst Charlie Tizzard and I got the experiment ready for the already delayed optimisation tests for the EROS tool.

I was surprised to find Julie was at the manor with her father when I returned. She'd been at the bank's regional office in Poole and had taken the chance to have another to talk about the Egliston offer. She and Charles had obviously been having a heart-to-heart talk and he didn't say anything but glanced at me and shrugged with a wry smile on his face. This time she seemed to be approaching things less emotionally than at our quick meeting in London, I thought.

"Harry, I've thought a lot about your offer from Egliston. From the bank's point of view, they've lent you lot of money and the deal would safeguard its investment in your company. I assume you would wish to carry on with that. I'm wearing two hats. As the Bank's investment portfolio representative I must clearly support the continued collaboration with Bakuoil and Summerfield even though they have changed ownership. If you don't take Egliston's offer, the window of opportunity for your invention could be missed. My Head of Department agrees and formally as project banker I must advise you to go ahead."

I was beginning to think I was out of the emotional wood but she was still standing, arms folded, glaring at me, but she then changed tack. "Personally I think you would be making an error and not just because I think he's a shit. I ask myself why he should be so personally interested in your invention. In his scale of interest it's chickenfeed, with due respect to you. There must be something else that's driving this. It might be because he was dazzled by your performance at high table, do you think so?"

She looked very cute now that her adrenaline was flowing. I must say though, like her, I was baffled as to the reason for his interest but I wasn't going to admit it, especially now she was being sarcastic. I decided to dig my heels in because I thought I was right.

"Your bank's right, the chance to use my invention in the Bakuoil Sea field is a chance I don't want to miss. The tool is ideally suited to the geology of the field. If it's going to work anywhere it will work there and I'm not going to question Egliston's motives. If I see it's going the wrong way I'll quit." I said with more confidence than I felt.

"So be it, I assume you'll be moving out of here, it would be wrong from both Dad's and my point of view and I may say, yours, to stay. Egliston's done a great wrong to Dad and you've said yourself that he is probably up to his ears in smuggling or something. This will affect our personal relationship as well and I think we'd better not meet again until I'm ready." This was a side of her personality I'd not seen before.

The conversation didn't go on much longer, anyway it was somewhat one-sided as I realised whatever I said would be wrong. She went back to her office saying she would be in touch about the project. Charles was clearly upset, just as I was.

"I can arrange for some other place for you to stay in the village of Wool if you like. Regardless of your working for Egliston I'd like to continue our friendship." he said sadly.

I thanked him and accepted his offer. I was upset about Julie's attitude but I wasn't going to give way.

Chapter 9. Summerfield under change

A telephone message from Campbell was waiting for me at the laboratory the next day saying I was urgently required at the Summerfield site in Oxford and asking me to drop all work and get there as soon as I could. I'd been expecting a development like this and rang his secretary to say I'd drive there immediately. Presumably they would have a contract for me to sign and we could discuss the next steps.

I was admitted to the manager's office on arrival. It wasn't George Ellis, Joe King's boss whom I'd got to know quite well, who was sitting in the chair. The individual was of Germanic appearance, square faced with a crop of fair hair and the build of a rugby back player. His face was pockmarked and brown like a pickled walnut. His demeanour quickly dispelled any idea of familiarity. He shook hands with a grip of steel.

"Let me introduce myself, my name is Johann Gluck. As of yesterday, George Ellis is no longer with the company and I've been assigned to this post for the time being. I'm from Egliston's central office. George felt that his future would be best served elsewhere." he said with a slight sneer "Please sit down."

I was taken aback. It was George who had been my champion with the company and but for his enthusiasm it wouldn't have got off the ground.

Gluck shuffled some papers on the desk.

"Lord Egliston seems for some reason to be enthusiastic about your project and I can assure you that our technical and financial backing will continue. I feel, however, that the pace of the project needs to be pushed with some extra vigour and I've told Joe King to get things moving. There's been too much time spent messing around when the tool appears to me to be ready for a large-scale trial. I'm making arrangements for the Bakuoil side of the project to be brought forward and I want a number of your tools made".

I protested that I thought the development hadn't gone far enough to fling us into a full field trial, but he stopped me in my tracks.

"You must get used to the Egliston way of working. Here one person takes responsibility for a project and things move, either that or he moves. You are responsible as technical manager for the technical success, the operational tests and the deployment in our oilfields. You will have authority to do whatever is necessary. I shall be touching base with you regularly. We will take risks and it will be your decision. I'm arranging for you to get a visa for visits to our bases in Baku and possibly Pakistan and Tehran. You will have to make a preliminary visit to Baku to liaise on the support facilities at that end. I expect that to be in about four weeks' time."

"By the way, this is your new contract. You will see it is with the Egliston Corporation and not Summerfield so that it covers work here and with Bakuoil. It is as you see very generous financially. However, you will probably gather that working for the new management will place more demands on you than before, including non-technical matters. I would be grateful if you will read it through carefully and I'd like it back within three days."

The interview was over very quickly and I was dismissed to seek out Joe King. He was in his office sorting through his papers.

"Hi Harry, I hear your project's got the blessing of our new owner. That's about the only good thing so far.

Several of our managers and one or two engineers have been given their marching orders because their faces don't fit. Tell the truth, I'm thinking about going before I'm pushed. What happened when you went to see the great white chief?"

I ran through the story and said I'd just been offered a contract that I intended to read through that afternoon.

"Beware an English aristocrat bearing gifts" was his response. "I hear your project is under high priority and that you're scheduled to go to Baku as soon as the tool is ready."

I was grateful to hear that Joe was still on the project and was prepared to stick with it at least for the time being. I hadn't read my contract yet but I knew I would sign it. It would be the opportunity to forge ahead and although I didn't like Egliston, I thought I might learn something from his organisation.

We sat down and worked through our programme for the next three weeks that would hopefully get us to the stage where we could carry out a test in the Wytch Farm oil field. I then sat down to go through the contract. The good news was that my intellectual property rights would not be affected. Bakuoil would retain preferential rights for the use of the instrument for two years.

The bad news was that I would be required to carry out unspecified work over a two-year period associated with the exploitation of the tool and other duties that the management might require. I would effectively be an employee of the company with only two months each year available for my own purposes. Confidentiality was highlighted as a key requirement. The salary was large and with a substantial bonus at the end. In retrospect I should have asked more questions than I did, after all, viewing it dispassionately it was over the odds for what the company would get out of it. Anyway, I signed.

Chapter 10. The Egliston Corporation

Harry was, of course, not privy to the following events.

The residents of Kingston village were used to the sight of sleek black chauffeur driven cars with darkened glass windows squeezing their sinister way up the narrow main street of the village and then heading out on the narrow road towards the coast and Egliston Hall. Most didn't give the big cars a second thought because of the increasing numbers of affluent people who had bought second homes in the vicinity. Executive helicopters on their way to the Hall might briefly cause people to look up as they clattered past, but there again they might not.

Even so, that day in April two years ago was exceptional in the number of visitors to the estate and locals were driven to speculate what was happening behind the screen of security. In truth, the villagers knew very little about Egliston Hall, as most of the information in circulation was only speculation.

Locals were not employed on the estate. All staff members were outsiders recruited in London or abroad; many were foreign nationals and all were told by their employer not to fraternise, as part of his obsession with security. This irked the landlord of the Scott Arms who would otherwise have rapidly gleaned valuable snippets of information as well as hard currency from staff refreshing themselves at the bar. Of course, rumours were rife on what went on in the place, ranging from tales of international chicanery to stories of wild orgies. The high security fence surrounding the estate and the security surveillance equipment were very effective in maintaining privacy.

Today's agenda at the hall covered a major event in the year's calendar of the Egliston Corporation and there were definitely no orgies, although there would be some corporate chicanery. Lord Egliston himself was chairing a series of meetings of executives concerned with developing business in countries that had been part of the Soviet Union but were now in principle independent, such as Georgia, Azerbaijan, Armenia and Uzbekistan.

Most of the business to be discussed that day was legitimate by the standards of international business; nevertheless Egliston's executives knew how to avoid seeing things that didn't concern them. If certain commercial doors opened they would take any business opportunities that came their way and they didn't enquire too deeply into the reasons why. There were also off-balance sheet items that managers did not probe into if they wanted to keep their jobs. During the day there would be another smaller meeting that would be kept firmly secret from the other executives. James Frobisher, ex-SAS, ex-mercenary and now businessman was the primary attendee at this meeting.

One item for discussion in the plenary meeting was the Corporation's move into oil and other businesses in the Caspian area countries through the proposed purchase of the Bakuoil Company and the Summerfield Tools Company. Strategically, petroleum exploration and production were seen as key lead areas for expansion. The West's oil supplies were unhealthily dependent on the Middle East with all its political uncertainty and the growth of fundamentalist Islam. The old Soviet Union countries were not free of uncertainties but the stabilising influence of Russia was still there and judged to be beneficial. Though the political risks were large, so were the potential payoffs. The region could overtake production from the Arab countries in the years to come and Western companies both large and small were elbowing their way in.

Clearly the Egliston Corporation had to be part of the action if it was to become a major player in the region. A foothold would also be useful for a host of other opportunities for a resourceful enterprise.

Egliston kept an iron grip on the management of the Corporation and gave no indication that he would ever release it despite having prepared his son Nicolas, now aged fifty, for leadership. He had sent him to the physically tough Scottish public school, Gordonstoun, where he had thrived in the Spartan conditions. He did not make close friends and became close only to those he could use in some way. His mother had died when he was ten and even at that time he showed no emotion at her passing, becoming more and more self-sufficient as he passed through his teens. Eventually he had left the school in his third year by mutual agreement having become 'persona non grata' through aggressive behaviour towards other students and lack of dedication to academic work.

He was nevertheless very bright and his father brought him into the business and for two years put him into various ground floor jobs round the corporation before sending him to the Harvard business school. Since that time he had served at various times as hatchet man to his father, CEO of several of the Corporation's businesses and now as business development director for the Corporation. He had a reputation as a hard man, emphasised by his sharp features, large frame and apparent inability to smile.

He had never married, not because of his sexuality-which many questioned in secret-but because he believed it would prejudice his effectiveness in business. Egliston himself had pressed him to make sure he had a son and heir to his title, to no avail. He had been very successful in extending the scope of the Corporation and had recently made expansion eastwards his forte. No one knew his inner thoughts but he must have been desperate for his chance to take over from his father and, if he was at all human, would be getting frustrated at the delay.

He had prepared the strategy paper under discussion that defined how the various business thrusts in progress linked together with the Corporation's existing work and where he expected things to develop over the forthcoming years. His presentation was persuasive and effective, bringing in the CEOs of the various businesses involved adding their views as required. Lord Egliston was of course behind the plan, otherwise it wouldn't have seen the light of day, and he showed Nicolas no favours in the discussion, seeming to delight in belittling him in pointing out weaknesses.

Nicolas was as sharp as his father, however, and was quite capable of fighting back. The other executives knew well to keep out of the crossfire between the two.

The main thrust of the paper was that the proven, probable and possible oil and gas reserves owned by Bakuoil were large and operations were already under way in Azerbeijan, Iran, Kazakhstan and Uzbekistan, providing a good cash flow. Bakuoil was also a leading partner in a consortium to build a pipeline through Georgia to the Black Sea. Most importantly the main shareholders in Bakuoil wanted to sell. It was a marvellous opportunity for the Corporation.

The idea of buying the Summerfield Tools Company was commercial security. Egliston didn't want the large Schlumberger or Halliburton Service Companies, which had most of the oilfield service contracts round the world and which would otherwise be the main contenders for the business, to know what was happening in Bakuoil. The meeting eventually endorsed the paper after Egliston had over-ridden objections from some executives concerning the financial and political risks involved.

At the close of the discussion, much to everyone's surprise Egliston announced that he had anticipated the outcome of the meeting and that arrangements for the oil deal had been finalised and would be announced within days. It was a clear demonstration of his control over his empire.

The whole business agenda was completed after four hours of discussion and most of the executives were dismissed to their limousines and helicopters, leaving just the two Eglistons, Frobisher and two of his staff. Frobisher looked like the ex-Sandhurst-trained officer he had been.

Tall, sharp-faced and with smoothed back dark hair, he had a commanding presence. He had left the army with the rank of Colonel after duty in many areas round the world. Some of his service had been with the SAS in the Middle East and the USSR, about which he would not talk, but was in fact the main reason for his employment by Egliston. He was the CEO of Wealdon Security Executive, one of the smaller and less well-known parts of the Egliston empire. Its function was in practice to provide military expertise and equipment to clients who were or would be in the position of helping other parts of the Corporation in its business.

In the past help had been given to certain African countries on the understanding that mineral exploration licences would be forthcoming once the Executive had successfully done its work. Most of its work was, however, with recognised regimes and it had avoided adverse publicity for activities that were clearly illegal although some sections of the left wing press had voiced criticism.

After dismissing the secretary who had been minuting the earlier discussions, Egliston opened the meeting.

"You now know the strategy for expansion, gentlemen. We have to talk about how we might lubricate the process and give ourselves a competitive edge. Frobisher, you heard the comments made earlier in the day about political risks. I am depending on you to make sure everything runs sweetly for the Bakuoil enterprises. Your men must make sure that the Georgian and North and South Ossetian governments are given all help subduing these dissidents who are sabotaging the progress of our pipeline. We are in the middle of a deal on royalties with the governments, the outcome of which is subject to your success. Give me your assessment"

Frobisher gave a succinct report in the clipped tones that seemed to fit his persona, standing easily facing his audience without using any visual aids. He exuded confidence and his assessment seemed to satisfy Egliston judging by the absence of interruptions.

He concluded by saying:

"As you know, the oil exploration work in Georgia was held up by interference from the local Mafia as well as some rebels supported by Russia but it's on the move again now I've reached an accommodation with them. They are too strong to oppose and co-operation is more effective. We shall also have to help them getting certain goods into and out of the country. They link up with the Mafia elements in the Russian Federation that are helping us get restricted goods into Azerbaijan and Iran. We shall have to make agreed payments to them for certain services.

"I told you about a small security problem we had. There were two geophysicists who became involved in one of our mopping up operations with the rebels and who threatened to report to the British Consulate in Baku. Fortunately for us they had an accident in travelling back, reportedly ambushed by rebels who had a dislike of Westerners. We shall not now be troubled by them," he said with a cold smile.

Egliston interrupted;

"You mentioned the 'restricted' goods, Frobisher. A key element in getting into new countries, particularly certain Islamic fundamentalist ones: is supplying them with uranium235 and plutonium. It will be desirable to store the material back here in the UK whilst the negotiations are under way. I don't want to hear about problems, I'm sure you will avoid political embarrassments. You know I'm prepared to spare no cost in your enterprise so don't complain about lack of resources. This oil company take-over will give us excellent cover to take delivery of the advanced military equipment and fissile material from dissidents in the Russian Federation and get it to our customers round the world.

"Our new MD for Bakuoil is Ivan Klanski and you will work with him to set up a foolproof route for the goods."

Turning to his son Nicolas he said, "It's up to you and Frobisher to set up these covert operations. It will be necessary to put key people into the oil operation who understand our business and know how accommodate your activities. Let others go. I don't want any trouble so make the departures amicable if possible. Of course if necessary you have freedom to use whatever means you wish to achieve our ends"

Nicolas Egliston then gave a detailed account of the plans for the next six months including the way in which

Bakuoil resources would be used in the smuggling operations. He introduced his two companions who had not contributed to the discussion.

"These two gentlemen whom I have worked with in earlier years will not appear anywhere on our payroll. They will in fact be employed by other companies but will act as our ears in competitors' or other organisations."

In conclusion Egliston said, almost as a throwaway remark,

"By the way, I plan to bring in an engineer called Aldborough. He has some good technology for which Bakuoil has a licence and if my judgement is correct he might well be useful for other purposes once we get him compromised. Nicolas, I've spoken to you about this. I don't want you near him for the time being."

Nicolas nodded and asked who was handling the British government angles.

"I'll handle those idiots in the DTI: they seem to think they own the British oil companies. We might even get them to help us with the governments in the Caspian but I doubt it." snapped Egliston.

The executives were all gone within the hour leaving Egliston to himself. He sat staring out to sea as the sun faded in a red splash of colour framing the Island of Portland in the distance and allowed himself a congratulatory smile on the success of the day.

He then rang for his valet to get his clothes and a shower ready before a helicopter journey to Oxford where he was due to have dinner at high table at Stirling College in recognition of his endowment of a chair in engineering studies. He would meet that old fool Hans Reise and the DTI minister. It would be interesting to bait the minister about government's lack of help to exporters in the Far East and to gloat over his take-over of the Bakuoil Company without their knowing he was even bidding.

Chapter 11. Whitehall

Harry would soon become aware of the following occurrences.

Brigadier 'Sandy' Rushton pushed back his chair, and deep in thought, glanced out of his window overlooking Horse Guards Parade just off Whitehall in London. The preparations for the Trooping of the Colour celebrating the official birthday of the Queen were in full swing with troops practising their marching routines in the bright sunlight and the band competing against the noise from the construction of the scaffolding for the spectator stands.

The tall, fit thirty five-year old Scot with thick red hair greying at the temples and a face prematurely lined by exposure to extremes of temperature, wind and rain was in thoughtful mood. Although a man of action, he had a deserved reputation as something of an intellectual as well. He had been assigned for the last two years to liaison with MI6 since returning from active service with the SAS. The name on his door implied he was responsible for strategic studies with NATO, a cover role that in practice filled only part of his time. His particular brief was monitoring the proliferation of high tech weaponry and Weapons of Mass Destruction (WMD). To that end anything that happened in Iran, Pakistan and the Caspian interested him immensely.

He turned away from the pageant of colour filling the Parade and his eye fell again on the Financial Times report of the take-over of Bakuoil and Summerfield Tools by the Egliston Corporation based in London. That Corporation was one that he had been watching for some time following reports from contacts in the Caspian countries that it had been developing business ventures over the last two years with a variety of organisations, some of which he knew were involved in terrorist and smuggling operations. He had no direct evidence that the Egliston Corporation or anyone within it was involved, but its growth in Africa and now in Asia over the years had been ruthlessly executed and he would not be surprised to find a link.

The part of the organisation that he had watched most closely was Wealdon Security Executive, a company that provided military services mainly to unstable third world countries as well as providing mineral and oil exploration services. An old acquaintance of his from the SAS, Colonel Frobisher, had set up the company with finance from the Egliston Corporation and this had sent alarm bells ringing in Rushton's mind because of Frobisher's time spent as a mercenary. Why Egliston's had a need for such a business was not immediately clear but he could guess. So far as he knew they had managed it very carefully such that no international scandals had emerged.

He went back to his desk and rang a contact in the Department of Energy for background to the take-over.

"It took us by surprise" was the response. "Egliston himself is a golden boy as far as some of our leading politicians are concerned because of his British base and because of the well chosen consultancies and travel opportunities it offers to those with influence in government and the opposition. He has some of the politicians eating out of his hand. He, or at least his son, now seems to be putting a lot of marketing effort into expansion into countries of the old Soviet Union like Georgia, Azerbaijan and Kazakhstan. The oil reserves there could rival those of the Saudis in years to come and he needs a foothold. On the other hand there's scope for what one might call under the counter trade, but that's your field old boy"

It was indeed. Rushton decided to find out more about the take over. He knew that the area around Azerbeijan had a staging post for drugs and high tech items from the old Soviet Union, smuggled from disaffected and greedy scientist and military sources. That might be part of Egliston's hidden agenda. Perhaps it would be a good idea if he ran a check on the personalities involved. He might be able to recruit informants in the companies taken over and see who was being injected from the Egliston organisation into them. His man in the British Consulate in Baku was Terry Colliston who had already identified a number of Egliston men who had been active in the country. He picked up the phone again and dialled on to the secure line to Baku to give Terry some more instructions.

****

When I returned to the technology centre the day after my interview with Egliston in his London office I was surprised to find a well-built red-haired individual with military bearing sitting in my office reading my Times newspaper. I noted that he had had the cheek to do the crossword. In such a security conscious outfit as Winfrith

I would have expected personally to authorise any visitors wishing to see me, but before I could ask who the devil he was he stood up.

"Apologies are in order for this intrusion but it is important", he said with a precise authoritative voice. "My name is Rushton, Brigadier Rushton."

He did offer his hand but didn't offer a business card.

"I work with a government external security department advising on trade matters. If you wish, your WTC security man will vouch for me."

"I think I will check if you don't mind" I replied and rang Patterson, our security officer, a retired major from the Marines. His reply was positive, in fact he strongly advised me to take Rushton very seriously indeed. I offered Rushton a mug of coffee and somewhat bemused by this James Bond charade asked him to tell me what was happening. While waiting for the kettle to boil he pulled some papers out of his briefcase, arranged them and sat down.

"Incidentally this is not an official meeting and I must ask you not to tell anyone that you have seen me." Rushton went on. "I wish to make you aware of a few matters that concern me and will no doubt affect you whether you like it or not. I am aware of your background from your dealings with the Energy Ministry and your research into oil recovery. I have been given to understand by them that the Egliston Corporation has taken over sponsorship of your work after the takeover. They also tell me that you might be offered a personal contract with Egliston's for duties not necessarily restricted to the oil work. You may not be aware of what you might be letting yourself in for and I'm here to tell you a little of what concerns me and indeed, to seek your help"

By this time I'd got over my initial surprise and composed myself. The best plan was to let him talk until I had a clearer idea as to what he wanted and what else he knew about me.

"Can you confirm that you are likely to be formally under contract to Bakuoil to provide services in their Azerbaijan oil fields?" he began. I nodded, wondering how much more he knew.

"The Egliston Corporation generally operates quite legally in the countries where it works. In fact government ministers highly regard it as a model of British enterprise and Egliston himself as a great ambassador for the country. However, in some countries commercial practice has rather flexible limits euphemistically speaking and Egliston's makes full use of these. Most other foreign companies do anyway. That is something that doesn't worry me too much as long as our government is not embarrassed or the country's security compromised. They went very close to the wind recently when their subsidiary, Wealden, gave military assistance to a rogue state in Africa in return for mineral concessions for one of the Egliston companies. We have suspicions that he is sponsoring activities that are definitely illegal but so far we have no hard evidence. It could happen in the Caspian as well and I'm sure from what I've seen and read about you, Dr Aldborough that you would not wish to be associated with these activities"

I was not surprised to hear that Egliston might have his finger in illegal activities. He was a first class bastard in private life and would be even worse, I suspected, when commerce was involved. He had apparently succeeded in keeping his nose clean for decades, assisted by his tentacles inside the government and the civil service. However, I could see no way in which my technical role could get involved in cloak and dagger escapades.

"Brigadier, I appreciate your concern, but I've seen nothing that would deter me from going ahead with this contract. The people I've worked with in Summerfield's certainly are unlikely to be involved in activities such as you describe. I'm scheduled to go to Baku shortly for planning exercises and you can rest assured I shall stick to technical work" I said somewhat pompously.

"So be it, I've warned you," he murmured, handing me a card that simply had his name and telephone number on it. "You will be dealing with ruthless professionals who would not hesitate to compromise or even kill you. I have two things further to say and then I shall go. First, the telephone number on that card is on a secure line in Whitehall. You can speak to me directly. In Baku, if you have need, ring the consulate and ask for Mr Terry Colliston, the trade attaché. Confide with no other person in the consulate. Secondly, in order to set your alarm bells ringing you might wish to ask discretely about Bob Denver and Dave Ross whom you might have come across when you were with BP. They recently approached one of my associates in Georgia where they were prospecting for oil. They got involved with Nicolas Egliston out there, and phoned Colliston saying they wished to blow the whistle on what he was doing. Unfortunately they disappeared before he could meet them. We assume that they are dead."

He wished me good day and went. I didn't at the time take this cloak and dagger stuff too seriously. I reasoned that the staff changes that had happened at Summerfield and Bakuoil were to be expected with a new management and were unlikely to be sinister. My views on Egliston personally had been obtained through

Charles and Julie and would be coloured. He was a ruthless character who would take business shortcuts. So what, that didn't make him a criminal! Anyway I savoured the fees I expected from my employment with Egliston's.

Chapter 12. Back to the workbench

A day or two after my conversations with Charles and Julie I'd moved out of Norden Manor into Woolbridge Manor Hotel, a large old stone building converted into a hotel near to the technology centre. Sitting next to a picturesque old bridge across the River Frome well away from the nearby village it would suit me fine. It was a little gloomy but was comfortable and near to my work. The proprietor told me it had achieved somewhat questionable literary fame by being the house in which Thomas Hardy, the novelist, had based the wedding night of Tess of the D'Urbervilles. He also told me not to damage the old bridge outside as there was still an old sign threatening any transgressors with transportation to Australia. That really was a threat! I truly was in deepest Dorset!

Another manifestation of deepest Dorset, Charlie Tizzard, appeared at my office door soon after I arrived at WTC.

"You ready for the experiment Doc?" he ventured in his Dorset accent. I was. There was little time left to optimise the tool operation before my journey to Baku.

The day went smoothly and we'd made a lot of progress optimising the operating conditions before it was time for Charlie Tizzard and the rest of the general workers to go home. I decided to stay on and start the analysis of the results to get all the data to Summerfield's as soon as possible. I also had in mind to see if I could investigate whether any sign of the flashback I suspected I'd seen could be reproduced without causing another piece of the rock to disintegrate. At least it would take my mind off Brigadier Rushton and his conspiracy theories.

I knew now how far I could take up the power levels without going outside the envelope of safe operation. I intended to vary the settings of vibration frequency, electric field and power level. I turned out all lights inside the cell and turned the CCTV on to high sensitivity. Two hours passed. I was about to pack up as I'd seen nothing of interest when I tried doubling the frequency of the ultrasound, way above anything I would use for the oil recovery usage.

Almost immediately the vibration sensors showed a large response. I must have hit a resonant frequency in the system. On the screen a faint glow appeared near the rock as though it had an aura. Then there was a sign of movement and a very faint figure walked past the rock. When moving he was a blur but when he stopped I saw he was dressed in a cap and had his trousers tied with string just below his knees.

I could feel my heart pounding. It was just like the photographs in black and white one sees in books of the thirties and forties. He then walked away and I saw nothing else apart from the glow, for at least half an hour. I was thrilled to the core. This was it! I'd most likely seen a genuine flashback across a gap of some sixty years. I wanted to tell somebody immediately.

The implications were enormous. History would be an open book, crimes could be solved, and I could make my fortune! Hunger was forgotten and I spent the next few hours scanning for further signs of life, and was rewarded with images of sundry workmen passing by the rock. In one case one appeared to relieve himself against it. The images were not clear but maybe that could be improved.

Hans Reise was in Oxford when I rang to tell him the news. He was incredulous to say the least and after a great deal of persuasion said he would drive down the next day. My main worry was keeping my discovery quiet until I understood it better and I'd got Hans's opinion. I certainly wasn't going to tell Charles until I was absolutely sure. I locked up the CCTV tapes – I didn't want Charlie Tizzard to see them - and went back to Woolbridge Manor to sleep on the discovery. The work on the oil recovery method was driven right out of my mind.

True to his word Hans arrived the next morning eager to see for himself. He was clearly excited and was chattering ten to the dozen.

"Harry, it is vital that you keep all this completely secret. Does anyone know but you and me?"

I assured him that I had no intention of making a fool of myself by telling the world, until I understood what we had found.

"No, no my boy, my worry is the dead hand of government. This has such wide implications that I would expect the military to put the whole project under a secrecy blanket. You'd lose control over the whole thing. It happened in the 1950's with the pioneers of laser development and they lost out to others who tried an approach outside the security blanket. Quite apart from the government there are some unscrupulous guys out there, you could get yourself killed."

He was like a small boy with a new toy and I left him to it while I made sure that the laboratory assistants were given work to do well away from the equipment.

To my relief I was able to get flashbacks similar to the ones I'd seen the previous night and Hans was spellbound. I couldn't drag him away.

"I'm really excited about your findings. The implications are enormous!" he enthused. "There've been many reports of sightings of what one might call flashbacks, many of them reasonably well verified. I've read in military briefings, of World War 2 planes being sighted over the Fylingdales nuclear attack early warning station, which haven't been detected by the radar, for example. In other case there were sightings where there was the presence of high power radiation"

|If you've described it to me accurately you might indeed have accidentally generated gravity waves of sufficient power to couple the present with a past time briefly. Perhaps you hit a natural frequency of the molecular structure of crystalline rock in that chunk of stone in your laboratory so that the whole lot was vibrating in resonance. With thirty tonnes of rock vibrating in tune the gravity wave generated might be of sufficient power to create a link to past events in the vicinity of that mass of rock. But why you should home in on that particular time in the past, I don't know."

Hans had obviously done some thinking about how we could work under secure conditions. He clearly wanted to take an active part.

"Harry, I have a proposal for you. I'm reasonably wealthy as I mentioned before and I would like to finance your research. I'd do any necessary theoretical work. I am convinced that gravity waves are a key feature of the process that produces flashbacks. I believe that although gravity is very weak in relation to electric and other forces in the dimensions we are familiar with, in other dimensions necessary in theoretical studies, it can be strong. In that case gravity waves can be amplified. We would have to find ways of generating gravity waves using transportable equipment," he explained. "I know that you're under pressure with this oil project of yours but we can subcontract some work such as instrument development".

In a sense I was relieved that Hans was so interested and willing to throw himself into understanding what we'd found. I had to carry on with the oil work because it was so commercially attractive but on the other hand the potential for this time shift project was so tremendous that it needed to be investigated straight away. Hans seemed utterly trustworthy to me and had the resources.

We parted after he had made me promise to tell nobody about the discovery. He would set up funding and make time in his schedule. We discussed ideas for making a portable tool for generating gravity waves so that we could get away from the constraints of the need for tons of rock.

A week later I'd finished the tests needed for the first phase of my oil company contract work and sent off the results to the Summerfield laboratory where they would make up equipment to be used in a Wytch Farm oil well. This design and construction work would take about two weeks, leaving me with some time to follow up the gravity-wave work.

Hans, who had been pressing me to join with him in following up the time flashback work asked me to visit him in Germany where he had a house in which he used in the periods outside Oxford University term time. His home was in Heidelberg, the ancient German university town.

I decided to drive there using the Channel Tunnel link rather than fly, forgetting quite how far it was. Eventually I arrived late in the afternoon, driving through the old town with its picturesque Old Bridge across the river Neckar, and with the castle dominating the hillside. My destination was on a road, the

Schlosswolfsbrennenweg, skirting the hillside above the castle. Hans's home turned out to be a large Gothic style stone house at the end of an upward winding driveway flanked by conifers.

Hans was there to greet me.

"What do you think of my house? It is one of the things I value most in my life because it is where I was brought up and it is where I can think clearly. I come here whenever I can. Did you have a good journey?

He led me round to the imposing front of the house looking out over miles of forest.

"Isn't that beautiful," he went on" Here one can recharge the batteries of one's soul ready for the next term at Oxford. There's no point in lacking home comforts. I've an efficient housekeeper to feed us."

The main living space was a split-level oak-lined room festooned with old sporting trophies and with a roaring fire in a three metre wide hearth and it was there that we settled down after I'd been shown my room. It reminded me of the Manor at Norden but that was at least three centuries older.

I was rather tired after the long drive and it was very relaxing to sit

and catch up with university gossip before dinner. Hans brought me up to date with his thinking on my discovery. He was even more convinced that gravity waves played an important part in linking the radiation field at the present with the past. The stronger the waves and the more precise their frequency, the stronger would be the flashback and the ability to 'tune - in to a specific time. He then went into a discussion of quantum theory that lost me completely.

The hausfrau, Katrina, turned out superficially to be rather forbidding and didn't speak English. My German was rather poor and I couldn't raise a smile from her with my attempts to be friendly.

"Don't bother." said Hans sympathetically "She makes me feel like a boy at school as well. She is marvellous with the cooking and runs the place like a military operation." He went on: "I'm planning to spend four weeks here before I to go back to Oxford. We have to agree on a detailed research programme to understand what you've found and to improve the process. I'd like to look at the theoretical side of the subject, particularly the quantum implications, and I'll be spending most of my time thinking and using the Heidelberg University's supercomputer. I can get you an introduction to the engineering workshops and the library. What are your plans?"

If Reise was correct about gravity waves being responsible for the time flashbacks it would be necessary to find a way of generating them more efficiently than getting a sonic resonance with a massive block of stone and my ultrasonic generator. I knew that there was an international astronomical project under way to detect gravity waves generated by exploding stars and black holes. These relied on detecting movements of the order of distances between individual atoms. The wavelengths would be much longer than those involved in the quantum processes we were interested in, according to Hans. The flashbacks we had produced at Winfrith were associated with mega-or giga- Hertz ultra-sound frequencies.

Hans had suggested a method. A large single crystal of a heavy metal derivative such as a depleted uranium metal or salt, at liquid nitrogen temperatures, might be persuaded to vibrate in a single quantum state when driven by a combined magnetic-ultrasonic power source.

I hoped that by producing a situation where gravity waves from atoms all reinforced one another and were amplified, I could succeed. I'd already had some ideas on this subject and believed I had the answer. Instruments known as lasers and masers produce powerful coherent beams of light and microwave radiation.

What was needed was a device analogous to a laser that instead of generating a powerful pure beam of light would do the same thing for gravity waves. At certain frequencies the waves would be amplified and emerge as a beam.

Hans agreed with my ideas and I spent the next week refining the design of a test generator and visiting companies in Germany that might construct a trial wave generator. Hans got together a team of technicians from the University low temperature physics department to test the ideas and if successful to assemble a prototype generator. I would try and keep in touch by e-mail. Hans also had a network of contacts that would be very helpful in applying the necessary pressure to suppliers to complete the work to the tight schedule we had set.

I was left after a couple of weeks, before the results would start to come in and decided to ask Julie if she would take a few days to sample the delights of the beautiful old town of Heidelberg with its 'Student Prince' musical memories. It might heal our fractured relationship. I also needed to talk to someone other than Hans about the flashback discovery.

To my surprise and delight she agreed, having a break in her hectic schedule and, surprisingly thought it a marvellous idea. Two days later we were strolling across the Alte Brucke after doing full justice to Weiner schnitzels and cherry pies in a beer hall near the university before going to a 'son et lumiere' performance at the castle.

We hadn't spoken much about my dealings with Egliston, partly because we didn't want to spoil the magic of getting together again and decided to put any discussions on the back burner until I found more about the job I was supposed to do. What we did talk about was the flashback project. Julie was very thoughtful as we sat drinking a glass or two of schnapps after the schloss festival.

"I can't understand why Hans wants to keep so quiet about this, you really should be getting a patent." she said. "He's spending a fortune on it. I estimate he's committed at least half a million euros with the programme you've agreed on. He can't be so wealthy that he is doing it for pure science. If I were you I would be looking over my shoulder at what he has in mind and whether there is anyone else involved."

"I think he is genuine." I replied, "His standing in the academic and quasi- government circles is second to none. He's very well off and has no family to spend it on or leave it to. This is Nobel Prize stuff potentially and I know he would dearly love to have such an award. Besides I think he is right about the dangers of government interference."

"I beg to differ." she said, "You're too close to him to see clearly how his mind really works. I'm also very suspicious about how he acquired so much money from legitimate interests."

She had me worried because in her banking job she had developed an intuitive insight into the motives of entrepreneurs whatever their apparent credentials. She would make a good Poker player. Nevertheless I'd valued

Hans as a father figure for many years and I had developed a trust in him. I agreed to keep my eyes well open and we dropped the subject.

Later in the evening after Hans had gone to bed we talked over our differences and under the influence of a bottle of spätweis wine we both took on a benign view of the world. Julie pulled me into her bedroom as we passed it and under the soft fetterbett our relationship took on a much more intimate turn. Julie's libido left little to be desired and she gave the impression that her repressed feelings were no longer - well – repressed. We made love until daybreak appeared through the curtains.

I was surprised to learn from Katrina the next day when I persevered with my German that the house had once belonged to a minister of the Third Reich and had been acquired from his family by a company with which Hans was associated, only ten years ago.

Why hadn't he spoken about this, I wondered; he had intimated it had belonged to his family for a long time? I resolved to question him discretely about it when the time seemed ripe; perhaps Julie was right to be sceptical. The next morning Hans was eating his breakfast outside in the early morning sunshine when Julie and I joined him.

"This is a beautiful house is it not?" he asked, not I suppose, expecting an answer from us. "With this view of the Neckar below and the carpet of dark green forest for kilometres into the distance I wouldn't want to be anywhere else – even Dorset."

With that he turned to Julie and said, "You probably have the same feelings for your home with its family history that I have of this house. Like yours it has had sad times. You probably wonder why. It is because this was my family home up to the late 1930's. We were a Jewish family and my father was a banker here in Heidelberg. I was sent to England when the Nazis began their pogrom but my parents stayed here, hoping that they would be spared as my father had strong international links that would be useful to the Reich. They were wrong."

"Even today I don't know what happened to them. Neither do I know what happened to our family art treasures. There is a link to your uncle, the Lord Egliston, which one day I shall tell you about, but not now. I tell you this because I can see that you, Julie, do not trust me."

Turning to me he went on: "I'll keep you informed my boy, there really isn't much you can do here until your wave generator is delivered. Bear in mind the need to keep all this quiet."

Julie looked at me with a raised eyebrow but said nothing.

We flew back home the next day.

Chapter 13. Professor Reise's business associate

Some considerable time later Hans told me about his duplicity with respect to the financial backing of the project. This was the gist of what he said.

The secure telephone in Lord Egliston's penthouse office overlooking Nelson's statue in Trafalgar Square rang, bypassing his secretary. "Yes?" he growled.

"Reise here," came the reply. "Are you alone? I'm ringing about that scientist Harry Aldborough whom I recommended to you for project funding. I was glad to hear you've taken him into your organisation. I'm sure you won't regret it."

There was a long pause before Egliston replied.

"I've got reasons of my own for taking him on and I'm taking your word for the profitability of this improved oil recovery research of his. Anyway I'm throwing him in at the deep end. He's off to Baku next week. What do you want? I thought you wanted our business activities to be kept quiet. The more you contact me the more chance there is they will leak out. Your information on good scientists and research projects has been very profitable so far but there are limits."

"Two things." Reise went on, ignoring Egliston's reproof. "First, I advise against exposing him to any covert side of the Baku operation of which I'm sure there is one. I don't think he would fall in line."

"That's my problem not yours Reise. He's getting paid a lot and by the time he realises what's going on it will be too late for him to back out. What's the second problem?"

"Not a problem but a possibly exciting discovery. There's the remote chance that he has stumbled on a way of getting visual flashbacks of past events. It's a remote possibility and it will cost a lot to develop. The commercial implications will be obvious to you. To take it to the next stage will need about half a million dollars. Are you willing to back my judgement?"

"You really are on a wild goose chase now! I'd have thought you would have known better. Your time-travel literature has softened your brain you old fool." Egliston paused. ", I'll forward the money to the usual Swiss bank account. Keep me informed; I can't spare any more time to discuss this".

He rang off, "Bloody scientists!" he said shaking his head.

Reise smiled, he had his own agenda. The prospects for success were high in his judgement. He needed Egliston's money for the project because his own business dealings had cut down his liquidity. What he did not want was for Egliston to get control of the invention. He also pondered that he might be on the way to a Nobel Prize. The demonstration of gravity waves and the possibility of producing a device that would amplify them, just as had happened with the Maser in microwave work, would make him famous. One might be able to make a gravity wave telescope that would detect supernova invisible to other instruments. In a few weeks he would report to Egliston that the project was a complete failure because he knew from previous experience that Egliston would accept that. He relied heavily on Reise's judgement on the outcome of research, which in the past had been very good. It was essential to keep the whole project secret until scientific papers could be produced that put him well and truly in the forefront of the discovery.'

Chapter 14. Azerbaijan

Maiden Tower

While I was with BP I'd wanted to visit their Caspian Sea projects but the chance never came. I was now looking forward to going out there because that's where much of the oil industry action was taking place. It would also be the focus of oil production in the future rather than the Middle East. The opportunities for my EROS project would be great there. I also had a schoolboy desire to see a place where the West meets the East: silk routes, Genghis Khan and all that.

Baku, the capital of Azerbaijan, sitting on the shore of the Caspian Sea, is at the centre of the regional oil activities with both major and minor oil companies having established bases there. It is also a gateway between West and East for a whole range of commodities that move with a minimum of government interference following the break up of the Soviet Union. As a result there is an atmosphere of the Wild West but with advanced technology mixed in.

Summerfield had booked my flights to Baku via Moscow. The first leg by BA to Sheremetyevo airport in Moscow passed without incident, but I found after an interminable delay through immigration and baggage check, my onward flight from the Vnukovo airport South of Moscow had been cancelled. I also found I'd been booked by the agents into the 'Mez' hotel, seemingly a poor man's Regency Hyatt, overnight.

In the crowded bar after a meal alone, I unloaded a few of my dollars to drown my frustrations and struck up a conversation with a square-faced Russian businessman who introduced himself as Pietr Roscoff. He seemed for all the world like the president of yesteryears' Nikita Kruschev, bald headed, diminutive and extremely garrulous.

"You're going to Baku also?" he said in impeccable English after hearing about my troubles. "So am I. We'll share a taxi to take us to the airport. I'll take you in hand and make sure you get there with Russian efficiency," he said with an attempt at humour.

We chatted and drank many shots of vodka for a couple of hours and when I departed for bed I had the uncomfortable feeling that I'd been interrogated. I realised I knew next to nothing about him. He, on the other hand, would now know everything about me including the colour of my socks.

True to his word, early the next morning, before I had any chance to get anything to eat, because none of the restaurants seemed to be open, he buttonholed me again. We got a taxi round Moscow's concrete potholed orbital road to the regional airport.

On arrival, starving, I made the mistake of eating from the snack bar in the main terminal. I found later from Pietr that I should have used the VIP lounge. Obviously Russian food bugs had got at the sandwiches so that my stomach was in total revolt during the flight, griping in concert with the bucking of the aircraft. Allegedly vodka would kill off any bugs according to Pietr. The absence of a working seatbelt and refreshments seemed minor problems in comparison.

During the flight Pietr carried on with his verbal probing, which was now, more penetrating and I began to wonder whether our original meeting was such an accident. On arrival in Baku he managed to pull sufficient strings to get us into the elaborately carpeted government ministers' waiting room at the airport while Summerfield's car was sent for. During the flight he had admitted to being ex-RFU but was now a businessman. As we parted, the car having finally arrived, he took me aside and with a completely different approach said earnestly,

"Dr Aldborough, a word of wisdom to you. You are a clever man. I strongly advise you to stick to your research. This is a wild place and your activities might not meet with my country's or other people's approval". With that, he disappeared leaving me wondering what the devil he meant and feeling completely uneasy.

The driver of the car sent to meet me also offered me a slug of vodka as a cure for my stomach. It was the last thing I wanted – did everyone think vodka was the answer to everything? The drive to the city past a forest of derelict oil derricks sitting in pools of thick black oil didn't improve my appetite either.

Baku itself, once we had passed the ubiquitous statue of Lenin, was a strange mixture of pre-communist elegance, communist concrete, and modernity.

Once in the Hotel Moskva I turned the air conditioner on full and tried to sleep away the churning in my stomach, despite the loud mechanical racket. I was eventually woken from a broken sleep by the room telephone some nine hours later. My contact assigned by Summerfield was in the lobby to greet me and show me the sights, a mandatory exercise for foreign newcomers. Farouk al Tehrani was an amiable energetic Azeri of Iranian origin who took me to his home for breakfast. Life took on a rosier hue as my gastric problems receded.

"We must call in the company office first to get your pass. The rest of the day is free because the key men are in a meeting all day with a guy from your Egliston's head office who is bothered about the security or lack of it round here. I'll give you the standard Intourist tour. First we'll go to the memorial to the twenty-six commissars you Brits murdered here years ago, but don't worry, we forgave you long ago." he said with a grin.

The day passed quickly with visits to the 'everlasting flame', prehistoric rock carvings and the town itself. In the evening we ate at a converted caravanserai in the old town and drank a sizeable amount of vodka toasting the project, our families and the world in general.

"A little advice," said Tehrani finally when he felt we knew each other reasonably well. "You will find some impatience with your project amongst the local crew. The new manager of both Bakuoil and Summerfield set-ups is Klanski, brought in with the take-over. He just wants to keep the oil flowing, and he accepts your test programme because head office has told him to. Also, there are new projects going on here, which are under wraps, and it doesn't pay to ask too much. Stick to your project and turn a blind eye to things you might see out of the ordinary"

I was beginning to wonder what I'd stepped into because Farouk wouldn't expand further. Everyone seemed to be giving me advice and keeping quiet about what was really going on.

The next day he took me to meet the manager Ivan Klanski, a humourless Russian who clearly wished I was anywhere but in Baku. He had been put in place by Egliston and would presumably be fully engaged in any illegal activities that might be going on.

"You're the whiz kid Brit I suppose," he growled, with a forced attempt at civility. "Tehrani here has the job of wet nursing you through the next three weeks. We've a number of projects going on that involve other companies. These are tight commercial security jobs and I don't want you poking your nose in"

Turning to Tehrani he said "I'm holding you responsible for our friend here. I want to know if there is any trouble, as soon as it happens. I also want a daily report on the project"

Again, to me he said, "Your equipment has been sent to the rig factory south of here along the coast. You are assigned rig area 12. There are security guards on twenty-four hours a day, so you should have no problems with thefts. You will, however, have trouble if you wander into other areas, so don't. Now I'm due at a meeting. Good morning"

Tehrani had a beat-up company Toyota pickup truck in which we drove out of Baku along the semi arid coast. After a half-hour's drive we arrived at a factory originally built by the French years ago to mass-produce offshore rigs for the old USSR oil companies. It had only ever succeeded in producing at half design rate and now a large part of it was used as a maintenance area supporting a whole variety of offshore operations.

After Tehrani had expertly navigated some petty bureaucracy I was formally allowed to go in and eat at the canteen although Tehrani advised me against it. I hadn't eaten breakfast and was starving but after my experiences at the airport I took note and stuck to hot foods.

Afterwards we made our way to the rig bay 12 assigned by Klanski and to my horror I found my equipment was dumped in a heap and covered in brick dust from some building repairs nearby. We were supposed to have two process workers assigned by Summerfield's to safeguard things but of them there was no sign.

"Everything seems to be running normally," remarked Tehrani with a wry grin.

After losing my temper with the factory supervisor and helped by Tehrani, a posse of sullen fitters was pulled together to assemble my equipment in another test bay well away from the noise, dust and activity.

The next few days we worked from dawn until late to get it working and coupled to the actual "tool". This EROS tool looked from the outside like a simple 4-inch diameter stainless steel tube but contained a complex array of sensors and the ultrasonics/electric wave generator itself. In use it would be lowered down the well production tubing to depths of up to three kilometres into the oil-bearing formations.

Late one night while we were waiting for the computer to process some test information I wandered around the factory to see the massive steel assembly lines for the drilling rigs. I hadn't really taken Klanski's warning seriously. Tehrani had gone into Baku to collect some tools.

Whilst I was in one area filled with Russian-made equipment that I found interesting, there came the noise of a shutter door opening about fifty metres away. I turned and saw a lorry being driven in. I pulled back into the shadows; suddenly aware of the risk I might be taking if Klanski were to be believed.

The lorry contained ten so-called "tools" used for making measurements down well bores. As each was unloaded a worker used a radiation counter to check it before it was taken into a secure shielded cell.

At the time it didn't strike me as particularly strange as radioactive materials are used in some of the tools for measurements of the rock properties. What was strange was the presence of two guards with automatic weapons at the ready. When the chance came I slipped back to our compound. A minute later one of the guards I had seen burst in waving his Uzi machine pistol.

Whatever language he was speaking I was under no doubt about the drift of his meaning. I was taken outside and told to sit down with my hands on my head.

"You will wait there. If you move you will be shot" he said in broken English. There was a discussion between the guards with much waving of arms and glances at me. One guard drew his finger across his throat somewhat ominously, after which the other guard led me to a motorboat. It was clear to me that I was probably going to be killed and disposed of before I'd even started my job. He had seen me and clearly thought I was some spy.

Tehrani, who might have sorted it out, wasn't there to help. As I got to the boat I saw my chance. The guard had expected to find someone in charge of the boat and made the mistake of turning away from me. I hurled myself at him to get him in the water and we both fell off the jetty.

When I came to the surface I saw that his gun had fallen on the stern of the boat, which was nearer to me than him. I started to swim but my leg had become tangled in a rope and I couldn't break free before the guard reached the gun. To my horror he let off a three shot burst that passed over my head. There was then another burst and I thought I'd had it. I hadn't: the guard was trying to get back on shore where Tehrani stood, holding an automatic pistol. He had shot the gun out of the guard's hand.

He delivered a flood of Russian invective and after a deal of argument with the guards he led me back to the compound while the guards sullenly returned to their work. It was a first taste of the potential violence in this area.

Tehrani said nothing until we were back in our compound.

"I perhaps did not emphasise enough the need to keep out of things that are not your concern. It's lucky I returned sooner than I had intended. I've said to you before that since the take over by Egliston's there is a continual threat of violence. Clearly there is some illegal activity going on. Here it is best to keep away from other Egliston projects and not ask questions. I have a family and I don't see or hear anything I shouldn't"

The next day we were summoned to Klanski who told us in no uncertain terms the error of our ways. Someone had been quick on the telephone. He also told us that offshore tests to measure the oil formation properties were scheduled later that week and that a Summerfield boat would take the kit directly from the factory to the rig twenty kilometres offshore. We would follow later.

An e-mail from Rushton was waiting for me when I eventually logged on to my laptop asking me urgently to collect, in person, a message he had sent via the British consulate in Baku. Later, having found my way across the town to the consulate, I was directed to the trade attaché's office. The guy behind the desk seemed a man of few words and after making sure I was who I said I was, handed me a letter, which he told me not to take away but to return to him when I'd absorbed its contents. The message read:

"Klanski, the general manager is a new man brought in since the take -over. Our contact reports that he is probably a linkman in smuggling operations. There are reports of boat traffic, which is unlikely to be oil related, operating between Kazakhstan, Uzbekistan and the rig you will be working on. We believe that U235 is being smuggled out of the old Soviet Union through Summerfield's facilities but have no idea where it goes or how. Keep a log of all traffic and of any non-oil activities. I also have reports that someone has been asking questions about your background in Dorset and the work you are doing there. I have told the WTC security to monitor your equipment 24hrs a day. To my knowledge your links with Charles MacLean have not been discovered"

I solemnly returned the note to the official who put it into his shredder.

I was beginning to get worried, first Roscoff and now this message. Everyone seemed to know what was happening but me. At least Julie was not involved yet.

I decided to see more of the sights while I had a few free hours. Baku, seen superficially, appears like a Mediterranean resort with a long promenade sweeping in a wide arc round the bay. It's only when you get closer you see that it isn't a place for holidays and with little provision for the tourist. A small funicular took me down to sea level, for which I had to purchase a five Kopek piece, which was solemnly taken back at the bottom. The locals were friendly but uncommunicative and I was given a cup of tea at a sea front café for which payment was waived. Eventually I arrived at the Maiden Tower, an ancient defensive castle and part of the visitor's Intourist circuit.

There was a crowd of children dressed in white uniforms with red neckerchiefs, milling around outside. I was, however, alone as I went up the three flights of stairs to the top of the tower.

The panorama was quite breathtaking and I was leaning over the battlements looking out over the Caspian Sea when a sixth sense made me turn round.

A man was running at me, presumably to push me over the edge. I don't know why I reacted so quickly but fortunately I did and managed to use his momentum in a Judo throw, which sent him on to the stone courtyard twenty metres below. In double quick time I rushed downstairs to see my erstwhile assailant. Before I'd had time to look a hand grasped my elbow, pulling me away.

"Dr Aldborough, I suggest we leave here quickly." It was Roscoff. "The Azeri authorities can be rather tiresome when dead bodies are involved"

The man had fallen on the side away from the tower entrance and nobody else seemed aware of what had happened. I decided to take his advice and left quickly with Roscoff. We went into a large hotel lobby nearby.

"It would appear that someone has taken a dislike to you," he said after he'd bought me a drink and parked me at a table. "I warned you that this was a wild place. I don't suppose the attack was personal, more likely it's because you're British or work for Summerfield or both"

"Who are you and who are you working for?" I stuttered beginning to get over my adventure. "I guess you aren't a businessman?"

"Perhaps not," he said. "From my point of view you are a scientist, you work at a nuclear research establishment and are very much financially involved with Summerfield. You are in Baku at a time when the Russian government is concerned about illegal smuggling activities involving some oil organisations in this region. I don't know who tried to kill you, but it seems to me that someone has put two and two together and made you an agent in smuggling of nuclear materials"

I had to play ignorance.

"I'm sorry to disappoint you, Pietr, but my role here is purely commercial. I'm using the nuclear research place in England as a commercially secure laboratory to do my oil research. I don't know the first thing about nuclear materials technology. If your organisation cares to look you'll find that my research is partly government funded and genuinely oil related".

He looked at me in a disbelieving way.

"Maybe, you might or you might not know anything about this. I don't want you to have an accident. Some other people are not so discriminating. I shall however be watching you like a hawk"

With that he rose and left me to my shaky thoughts. Outside across at the Maiden Tower, police cars and an ambulance had arrived. My assailant was apparently dead judging by the stretcher with a sheet pulled over his face.

Clearly I needed to bring Colliston up to date with developments. I hadn't envisaged this sort of hostility to me personally. Rapidly I went to the consulate where I demanded to see Colliston. He was there, fortunately, but was not amused at what had happened and at my unannounced visit to see him. I assured him I had taken action to shake off any followers on the way to the consulate, at which he shook his head

"This is most unfortunate. We were hoping that you would be accepted as a bona fide oilman and not be a target for any of the ungodly people round here. Someone has linked you to Summerfield's smuggling.

Then there is this Roscoff whom I know well. He is still with the Russian RFU. They are presumably just as concerned about the smuggling as we are. I'll check with the hospital to see whether they know who the man was who tried to kill you. It could be that the Russian Mafia is involved and wants to send a warning shot across Summerfield's bows. In the meantime you must not tell anyone about your adventure. Another thing that bothers me is that you don't know the first thing about surveillance. It wouldn't surprise me to find that you have been followed here. You had better work out a plausible excuse for this visit"

I thought the word 'unfortunate' was a little mild but he then suggested that he might organise someone to watch my back now that I had become a target. I left him in no doubt about my feelings on the matter.

Despite what Colliston said about keeping quiet I told Tehrani about my scrape with death. He was very concerned.

"Two geophysicists, Denver and Ross, working on one of our projects disappeared some time ago in Georgia. Rumour has it they were killed because they had come across some smuggling activities. We don't know who did it. I advise you not to go out alone from now on."

This was the second time I'd heard of these two unfortunate geologists. In the next two days I did precisely what Colliston had advised. Most of my time was spent offshore or at the rig workshops and I avoided any sightseeing. When the time came for me to return to the UK it was with a sense of relief I boarded the plane for home, this time via Istanbul rather than Moscow – thank goodness

Chapter 15 - Whitehall puts on the pressure

I was not aware that Rushton had been busy on my behalf. He had spent an hour on the phone to Baku being briefed by Colliston on my experiences and on his investigations into Egliston Corporation activities in the Caspian region.

The situation was getting more complicated at a faster pace than he'd anticipated. The appearance on the scene of the Russian RFU in the form of Roscoff was not surprising, bearing in mind that Azerbeijan was still considered by them to be in their backyard despite the breakdown of the Soviet Union.

Rushton was cheered that Russian Intelligence was at least concerned about the smuggling of fissile material from the area rather than turning a blind eye to it. Whether that concern was prompted by the need to stamp on nuclear proliferation or competition to its own sales he did not know. Certainly there was evidence from elsewhere that Russia was selling nuclear technology to pariah states like Iran.

He decided to get Colliston to make contact with Roscoff to discuss mutual interests, like keeping me alive. Egliston's men were obviously competing with established local illegal activities and presumably it was the Mafia who wanted to send a clear message to him to stay clear by staging the attack on me.

I had now to be brought on board and to be made to realise the risks I was now facing. It would also be prudent to give me some instruction on how to look after myself. As soon as I returned to the UK I would be briefed before I met anyone else. Rushton picked up the phone to speak to the immigration authorities.

As soon as I landed I would be taken to a secure office at Heathrow, where Rushton would be waiting and this time I would be told clearly and forcibly what was required of me. 'Bloody scientist' I imagined him saying!

****

When the BA flight from Istanbul joined the stack of aircraft above the Home Counties waiting for air traffic control to give the go-ahead to land I began to relax. The sight of green fields, hedges, and cars down below driving on the left hand side of the road was welcome.

My reception in Baku had been more exciting than I had anticipated and I was looking forward to picking up things at home where I'd left off. I was desperate to see the progress with the gravity wave generator, to seeing Julie and to feeling safer than I had recently. As the engine revs picked up and as the pilot announced the imminent landing I settled back in the seat.

I quickly retrieved my baggage from the carousel – for once it was one of the first to appear - and hurried to immigration control, expecting to be waved through on the nod. The official studied me closely, scanned my passport and with an inscrutable face asked me to step aside, nodding to a colleague nearby.

"Will you follow me, Dr Aldborough?" he said quietly and refused to say more.

I was led into one of the fluorescent tube lit boxes that pass for offices at Heathrow to be met by Brigadier Rushton himself.

"Welcome back to the UK, Dr Aldborough." he said grimly. "I think it would be in your best interests if we had a heart-to-heart chat, please sit down". There was certainly a change in his demeanour since we last met.

At once all the trauma of the past three weeks came back to me and I meekly did as he asked. He did offer me a plastic cup of lukewarm coffee.

"When last we met down in Dorset I think you didn't really take on board what potential danger you could be in by rubbing shoulders with the Egliston crowd. You now probably have a different view. I hadn't expected people to be trying to kill you but that's par for the course in that area." He pursed his lips wryly.

"I've had a good briefing from Colliston on the situation in Baku and I'd like to hear what you propose to do now. You will probably accept that Bakuoil under its new management is engaged in clandestine activities. Your own work might be perfectly legitimate but you will realise now that others don't necessarily see it that way."

Rushton fixed me with his steely blue eyes.

"A man has died because of you, as the Mafia sees it, and they will be after revenge, quite apart from getting at the Egliston Corporation. Even if they realise you are not involved with nuclear smuggling they will still view you as a legitimate target in their struggle with Egliston. Of course Egliston himself will be unlikely to lose any sleep over your safety if you become a liability rather than a technical asset to them. You will essentially be on your own. I want you to understand clearly the situation you are in"

I was expected to grovel at this stage.

"The fact that I've had two attempts on my life hasn't escaped me. I have to continue with my oil

130

contract or I will probably lose any prospect of exploiting my invention. What's your suggestion?" I said "The fact that you're here means you've something in mind".

"Correct." he said allowing himself a small smile. "I want you to continue with your Bakuoil project because you will be in a prime position to spot any smuggling. We don't have a better chance of nailing Egliston. Your continuing safety does, however, concern me. We know about the Russian, Roscoff, from the past and look on him as part of the opposition but in this case he is an asset. His interests appear to be the same as ours. Colliston has spoken with him and he will probably be able to help more consistently in watching your back when you return.

"That won't be enough to keep you in one piece however. I want to educate you as much as I can in tradecraft, such as making sure you are not followed and evading people trailing you. You should also learn the rudiments of firearms even if you don't carry one. I will get the SBS people in Poole to give you some training over the next few weeks. My main concern as you will realise is getting intelligence on what is happening inside the Corporation particularly with regard to smuggling of fissile material and high technology; where is it going and where does it originate"

"You will tell nobody what you are doing for me and that includes Miss Julie MacLean and Charles MacLean. If they don't know anything they can't let information slip. Colliston will continue to be your contact in Baku and in Britain I shall be available. I know you are being paid a high retainer by Egliston's because they want you to keep quiet about any activities in the organisation whilst at the same time benefiting from your invention. They will attempt to compromise you so they can keep you quiet. I want you to accept any such attempt and make them believe you are reliable in that respect."

"I don't have much choice, do I?" I said with resignation.

"Good man, you'll be contacted in Dorset in a day or two" he concluded

He didn't offer me a lift into London, and I made my own way to Egliston's office near Trafalgar Square where I'd been told to report to Campbell as soon as I returned. I did look to see if I was being followed but saw nothing. If what Rushton had said was correct that didn't mean I wasn't being followed.

****

I felt very scruffy as I went up to the Egliston reception desk as I hadn't shaved for twenty-four hours. The receptionists obviously thought so as well and directed me to an executive washroom where I was assured shaving facilities were available. Campbell wasn't immediately available and I was asked to come back in an hour. Clean and polished and fortified by a double espresso, I presented myself back at the desk at the appointed time.

"Come in, Harry," was the response from Campbell when his secretary ushered me in, a much more civilised response than on the last time I was here. The permanent scowl lined into his features belied his attempt at geniality.

"I shall expect a written report from you on the field tests as soon as you can. I've spoken to Klanski and got the main gist of what happened over there. I understand you've got the operating system set up and the local people know how to get things ready for the field operations. However, Klanski also said there had been a few other problems that had given him some grief and I want to know from you directly what happened."

I had to be careful what I said. As far as I knew, nobody in Bakuoil knew about my contacts with the Consulate. It was solely of the problems Farouk and I had had at the rig factory they had been told.

"We had a brush with the some security guards who were part of Bakuoil's operation while we were setting up the kit. They would have killed me unless Husseini hadn't come back unexpectedly. I objected strongly to Klanski – it certainly isn't what I signed up for."

"The armed guards are unfortunately a necessity in that region." said Campbell. "You'll have to accept that. There is an illegal trade in oil field tools that the Mafia runs. I'm sure Farouk advised you not to ask too many questions. The Azeri government can be very tiring and it is in our interests to restrict what they're told. The hangover from the old communist regime persists and they like to interfere and control to the extent that we can't get on with our work. Also Klanski said you spent a time at the British Consulate. Might I ask why?"

I had obviously been followed. I thought quickly. "Yes, I wanted them to set up visits to research institutes to see what is being done out there. They might well have information that would help me understand how local geological conditions might affect my work. In return I would offer to give a few lectures to students. It would be beneficial to Bakuoil. " I replied, hoping I sounded genuine.

"I would prefer you not to have too much to do with the diplomats." snapped Campbell. "They don't help us much: their main interest is in diplomatic cocktail parties and bureaucracy. Anyway Klanski will arrange any contacts with the local institutes. You should not do it yourself. Keep clear of the Consulate. Data security is vitally important to our interests out there. Sometimes we have to bend a few rules to get the work done, as I'm sure you realise. With the retainer we pay you we expect that you will not make any waves. Do I make myself clear?"

He then spelt out clearly what technical tasks he expected me to work on before my next trip to Baku.

"Thank you for your co-operation Dr Aldborough. This company rewards discretion and achievement from its staff." were his closing words.

Julie was out of town so I to the next train down to Dorset and to the Manor at Wool.

Chapter 16. Gravity Waves to Order!

Alte Brücke, Heidelberg

A message from Hans, in Heidelberg, was waiting for me when I arrived at the Technology Centre after my Azerbeijan adventure. It said that he had had a breakthrough in the generation of gravity waves and he was planning a design for a prototype essentially based on the principles we had discussed previously.

The process did involve quantum effects and the simultaneous use of mechanical and electric vibrations. He was sure that by varying the frequency of the waves it would be possible to tune in to any time in the past. The process was mathematically highly non-linear and was described by chaos theory.

Equipment had been set up at a secure laboratory in the University of Heidelberg. He pressed me to go over there and work with him on its commissioning if I could do so. It was essential that I was in at the work at this time and I accordingly rang Johan Gluck at Summerfield's to report on what had happened in Baku and to tell him I would be out of the country.

He already knew about the attack on me and had been briefed on the tests on the tool in Baku. He didn't seem surprised at developments and said that Joe King was incorporating the modifications into one of the prototypes. It would be ready for a further test in the Wytch Farm oil field in about a week. There wasn't much I could do in Dorset and I set off for Heidelberg, this time by air.

Hans had quite an impressive laboratory set up. His ideas on how gravity waves are effectively amplified by transmission through another dimension appeared correct. The gravity wave generator was mounted in a strong steel frame and coupled up to a high wattage power supply. On the opposite side of the room ten metres away was a similar set up acting as a wave detector.

"It doesn't look very portable at the moment, but I'm sure we can work on that once we've established the principles." Hans said excitedly.

We worked all day getting it ready for the test and eventually brought up the power. If our theory was correct, the whole system would start to resonate and produce gravity waves at particular discrete settings.

Hans peered at me with a mischievous smile. "I do not expect the gravity waves to be harmful to us but it would be prudent not to stand in the path of any beam that is generated. You remember Lord Rutherford's assistant who used to test radioactive sources, before they knew about the risks, by the feeling they generated in his thumb? He lost it."

I agreed it might be prudent but the gravity changes would still be very small.

"Don't fear my boy, it will work first time!" Hans exclaimed. He was right. The detectors showed a measurable response at the wavelength he had predicted. The amount of power absorbed by the instrument was about fifty kilowatts and we had to turn it off before heating could cause a failure.

It looked a fearsome sight, with the liquid nitrogen fumes curling round the throbbing equipment. I half expected to see a time flashback but of course that was unlikely in those surroundings.

"My God, I didn't expect that so quickly!" he said.

It was a considerable achievement simply to be generating and detecting gravity waves. Their power levels were still extremely low and might not be enough to cause flashbacks. To my knowledge nobody had done it before. Hans was adamant, however, that we must not make it public at this stage and had gone to great lengths to keep the experiment secret. Even his hausfrau didn't know. The laboratory workers had been sworn to secrecy.

That evening we discussed what the next steps would be. The conversion of the equipment, set up simply to produce a beam of gravity waves, into a device for generating time flashbacks would take some time and clearly I would be unable to help.

Once working he wanted to use it for time flashback experiments at his home in Heidelberg. The conditions would be good there for producing any such results. The building was unchanged structurally from the 1920's and was built with massive stone walls, which would strengthen any possible potential for success.

I, on the other hand wanted to get it back to Charles MacLean's manor at Corfe where I thought I had seen that flashback during the thunderstorm months ago. Logistically however it made sense to satisfy Hans's wishes and I reluctantly agreed. We christened the equipment 'The Torch', for our hope it would illuminate the past.

The next steps could not be done quickly and I wouldn't be able to stay to see them through because of my Summerfield commitments. I asked if Hans would mind Charles's coming over to help, after all he had started this whole idea. In my mind it would kill two birds with one stone. I knew Charles would enjoy it enormously and I'd felt I'd let him down slightly by joining Egliston's company. It would salve my conscience. Besides I wanted to keep an eye on what Hans was doing and Charles would be my proxy.

Hans agreed, somewhat to my surprise, because I'd anticipated he would be secretive if Julie's doubts about his motives were justified. Charles said he would come over immediately when I rang him up

A message was waiting on my mobile from Joe King saying that they were ready for the final prototype trials at Wytch Farm and asking me to return straight away. I wasn't able to meet Charles to discuss things before I left.

Chapter 17. The first flashbacks

I kept closely in touch initially to see whether Charles and Hans got on well together. To my surprise they did. Hans was clearly excited about the unfolding scientific and commercial possibilities. The production of a generator of measurable gravity waves, a previous obstacle to study, was an academic breakthrough in itself. The work would, when published, create a flood of interest in the university world. The further possibility of producing time flashbacks was mind-boggling.

Naturally with such a wealth of goodies, Hans wanted to get on to the next phase of trials as soon as possible. Charles told me afterwards in detail how things had gone. This was a summary of events.

'He could see clearly that Hans had a consuming personal interest in probing the secrets of his home, lost in the passage of time, as well as in the discovery itself. I had mentioned to Charles that the house was Hans's pre-war family home and that he had never known what happened to his parents in the Nazi era. Charles could see his point. He also would dearly love to see flashbacks of his own and his brother, Henry's, lives.

Hans organised the transfer of the gravity "Torch" from the university to his house. The equipment was cumbersome and needed the strength of two technicians to move it. They were obviously curious as to why such strange equipment needed to be brought into a domestic location but Hans led them to believe it was his eccentricity in wanting to do his research at home rather than at the university.

The main living room of the house, with its sunken central area and dark panelling, was chosen for the first test because this would be where most people would have spent much of their time while living there. The room itself had not changed significantly over the last sixty years, even the bulk of the furniture was the same. The conditions, according to Charles's ideas, were perfect for the production of a flashback. Hans had sent his housekeeper away for a holiday to ensure privacy.

Charles didn't know what to expect to see. I had not told him about my flashback discovery at Winfrith until I asked him to come to Heidelberg. He had seen a 'natural' flashback years before at the manor that was very fuzzy and ethereal but that might be completely different from that produced by the 'Torch'.

If the idea worked, would a flashback image be restricted to the extent of the beam of gravity waves or would it be best to direct the beam on to the massive stone walls and hope that the radiation field from the past would appear over a wide area? Hans believed that the flashback, assuming they actually got one, would be strongest where the beam struck a solid body but would be still be visible for some distance from it.

They waited until darkness fell so that any flashback scene would more clearly be visible. Hans insisted on a systematic approach, varying the power and frequency of the gravity waves. Charles felt slightly embarrassed sitting waiting for something to happen. The odds were pretty long against seeing anything. They sat there for an hour trying this and that, and drinking coffee.

"When was the house built?" Charles asked. "Perhaps we are tuning to an earlier time."

Reise waved his arms in frustration, "We could be completely outside the ball-park. It could be that some time-spans are outside our reach. Have you studied chaos theory Charles, you know, the butterfly effect – the flapping of a butterfly's wings in Peru could cause a storm some time later in the Caribbean Sea - that weather forecasters blame for the inaccuracy of their predictions? The path of space-time is probably chaotic also. After all, the smallest effect can completely alter the future; that's a feature of chaos theory. Chaos theory says that a point in space-time never intersects an earlier point, that is, we can't go back to the past but can come very close to it. If that's true we will be looking for those windows in space-time near to us or very far from us."

The search became a tedious process of trial and error. The breakthrough came one evening. Charles was suddenly aware of a glow centred on the area where the beam hit the wall of the room. He could see indistinct images of furniture and a beam of sunlight casting shadows on the wall. Reise quickly joined him and then a man in German officer's uniform came into view.

The flashback, for that was what it undoubtedly was, was indistinct. The figure sat down at a desk, writing. They sat there transfixed for maybe half an hour watching this rather static image before speaking.

"Eureka!" cried Reise. "We have to find out how to adjust this equipment to sharpen the image and to scan across a reasonable time. I want to find out the exact time in the past we are looking at. We are obviously in the wartime period. I'd hoped to see my family."

It was clear to Charles that Reise was now totally immersed in personal events that had occurred sixty or so years ago, rather than understanding the science. Reise seemed to forget Charles was there and for the next few hours sat varying all aspects of the equipment and its settings. He had found that he could scan across months and improve the image, but saw only army officers talking and relaxing in the room. Of his family there was nothing. Eventually he sat back, drained.

"I fear that my parents were no longer in this house, at least during the later part of the war. They would have appeared at least briefly if they were here. I wish I could tell by lip reading what was being said by these officers."

Charles felt he was surplus to requirements over the next week. He rang me in Baku where I had been sent immediately after the further tests in Wytch Farm, to bring me up to date but he could only speak in guarded terms in case the conversation was overheard. I was having problems of my own, which I in turn felt unable to talk about on an open line.

Reise sat from dawn until dusk scanning and watching, getting more and more frustrated. One morning his hausfrau Katrina came in catching them in the process of watching the flashbacks. Reise had completely forgotten about her return from holiday. There was no alternative but to tell her what was happening. To Charles's surprise she seemed unfazed by what she saw.

Reise suddenly started.

"Katrina, you are quite deaf. Can you lip read?"

When she nodded he hugged her and sat her in front of the equipment. The poor lady was then obliged to sit there as Reise scanned to various scenes he had seen before.

Charles's German was not up to the pace of the conversation and he spent time walking into the town, going on river trips and visiting Mannheim and Ludwigshaven.

One day on returning, Reise was distraught.

"I saw what I feared," he said. "My parents were killed by the Nazis. Katrina and I saw a conversation where it was discussed. I had thought that my father's position as a banker would save him. One of the Nazi party leaders took over the house and its contents. When I bought the house some years ago from the family of that minister, the deeds to the house showed that it had been sold to the German State, but clearly now I know that it was expropriated. I had been given to believe by a person in England that they had been allowed to stay. Clearly I was lied to."

Reise didn't go on to say who that person was. After that, his interest faded and he became withdrawn, although he continued to search for new flashbacks. Charles felt that now was the time to set his own curiosity to rights and to get Reise's agreement to ship the equipment to his manor in Corfe. He had his own skeletons to investigate. He broached the subject after breakfast one day.

Charles felt the time was ripe to satisfy his own curiosity. "Hans, you have found what you were looking for. I want to follow up my interests in my own family, to see my relatives who died long ago and to trace my brother's movements during the war after he came back from Colditz. Would you be willing to allow me to ship this equipment to my home? You probably need time to reflect and also possibly to develop a mark 2 version of the equipment."

Hans's reaction was dramatic. "No, that would be most unwise. You would be opening a Pandora's box that will not be good for you or for your family."

This took Charles aback. "Hans. Harry has told me that you visited the manor and knew my brother. You clearly know something I do not. I have a right to know even if the news is bad."

It took two days before Hans relented. "You will probably regret this for the rest of your life. Our friendship may not survive. However, I now accept that you must be permitted to do whatever you want. Take it. Please let me know what you find."

Charles desperately needed to talk to me but couldn't get through. In the end he sent an e-mail saying he was returning to Dorset with equipment and urgently needed to talk. I did not receive it. Reise was still strangely turned in on himself, saying he would be in touch in due course.

Katrina was at least happy to see the equipment go so that she could get the house back to normal.

Chapter 18. Discovery at the Manor

Charles was in contact with me as soon as he got back to Dorset from Heidelberg and I from Baku, frustrated that he'd not had the chance to discuss what had happened. It would be a week before I could get away from the rig tests to help him. The bulky flashback 'Torch', incorporating some modifications from lessons learned in Heidelberg, had been delivered to WTC rather than to Norden Manor.

Hans was developing a more advanced version for further use in Heidelberg and was now quite happy for me to keep the prototype in England. My assistant Charlie Tizzard was not let Charles have access to the 'Torch' as he now called it, without my say-so. Charles, of course, wanted to get access to it as soon as he could to see whether he could get it to excite time flashbacks. I arranged for him to have access to the 'Torch'.

As soon as I was able to meet him, Charles brought me fully up to date on the happenings in Heidelberg and on the depression that Hans had now sunk into.

The possibilities were mind-boggling. If we could tame this discovery, it would be possible to eavesdrop anywhere. History would become an open book, private meetings could become public knowledge, and criminals could be seen red-handed at the scene of their crimes. There would obviously be limitations, but it would have a profound influence in many areas.

It could make our fortune. It could also get us killed. I agreed with Charles that the most promising location for tests was the Norden Manor House because I was now convinced, like him, that the fleeting image I'd seen in the lounge that Friday last November was real, possibly brought about by the influence of the electric storm going on at the time.

He had anticipated the move and had had a three-phase supply installed at the manor to power the kit. I would have to convince Charlie Tizzard that the equipment was part of my oil research project that I wanted to work with on location but he wouldn't see why I needed to take it to the Manor. I would have to work out a good reason.

I had told Charlie Tizzard that I would be moving away from Winfrith in the next month and that it would be more convenient and cheaper to have the calibration equipment at Norden. I'm sure he smelled a rat but seemed to accept my explanation. He and other general workers at WTC loaded the equipment on to a site van and drove it to the manor.

The most promising location would be where I'd been sitting in the study and directed towards where I'd seen the image of the soldier. The heavy equipment was finally in position and Charles and I were left alone with it.

I didn't expect to see anything with the 'Torch' at the Manor until it was dark, because the images they had seen at Heidelberg were weak and there was no real reason why anything should be different here. The time eventually came to run up the power levels with the settings they had used before and with racing hearts Charles and I stood there expectantly.

Gradually we started to see pale images of furniture that we were able to sharpen up by redirecting the gravity beam at the stone floor. To our disappointment there was no sign of life. Because we were using the settings used in Heidelberg we assumed we would be scanning the same time in the past. As the evening wore on we tried other settings.

Eventually, bingo, a figure appeared seated at the table, much as I had seen in my after-dinner reverie that Friday long ago. He was writing, referring occasionally to what appeared to be ledger books. My heart was thumping as I hadn't really believed that the thing would work.

I turned round to Charles who was staring at the man.

"That's my brother when he was in his twenties!" he exclaimed. "We must be looking at a time before the end of the war because that's when he had moved out of the Hall to the family home here at Norden."

At that moment to our surprise another figure appeared, this time an older woman.

"And that's Nicole, the wife of my father's butler," he went on excitedly. "She died in an air raid in 1944."

We had observed for about half an hour this cameo unfolding in front of us when, in the flashback, Charles's brother rose, carrying his paperwork, and walked towards the far wall where he stretched out his hand to a decorative piece of carving on the panelling and moved it forward. A vertical panel moved down which he then pulled forward revealing a passageway into which he walked, closing it behind him. We sat there enthralled and eventually he returned carefully closing the panel behind him.

"I'd heard that there were hidden passages leading from the Manor to Corfe Castle, but I'd never believed the stories," said Charles, "Let's turn off the beam and see if we can find that tunnel."

The decorative piece of carving we had seen in the images was no longer there and it was some time before we found where it had apparently been sawn off and the cuts filled in with wax. With a few tools from Charles's shed we eventually were able to get some leverage on the residual wooden stump and to our excitement the wall panel broke open just as it had in the images. It took some strength to open it fully.

Charles got a torch and a passageway was revealed. We walked into it carefully not knowing what we would find. However, it was blocked by a roof fall some twenty yards into the tunnel at a point where it would be under the kitchen garden.

"It seems rather dangerous to me," said Charles, "I think we should pack up now and I'll get some workmen in to shore up the roof and dig our way through."

I agreed with him. We'd clearly proved the effectiveness of the gravity beam and had calibrated it to reveal events about fifty-six years in the past. Charles, although thoroughly excited, was worried about telling anybody what we had seen. There might be skeletons in his family cupboard and he wanted to do the digging work before moving on. In retrospect, it turned out to be a very fortunate decision. I didn't want anyone to know either.

****

Charles got a local builder to do the excavation work starting the next day. Before he arrived we covered the flashback 'Torch' to look like a piece of bulky furniture under wraps and disconnected the cables.

According to Charles, there always had been rumours that there were such tunnels going from the Manor across to the now wrecked Corfe Castle. They had always been discounted as pure folklore because the Manor was Elizabethan and the Castle was reaching the end of its useful days at that time. Maybe my gravity beam would some day cast light on the archaeology.

When I arrived, the builder had shored up the first part of the tunnel and was removing the fallen masonry that cased the tunnel. The quality of the stonework was high and we were surprised that it had collapsed. Charles and I sat with coffee talking over the events of two days ago while he brought me up to date on what had happened at Heidelberg.

"I'm intrigued to know what's in that tunnel," he said. "My brother must have found the operating mechanism by accident or perhaps Nicole knew from my father." Just then there was a shout from the tunnel.

"Come and look at this"

We rushed in. Some of the rubble had been removed and a filing cabinet and an old radio transmitter revealed.

"Stop everything," said Charles suddenly. "If this is what it seems, that is a wartime transmitter. It might be booby-trapped. Look at those wires going into the rubble."

The tunnel emptied in double quick time.

"I'm going to get in touch with Bovington Army Camp to get them to give it a sweep for explosives. In the meantime please keep all this quiet, Fred." he said, turning to the builder, who assured him he would. "The last thing I want is the press round here. I need to ask my brother, Lord Egliston who lived here during the war a few pertinent questions"

To me in a subdued voice he said, "We need to be careful about how we say we found this place. If you are agreeable we'll say nothing about the gravity 'Torch'. Let's make sure that it's well hidden"

The bomb disposal squad was with us within a half-hour and evacuated the area, stopping traffic on the main road through the village. Charles's story was that we had found the passage while we were following up some old stories about such tunnels.

The officer, after looking round the scene for some time, asked whether there was a possibility that the collapse might have been caused during the war by a nearby bomb. If so, it was possible that there could also be an unexploded WW2 bomb in the area. That was then Gladys volunteered the information that a stick of bombs had in fact been jettisoned by a German plane over the village in 1944 and that it was a distinct possibility. She added that one of the Manor's servants had been killed at that time near to the house.

Now we had two possible dangers, a possible bomb and a booby trap. The squad went over the whole area with metal detectors, digging a hole in the back garden above the roof fall. Twelve hours later they had actually found a bomb in the Manor garden, and were able to defuse it. The next day they returned to the tunnel itself, gradually removing the rubble.

We weren't allowed near and had to sit biting our nails. Eventually the officer in charge came up to us.

"You were quite right to call us. The tunnel was booby-trapped with a grenade and magnesium flare in the filing cabinet, but the roof fall had fortunately broken the trip wire without setting off the charge. We'll take it away and dispose of it at Bovington. The contents of the filing cabinet are clearly those of a spy, reports of military activity, transmission details and so on. I've spoken to my CO and he'll put out a press release saying we investigated an unexploded bomb and have disposed of it. That's quite true in a way; it's just that we won't be mentioning the spy part. I'm taking away that cabinet for the spooks to investigate. You will no doubt be asked to cast some light on what has been found. The spy routinely booby-trapped his hide hole. What he hadn't reckoned on was his German friends dropping bombs on him"

Charles was clearly upset.

"The obvious deduction is that Henry was acting as a spy. He must have been turned when he was a PoW and his escape engineered. I suppose Nicole must have been part of it as well. She was German originally before she married my father's gamekeeper."

I resolved to tell Rushton directly when Charles was not there. If Egliston were involved in spying all those years ago he would no doubt be interested. I took the officer on one side and asked him to brief Rushton as soon as possible.

Charles must have told Julie about the findings immediately. He was very distraught at finding that his brother had been a German spy, despite all that had passed between them. The thought that his family name would be besmirched was another factor. She arrived the next day wanting to know all about it and the flashback results. I came into the firing line straight away in the light of these revelations about Egliston.

"Have you signed the contract with Egliston's company, Harry?" were her first words when we met. "You cannot in all conscience work for this man now."

This placed me in a dilemma. I was just as appalled as she was but I had signed the contract and had committed myself to helping Rushton to investigate the nuclear materials smuggling. Furthermore Rushton had told me to tell nobody what I was doing, particularly Julie and Charles. We had quite a ding-dong quarrel, with Charles trying to make the peace and it ended with Julie busting into tears and saying our relationship was definitely at an end. Overall, it was not a happy time.

Chapter 19. November 1939 – Nicole Taylor's anguish

Jurassic coastline

Nicole Taylor sat on the hard-backed kitchen chair staring at a steaming mug of tea on the scrubbed oak table in front of her. Turning off the radio she breathed a sigh of resignation to her fate. In front of her was a letter from her son, Frank, delivered several weeks ago. Mother and son had anticipated two whole years ago that Britain and Germany would be at war in the next few years and as a result she had sent him to live with her relatives in Essen.

Now it had happened. Neville Chamberlain, the British Prime Minister, had just made his fateful countrywide broadcast formally confirming that the two countries were at war.

The letter from Frank had said that he would join the SS, having come to the attention of senior Nazis through his membership of the Hitler Youth. He had written to her regularly, the letters having been posted to her by a diplomat at the German Embassy in London. In future Frank probably would not write because the embassy would be closed, although a neutral country like Spain might be persuaded to send on any correspondence. Had he stayed in England he would soon have been conscripted into the British army, a prospect that sickened her. Now he would serve their beloved Fatherland and would no doubt be part of a future invasion force.

Thank goodness, she thought, that he had taken so well to Germany, where he had gone to Heidelberg University to study law. She wished now that she had emigrated as well but realised she might have impeded Frank's progress. She was stuck here in England looking forward to the inevitable invasion by Germany, whenever that might be. In the meantime she had to tend as housekeeper the elderly Lord Egliston without the help of the servants on the estate. He had moved out of Egliston Hall, anticipating its requisitioning by the army, into Norden Manor. Most of the staff would soon be enlisted into the armed forces and the rest, mainly elderly, would be kept on to maintain the estate.

Her role was to act as housekeeper and general factotum at the Norton Manor with some part-time help from the village. Before the war, her job as housekeeper at the Hall had at least been interesting and she could also keep well out of Lord Egliston's way. Unfortunately now she was physically close to him and in addition he was demanding a lot of attention and she was constantly in demand. She loathed him.

The weeks rolled by and she carried out her duties like an automaton, looking forward to hearing again from Frank. After the rapid advance of the German armies across Holland, Belgium and France and the months of the so-called phoney war everything seemed to be going as she had anticipated.

One morning in late May 1940 her customary routine was interrupted by the sound of the morning post arriving. She rose, crossed the wide hallway and picked up the pile of letters lying in a heap at the front door, all of them as usual addressed to Lord Egliston. She put them on a silver tray - the old devil insisted on keeping up the way of life he had had in Egliston Hall before the war. One of the letters struck her eye as it had the letters 'OHMS War Department' on it. That was ominous. It might concern Egliston's eldest son, Henry, who had signed up at the outbreak of the war. He had been commissioned and sent with the British Expeditionary Force in France. She despised him as well as his father and wouldn't have been concerned if he had been killed. With a grim look she took the tray into the lounge where Egliston was smoking his pipe reading.

He took the letters without acknowledging her presence, continuing to read. She withdrew; the tea she had left on the kitchen table was now cold.

She then busied herself with house cleaning until she felt she had to go for a walk. The village was buzzing with apprehension about the way the war would. There were rumours that the German army had pushed the Expeditionary Force back to the Channel at a small coastal town called Dunkirk. It was possible that the army would be forced to surrender, leaving Britain defenceless.

Nicole rejoiced inwardly, but she did not join in the conversations because she knew there would be the usual foul comments about Hitler and the Reich. The morning passed until the time came to serve Lord Egliston's lunch of cold meats, bread and pickled onions. As usual he said nothing to her but, as she was about to leave, he spoke.

"Nicole, you no doubt saw the official letter this morning. I have to tell you it concerned my elder son, Henry. He is reported as missing in France. He could be a prisoner and was reported as being injured in battle. I hope to God he is all right. I would be grateful if you would pass on the information to the staff at the Hall. I don't care to do it myself. Thank you."

He was as usual, taciturn, bearing the traditional British stiff upper lip and seeming to show absolutely no emotion. Nicole, however, had seen him so often she could read his moods like a book, as she needed to avoid his habitual flare-ups of anger. He was, she knew, deeply affected. Henry had been the apple of his eye and had a similar personality. The younger brother, Charles was still a boy and had been evacuated to Scotland. He was a quiet thoughtful type and tended to be ignored by his father and brother. Nicole had a feeling of schadenfreude at Egliston's troubles despite her worries about her own son. It lifted her spirits for the rest of the day.

In the following weeks Lord Egliston developed the habit of taking long walks in all weathers across the broad plateau of St Aldhelm's Head to gaze out across the Channel towards France. He brooded about his son who was, he believed, a prisoner of war and not killed in action. Nicole on the other hand was elated. She had had a letter from Frank, delivered by hand from some unknown person. It was full of the achievements of the Reich and his own advancement in the SS. It also gave instructions on how to use a dead letter box to send occasional letters to him together with any intelligence information she could glean.

A desperate plan was forming in Nicole's mind, a plan which would cook, as the English would say, Egliston's and his son's geese forever.

People had often commented on the physical similarity between Henry and her son Frank. Now that Henry was probably a prisoner of war it would be easy for him to be quietly disposed of by his captors and perhaps for Frank to take his place. Some minor facial surgery, a bogus escape and simulated effects of the battle injury, shell shock or whatever, could hide the transition. Once back he would make the ideal spy, trusted by the

English as a member of the landed aristocracy and an army officer. It would of course be necessary to get rid of old Lord Egliston as he would see through the deception.

Dorset would be a likely invasion point and, were Frank to get himself into the local administration, he would be privy to intelligence vital to an invasion force. She knew now how to get messages to her son through the dead letter conduit and sent off her outline plan to him and waited for a reply.

Nothing came back as the days passed but then, a letter came, seemingly from Scotland. Frank had taken the bait and had clearly been very busy. Egliston's son was in fact a prisoner and had now been transferred to a secure prison used for men who might be useful for blackmail or prisoner exchange. The German High Command thought Nicole's plan had merit and had put planning into immediate effect. There was no timescale or details given but she was ordered to wait for instructions and to make sure she stayed as housekeeper to Egliston.

She had already the germ of a plan to kill Egliston. On his horse rides to St Aldhelm's Head he had taken to standing near to the edge of the three hundred foot high sheer crumbling cliffs, gazing out to sea. He would be so lost in thought he wouldn't hear her approach. How easy it would be to creep up unheard, hit him on the head and push him over the edge. There would be no evidence of her attack after he had impacted on the rocks below. His depressed state of mind was well known round the village and his death would be put down to suicide. She could ensure there would be no witnesses in such a remote spot.

Frank Taylor, who had changed his name to the Teutonic version Frank Schneider, had been noted by the SS as a valuable asset. His perfect English, his innate intelligence and his ruthless nature made him ideal material for a key position in the planned invasion of England and the subsequent occupation.

When his mother's letter arrived, the idea she put forward was to him a gift from the gods. He could return the treatment he had received from the MacLean family all those years, he could avenge his father's death and he could get power and money. With his skills of persuasion he sold the idea to his superiors who rapidly located the prisoner of war Henry Egliston and had him transferred to Colditz, where officers likely to be of use to the Reich were kept.

Henry had been severely injured in the leg and was also in a poor mental state. Frank was able to observe him closely over a period of months and had minor plastic surgery carried out to improve his fortuitous likeness to Henry. He had time to learn how Henry spoke and to copy his mannerisms although much of this he remembered from his childhood. He to pleasure in making him grovel, knowing he would be the one to pull the gun trigger when the time came.

Unknown to him, however, Henry who was no fool, realised that Frank, who had beaten him several times, would take any opportunity to kill him at some point although he knew nothing of the specific plan to replace him.

He knew he had to get away and through the camp escape committee was allowed to jump the queue for those wanting to attempt an escape. In those early days of the war the security was not as tight as it was later and he was able to escape dressed as a German workman who had been brought in to carry out repairs. His command of German was excellent owing to his time at University.

He made his way across the country to Switzerland and was transferred to England through an escape conduit.

Frank Schneider and his masters were furious at this frustration of their plans but neglected at that time to warn Nicole of the turn of events. She on her part had decided that she could not go on much longer acting as Egliston's skivvy and resolved that she would go ahead with her plan to murder Lord Egliston when the chance arose.

This came one day in January when there was a sea mist blowing in over the Downs and the visibility was down to about a hundred yards. Lord Egliston went off on his customary horse ride with his favourite dog despite the onset of heavy rain. Nicole followed on her bicycle at a discreet distance.

She was carrying an urgent message for Egliston that had arrived at the Manor a short time previously. It would be an excuse for her presence if he happened to see her following him and before she was in a position to strike. The dog would probably know she was there but was unlikely to react strongly to her. She had armed herself with a walking stick with a heavy silver head and planned to approach him from behind while he was deep in contemplation and to hit him hard enough to break his skull. She was a strong woman and had no doubts about her ability to do this and then to push him over the cliff edge.

Eventually he reached the cliff top, dismounted and sat on his shooting stick staring into the swirling mist with the dog beside him. The moment had come. She crept forward and was just six feet away when the dog barked and ran to her. Egliston turned and saw Nicole but turned back, ignoring her.

"Here is a message for you sir," she said.

"Another bloody message, why can't it wait?" he roared. "I don't want to see it yet"

Nicole stepped forward and with a swing brought the head of the stick round in a wide arc hitting his skull above his ear.

"You won't see it at all." she cried.

He was probably dead before his body slumped to the ground, blood spurting from the wound. The dog became very agitated and was barking wildly, facing her with bared teeth. Without thinking she swung the stick at it and smashed its head. Rapidly she pulled Egliston's body to the edge and with the stick pushed it until it overbalanced, falling towards the beach far below. The dog followed. Peering over the edge, she couldn't see either of the bodies through the mist and desperately hoped neither had snagged on any ledge on the way down.

She washed the blood from the stick in a rain puddle nearby and paused to think. There were no marks of her feet on the ground but there was a fair amount of blood. She hadn't anticipated that there would be such a mess and had no way of dealing with it. All she could hope was that the rain, which was now starting to come down fast, would wash it away. The horse had taken fright and had galloped away into the mist.

Once she was back at the Manor she made sure that all marks were removed from the stick and put it away. She would wait for some hours before she reported his absence to the police. By then at would be dark and it would be the next day before the body would be found. With luck it would be washed out to sea. The rain was still falling very heavily and she was confident there would be no signs of the murder. There was some blood on her clothes but these were easily disposed of in the blazing kitchen fire.

She reported after nightfall to the police that he had not returned from his ride, although his horse had just returned, but because they would not be able to use lights in the wartime blackout to search for him, no action was taken until the next day when a search party was sent out.

Nicole had told the police that he had probably gone on to the Headland. The next day the dog was found fairly quickly at the base of the cliffs where it had fallen on the sharp rocks. There was no sign of Egliston.

The police interviewed Nicole, who mentioned his depressed state and told them of his habit of spending time on the cliff top. Other people in the village supported her story, and the idea took hold that most probably he had committed suicide and the dog had instinctively followed him. Suicide was considered a disgrace at that time and the policeman tried to console her by suggesting,

"The official line will be that the dog ran over the cliff following a rabbit and that his Lordship accidentally fell off trying to stop it. There will be no mention of suicide"

His body was found washed up on the beach at Studland a week later. By that time the damage caused by the fall and the time in the water had hidden any evidence of the blows from the silver-topped stick. The coroner's enquiry gave the verdict as predicted by the constable.

The rain-soaked telegram that Nicole had taken as an alibi with her on her murderous mission lay unopened for a week. A London firm of solicitors responsible for executing the will left by Lord Egliston, was going through the papers left at the Manor. As the telegram was from the War Ministry it was opened immediately on their arrival in Corfe, and gave way to a flurry of excitement. Nicole was called in.

"This is very sad and ironic." the pin-striped individual leading the small team of lawyers told Nicole "This informs us that Lord Egliston's son who as you know was taken prisoner of war has escaped and is in hospital near London undergoing tests. They anticipate that he will be able to come here in a month's time if there is medical and care assistance available. The letter says that he will have to continue with medical and psychiatric treatment for the foreseeable future. I shall contact them immediately with the news of Lord Egliston's death. This clearly affects our work and I need to take advice."

The news hit Nicole like a sledgehammer. Why hadn't she had warning from Frank that the plan to kill Major Henry and to substitute Frank was imminent? Frank was now in London and would be here in the near future! Panic and elation competed for her emotions. The 'pin-stripe' was obviously taken aback by her pallid appearance and jumped up to give her a chair and rushed to get her a drink.

The team left shortly afterwards taking some papers with them, saying they would be back as soon as Major Henry was in a position to see them. They instructed an undertaker from Poole to start the arrangements for the funeral of Lord Egliston, and asked Nicole to take full charge of the Manor's household arrangements until future arrangements were settled.

There was no message at all from Frank over the next few days. She had expected a phone call but understood that as far as the outside world was concerned that Frank would have to be 'Major MacLean' in every visible way.

She did eventually receive a call from the hospital informing her as housekeeper to expect him to arrive the next day with an army driver and giving her instruction on the treatment he must receive. A nurse would be in attendance for the time being. It seemed an eternity to wait and eventually in mid-afternoon a military car drew up outside.

She had to maintain the part she was to play and steeled herself to show no emotion as she went outside to meet him. The WAAF driver who stood by to help her passenger out opened the car door. Her heart stood still. The person was exactly like Major MacLean, haggard and weak. She had not expected Frank's disguise to be so realistic.

The truth then dawned on her like a wave hitting her on the beach. This was not Frank; it really was MacLean. She started to faint, feeling nauseous, then taking deep breaths, regained her self control, and moved forward to help. He brushed her aside and slowly walked into the Manor with the WAAF in tow. The next two hours, in which she settled MacLean into his room, fed him and received instructions from the WAAF, were agony for Nicole. Eventually she went to her room and wept. What had gone wrong? Where was Frank? There were no answers. She must just wait and suffer.

Chapter 20. Walls have ears - 1940

Despite the constant warnings from the War Ministry that 'Walls have Ears!' the story that many scientists and engineers were being drafted in to staff a large new research site on the coast near to St Aldhelm's Head was widely discussed by the local population. The need to accommodate up to eight hundred people was largely responsible. The research to be carried out was kept a closely guarded secret but Nicole made it her business to find out. When Frank came, as he surely would, it would be useful information. Rumours abounded about the purpose of the research establishment, from development of poison gas to death-rays but she found out from a friend in Swanage, who had been allocated one of the scientists as lodger, that it was to do with a revolutionary method of detecting distant aircraft using radio.

The UK already had an array of early warning coastal radio tracking stations stretching from Scotland round to the Isle of Wight, she was told, and the Air Ministry wanted to develop equipment that could be used for use in aircraft and ships. She had no means by which she could pass on the information to the Germans but, like a squirrel gathering nuts and burying them, carried on finding out as much as she could, knowing that at some stage her son would return and deal with the battle-scarred Major Henry MacLean.

The friend in Swanage told her about her lodger. He was a research physicist from Oxford University, a Jewish refugee who had fled Germany two years before the war started. The friend had great difficulty getting the shy young man to talk but eventually she extracted his history. Hans Reise was the son of a German banker who lived in Heidelberg. The father had stayed in Germany, believing that his position in the community as a rich banker with contacts across industry would safeguard him and his family.

The young man desperately missed his parents, having been sent to Oxford to study and to get out of the way of the Nazis. Nicole assiduously noted all this intelligence. She found excuses to visit Renscombe Farm, on St Aldhelm's Head, around which the research site was being built. She saw the large radio masts rising into the sky, the barbed wire fencing enclosing acres of the headland and the presence of the military.

It was three weeks later that the letter arrived. It was from Frank, and it contained instructions to burn it as soon as she had read it. He knew about the death of old Lord Egliston and gave her the details of a new plan. He wanted to know details of the medical and psychological state of Major MacLean, to be sent by the established route through the drop box and Spanish Embassy. His masters would land him on the Dorset Coast from a submarine. He would make his way to the Manor, would immediately kill Major MacLean and would then assume his identity.

She should create an atmosphere in the village that suggested that for the foreseeable future the Major wanted to be undisturbed by visitors. Frank would deal with the disposal of the body. The signal that would tell her of his imminent arrival would be sent through certain phrases in a radio broadcast by Lord Haw Haw, the renegade British broadcaster, the day before Frank's arrival. She burned the letter and went about her daily routine with raised spirits.

The funeral of Lord Egliston had taken place and the body interred in the small churchyard in the village of Kingston where his forebears were buried. The gathering was small, consisting mainly of estate workers and local dignitaries. The mourners were led by Major MacLean, who spoke little to anyone and who returned immediately afterwards to the Manor. Villagers saw that he was apparently mentally and physically drained and suffering from shell shock. The stress of his escape had taken its toll on top of his already weak condition.

Nicole knew that Frank would have little trouble becoming used to his new life under cover of MacLean's disability. There had been callers from the army and from the local authorities paying their respects and wanting to find out what role he hoped to play both as the new Lord Egliston and as an officer once his sick leave was ended. MacLean really didn't want to know and lapsed into the life of a recluse. Nicole was very happy with this. It would make Frank's task in merging seamlessly into the role of Lord of the Manor easier.

Henry MacLean treated her with the same arrogance she had known of old, but she bore it with ease, knowing his days were numbered. He had begun to drink heavily and would retire to his study, where he would brood for hours on end. Most of his time was taken up with sleeping and he refused to deal with the solicitors executing the will.

The days went slowly by and as the time approached for Frank's arrival she listened every day to Haw Haw's broadcasts waiting for the phrase 'Macbeth will come into his own'. The time went on and nothing came, then one day the words were uttered. The weather was foul, with a strong south-westerly gale expected, which would make landing difficult, but it would decrease the chance of his being seen. Nicole unlocked the rear door of the manor and sat down in the darkened kitchen for her vigil on the appointed day.

About ten o' clock in the evening the house was quiet but outside the rain was sheeting down and there was an occasional flash of lightning. She had turned off the lights in the kitchen. If the door was opened no telltale light would get out and attract a visit from the ARP, the Air Raid Precaution men, who would be wandering about on the look-out for infringements of the blackout. Suddenly she heard gunfire, quite different from the thunder, from the direction of the coast. Her heart sank. The coastal batteries had seen something offshore. She prayed that it was not her son's submarine.

She settled back to wait while the thunderstorm continued, imagining the worst. Three hours later she was slumbering when the kitchen door to the hallway was opened.

"Why the hell are you sitting here in the dark?" snarled Major MacLean, "I've been shouting for you this last ten minutes. I need another bottle of whisky, bring it to me." He slammed the door and returned, limping, to his study across the hall.

Nicole rose and went to the bar in the lounge and returned to the darkened kitchen with a bottle of whisky. She heard a dog outside howl and her heart pounded in hope. The back door swung open and there was Frank silhouetted against the lightning. They embraced for a full minute and then she pulled him into the kitchen, locking the door and pulling down the blinds, before turning on the light.

"Thank God you're here," she cried, "Was that firing I heard at your submarine? I thought you were dead"

"The submarine and its crew are dead," he replied, "only I survived. The British don't know I escaped but there's a big search operation underway and I was lucky to get through. They might be carrying out a search operation in the village so I want to get out of the way as soon as I can"

Nicole grabbed his arm as she heard the door slam across the hall and a voice: "I'm still waiting for the bloody whisky"

"I forgot," she cried "I was supposed to get another bottle of whisky to Major MacLean. He'll be in here raising hell in a minute"

Frank pulled out his pistol again. "Better now than later" he said grimly, and moved silently across the hall to the study and pushed opened the door.

"About damned time," snarled the major. "Who the devil −" he began, and then paled as he recognised his nemesis.

Frank raised his gun. "I've waited a long time for this," he said. "Lebewohl, you bastard." and fired twice into MacLean's chest and stomach.

MacLean swayed without a word and fell forward across the floor.

"We've got to get rid of this body quickly in case someone calls." said Taylor. "You clean up the blood. I know just where we can put him while I work out how to make a permanent job of disposal". He crossed the study. "I found this priest's hole while I was doing some repair work here when I was a child. If I remember correctly... I move this piece of carving... and this bookshelf moves."

A crack appeared round the edges of the shelving and Frank forced it forward. As he had said, there was a musty-smelling cavity behind and what appeared to be a tunnel disappearing into the darkness. He dragged the body inside and closed the aperture.

"Now I'm going to clean myself up and then we must talk. I need to take over the fool's personality so that nobody knows."

Chapter 21. May 2001 - Return to Baku

Rushton was as good as his word. He arranged for me to spend an intensive three days handling firearms and learning self defence at the Bovington army camp near to the research centre in Dorset. It helped that I had represented my college at judo some years ago. The instructors delighted in giving me a hard time but it paid off in the longer term, and they showed me how to recognise and handle a number of guns that I might conceivably meet. In particular I was introduced to a Walther PPK and how to use it effectively in an ambush situation. This was to be the weapon of choice when I got to Baku.

"You will be given a Walther by the consulate in Baku and you will carry it at all times. If attacked you must be prepared to kill or you could be killed. Don't wait to ask the time of day; if you are under threat, aim to kill, and then get the hell out of there," Rushton insisted.

Another two days were spent on instruction on how to recognise and to shake off possible followers. How they expected me to learn enough to be effective when real agents take months to train, I did not know, but this was a lot better that than nothing.

The flashback equipment was now in full use at the Manor although it was a long and tedious process of working through each day in the war years. Unlike Hans, we didn't have the means to lip read. Charles was assiduously searching for more information on his brother Henry's life at the Manor during the war but had not found out any more about his spying activities apart from him going into the hidden room on a number of occasions.

To his surprise he had, however, seen a number of meetings between the young Hans Reise and Henry. It was clear that some of the later meetings were acrimonious, with Henry appearing to threaten the young scientist and Hans marching out of the room in anger. Both Charles and I knew from Hans's own words that he knew Henry, but the depth of antagonism between them was a surprise. Hans had told me when I was in Heidelberg that he did not trust Henry but had nevertheless worked closely with him after the war and had continued to do so to the present day. They must have had some type of bond. It made me uneasy about Hans and the close relationship we had in developing the flashback 'Torch': would he let me down, or worse, tell Egliston about it? It would seem that Julie's hunch about Hans might have some substance.

In the middle of all this activity the message came from Summerfield that they were ready to start full-scale implementation of my project in Baku and that I was to arrange to return there as soon as possible. Reluctantly, I left Charles absorbed in his research. He had tried to get flashbacks earlier than WW2 and was having difficulty going further back than the 1920's. Hans had warned that this might happen owing to the highly non-linear mathematical nature of the flashback process. We were reaching a technological barrier that needed theoretical help from Hans if it was to be overcome. Unfortunately I hadn't time to go into that with him, and in any case he was still in Heidelberg nursing his introspection. I would have to get Charles to press that topic.

As far as my love life was concerned my relations with Julie were still on ice and there was no way of changing that because of Rushton's embargo on saying anything about my role as a mole in the Egliston empire.

The journey to Baku via Moscow was this time uneventful. I had my own iron rations for the trip - no gut rot from flyblown sandwiches this time! Even the planes were on time by Aeroflot standards and no mysterious Russians accosted me. Farouk, true to his word, was waiting for me with his Toyota pick-up truck at the airport in Baku and took me again to his home for a meal before taking me to my hotel.

It was good to see his face light up when he saw me and it gave me a feeling that this time all would be well. It would be later when I realised how wrong I was! His family was as welcoming as ever and I began to feel at home. I had expected that the Bakuoil take-over and the Egliston shenanigans would dampen even his spirits and I asked him what had changed recently. At first he was reluctant to say anything, being a stoic sort of individual, but was eventually persuaded to open up.

"To tell the truth Harry, there's a sense of mistrust everywhere. The new management has imposed a veil of secrecy across our operations and several people have been sacked. We technical people are kept away from policy making, and operations are firmly in the hands of the new people.

I would advise you strongly to watch your back and stick closely to your project. The company has started exploration work in Kazakhstan and there is pressure on some of us to move up there. I'm not keen on going because the political situation there is more unstable than here and I don't want to leave the family. On the bright side, Klanski seems to want your project to be a success, which is a distinct change for the better."

I did not want to involve Farouk directly in getting evidence of smuggling but I would need to involve him to some extent if I were to get anywhere. We got down to planning the full scale implementation of my project and he brought me up to date.

"We shall be using your equipment in twenty wells. Summerfield has sent several spare tools, far more than we shall need. They are all being got ready at the rig factory where shall go first thing tomorrow. We are scheduled to go out to the rig in two day's time when it's shut down for maintenance," said Farouk.

Summerfield had appointed one of their engineers as project manager and my role would now be advisory rather than executive. He had worked out a detailed plan for the setting up and bringing on stream each of the Eros tools. All the tools were ready for action and the computer control system was operational. The oil-water separators on the platforms had been modified to cope with the emulsions that would be generated in the fluid produced by the tools.

I was relieved to know that we would shortly sail offshore to start our tests. At least I would be away from one lot of people who potentially had murderous intent although there might be another bunch out there at the platform! The two days passed quickly and we then got the go-ahead.

We embarked on a motor launch with a small team of operations staff. Heading eastwards we passed the Neftianye Kamni field, which was by now in its decline phase, having been in operation for about fifty years. I remembered seeing pictures in geography books when I was at school. It was an impressive structure with one thousand wells and over a hundred miles of trestle links, like an offshore town. Our destination was a newer field further out, unimaginatively named the 28th April field.

We lived on the rig structure that was small by North Sea standards, and the living conditions were

Spartan; the North Sea rigs I knew about being like the Waldorf Astoria Hotel by comparison. There were nonetheless about fifty men staying there at any time. Oil production had ceased temporarily for maintenance and we were able to get the tools downhole very quickly.

Once operations had restarted Farouk and I took it in turns to monitor the progress twelve hours on and twelve hours off. We were so busy that there was little time to think about anything but the job. Even the rice and unknown variety of meat, perhaps camel or lamb, served to us at most meals was eaten automatically. We were too tired to see what else was happening on the rig but there was a constant traffic of boats and helicopters. It just wasn't possible to keep a full log of the comings and goings as Rushton had asked.

By the end of three weeks we were almost on our knees. The tools were all working and the rig had been brought up to full production. We had demonstrated a twenty percent increase in oil production rate and the project was meeting all my expectations. Everything was going well and I needed to evaluate the results away from the frenetic activity offshore. Farouk and I decided to go ashore if possible and catch up on our sleep, leaving our small team to continue monitoring. Unfortunately no Bakuoil boat or helicopter transits were planned for several days and we would have to seize on any chances that came along.

Our luck was in. One of the rig staff said that he had heard that a launch would be calling in that night and we might be able to persuade them to take us. Duly at midnight the boat came and its skipper reluctantly agreed to take us ashore. It was loaded up with a fair amount of equipment as we waited to board. Two of the items caught my eye. They were two steel containers with the international radioactive symbol on them, and definitely not part of our equipment. The Captain saw me trying to get a better view and threw a tarpaulin over them. It wasn't the usual boat and we didn't recognise the crew but all we wanted was to get back on shore. Eventually all was ready and off we went at a fair speed. The night was warm and the visibility good. The lights from other oilfields miles away could be seen around us and I began to enjoy the journey.

About ten minutes into the crossing we were suddenly bathed in a beam from a brilliant searchlight on a larger boat that had appeared a few hundred metres astern. A voice speaking in Russian came over a loud hailer.

Farouk said, "They're telling us to heave-to for inspection. We're in the Azeri sector of the Bakuoil so it might be a government boat checking for contraband or even protection money. Anything's possible here"

At that moment, to my horror, our captain turned up power, the boat leapt forward, resulting after a few seconds in a burst of machine gun fire directed ahead of our bow from the pursuer. The captain promptly turned starboard in a shower of spray and raced away at full throttle. We threw ourselves down on the deck in case there was any more shooting. All lights were dowsed but the pursuing boat's searchlight was able to keep on track and periodically a burst of fire followed us, one round taking away the radar aerial.

We could see they were gradually overtaking us and it seemed only a question of time before we would be caught or sunk. Light from the gas flares of an oilfield platform that our boat was clearly trying its best to reach broke the darkness ahead of us. Another burst of gunfire and one of the crew screamed in pain.

Suddenly our boat veered to port sharply and we were running under the trestles of an abandoned section of the Neftianye Kamni field. The chasing boat, being larger, could not follow us directly and had to pick its way through gaps in the trestles. There was a crash as it collided with a part of the structure. The beam of light vanished.

"That should stop him," said Farouk. The captain obviously thought so and eased off the throttle. The injured seaman had blood pouring from a wound to the head and I tried to stem the flow of blood by pressing a towel I found in the cabin on it. Although the wound was bloody and the man in pain he was at least stable. Suddenly the searchlight reappeared, there was another burst of fire from the darkness and a row of bullet holes shattered the windshield. The boat swung round and I was nearly thrown overboard but saved by Farouk's quick reaction in grabbing my collar.

One of our crew men appeared from below with an RPG – a rocket propelled grenade launcher and, balancing precariously in the bucking boat, aimed it at the floodlight that was now fully on us. He fired: the other boat that by now was only thirty feet from us disappeared behind a brilliant flash of light. A blast of air passed over us and we could then see the remains of the boat on fire and no sign of its crew. We circled the wreckage but there was no sign of life. One of the crew now had a gun and I'm sure would have finished off anyone who appeared. A shout from the captain and we set off again.

None of the crew spoke to us in the calm that now had fallen.

"What the hell was that?" I asked Farouk.

"Better not ask," he said. "I'll say a bit more later when we're alone, lucky we had the RPG." Eventually the lights of Baku came up ahead and our skipper kept well inshore for the rest of the journey.

The captain came up as we disembarked and said in broken English: "I tell Klanski about this. You saw nothing: you tell nobody anything or you will have fatal accident." He had an AK47 that he waved around threateningly.

We didn't stay after landing and picked up Farouk's truck to make our way to my hotel. Farouk was clearly shaken.

"This isn't the first time we've had an incident like that." he said. "The Azeri authorities stopped a boat during daylight hours about a month ago and searched it, but there was nothing found that interested them. The Iranians occasionally get belligerent and insist in boarding when we venture into the centre of the Caspian Sea." He frowned.

"I don't know what started tonight's attack and I don't know why our skipper was so anxious not to be boarded. However I'm sure that boat tonight wasn't Azeri. Our crew thinks it's a Mafia operation. They're strong round here and some of the smaller operators pay them protection money. It could be that they've started targeting Bakuoil, or it might be that our guys had something on board that's worth killing for. Things have changed a lot since Egliston's to over."

"Anyway," he continued, I think it is as well to keep quiet until I've seen Klanski. I'm going to try and contact him now. I'll get in touch in the morning."

I decided to speak with Colliston as soon as I could and rang the number he had given me when Farouk had left. The call was diverted to Colliston's mobile, obviously catching him in bed. After I had told him there had been an offshore shooting incident he told me to lock my door and speak to nobody until he had seen me. He arrived quickly.

"I want the full story" were his first words. I went through what had happened, mentioning the steel containers containing radioactive material. He sat deep in thought for a minute or two when I'd finished.

"There are two things. First, your safety, we don't know who was responsible although it probably was the Mafia. If it was an official interception the authorities will be chasing Bakuoil, not you personally. If it is Mafia, they were after the fissile material not you. I don't think you're in any more danger than before, not that that is any consolation." He gave me a wry smile.

"You should carry on as Klanski decides because it is Klanski's problem. For God's sake don't mention the steel canisters to anyone. I'll take care of surveillance of comings and goings at the factory. As far as your health is concerned I will get a gun to you. I understand you know how to use it. You will also have someone keeping a watch on you although you might not recognise them. No doubt you will be going offshore again very soon and we can stand down these precautions." He rose.

"Sleep well. That's more than I shall be doing for the rest of the night," he said as he departed. Surprisingly, I did sleep.

Farouk rang me after I'd had breakfast room service.

"Klanski's told us to keep quiet about last night. It's not our business he says. This is a Mafia operation as part of a protection racket and the company will deal with it in its own way. He insists you are not in danger although that takes some believing." Then his voice brightened a little.

"Join me for a meal at the caravanserai tomorrow night, eight o' clock? Take a bit of rest and relaxation before we get back to the rig. I'm going to spend time with the family."

Chapter 22. Anna Kaplinska

64 Hussars' Memorial

I had the day to kill and decided to see some more of the sights of Baku and maybe go to the theatre in the evening. Walking along I thought I'd try out the tradecraft skills I'd been crammed with by Rushton's men, in scanning for followers. Pausing at shop windows while I looked around felt a bit silly; in most there was little for sale to look at, but I went through the motions, and of course saw nobody suspicious. As I went into the Lenin Museum, heaven knows why, I stopped behind a pillar and waited to see if anyone came in.

The only person who fitted the bill was a rather elegant young woman who seemed a little lost. She showed no reaction as she looked past me and then she strolled inside. My imagination was playing tricks. Anybody following me would be an ugly Russian 'heavy'.

I spent an hour or two there as I found the displays of Baku's past interesting and was surprised to find it was nearly midday. During lunch at the museum restaurant I was surprised to see the same girl ahead of me in the queue, even more so when she came to sit at my table.

"Good afternoon, Dr Aldborough, or perhaps Harry would be less formal" she said in a smooth Polish accented voice.

"Things like this only happen in James Bond films," I thought as I smiled in my most friendly way to this very attractive girl.

"The day seems to be getting better all the time," I replied. "You obviously know more about me than I do about you," I added, offering her a handshake.

"I'm Anna Kaplinska and I work with Pietr Roscoff," she said quietly, shattering my romantic thoughts. "He has asked me to make sure nothing violent happens to you. Don't underestimate me by the way; I can be quite lethal if I need to be. I think your British authorities have decided that your, their and our interests are best served by keeping you in one piece. All those big boys have put me in charge of your safety. What sights are you planning to see for the rest of the day?"

My outlook on the day brightened up like a firework going off. She took charge, showing me parts of the old city I would never have found myself. She was an excellent guide and indeed companion and we seemed to get on very well indeed. She might have been doing it for a job but for me it was great.

"When do you go off duty?" I asked.

"I've instructions to see you safely tucked up in bed," she said with a demure smile. "I'm back on duty tomorrow until Mr Tehrani takes charge of you again."

We ate at a restaurant that was obviously frequented by the ex-pat community, Western style food but with the inevitable addition of cheap 'caviar'. We drank a couple of vodka toasts to Anglo-Polish co-operation. To my surprise she also was a qualified engineer and it was the first time I had talked about my EOR invention as a chat-up line. True to her word she came with me in the taxi to my hotel and we went to my room door.

"Unlock it, Harry," she whispered and pulled a small pistol from her bag, swinging the door wide open and making sure the room was clear of intruders before letting me in.

"Time to say goodnight Harry," she said.

"You're welcome to stay," I said, hopefully.

"That's not in my job description" she said rather firmly. "Tehrani will call for you tomorrow morning. Believe me, despite what Klanski says there is a risk that the Mafia might see you as a soft target for getting back at Bakuoil. Don't go out unless someone is with you or you might be taken as a hostage. Yes, and one more thing; take this PPK, compliments of my employers."

She gave me a kiss on my cheek and left. Baku went up several notches in my estimation. I'm sorry to say I didn't have any pangs of remorse about Julie's absence.

****

Farouk arrived, as he had said he would, early the next day. I'd packed my offshore baggage beforehand and we drove in his van to the harbour where a small power launch was waiting.

"You met the beautiful Anna, I hope," he smiled." The Russians keep a close eye on what happens round here. They seem to think we're still part of the Soviet Union. Although she is Polish she heads up a small unit connected to the Russian Embassy that monitors the oil industry. In this case they seem to think that you are well worth protecting. She contacted me and said that they were willing to help me make sure you're not left alone now that we've evidence the Mafia is getting interested in our company." He paused and patted his left ribcage.

"I carry a gun and I believe you now do as well. I hope you know how to use it without killing yourself. I had another long session with Klanski by the way. Bakuoil's been threatened by the Mafia to pay protection money and have refused. That's why we are armed because he thinks there will be another show of strength."

I was glad to be in the relative safety of being offshore and back to work. The pace of work was less hectic now that the EROS tools were all working well and all we had to do was to monitor the results. At this rate I would be able to return to the UK and back to work on the flashback equipment. However, I would be able to keep tabs on comings and goings to and from the rig, of boats and helicopters and see if there was any pattern to the smuggling operations in the remaining time.

Klanski himself was dropped on to the rig by helicopter at this point, ostensibly to look at our results, and decided to stay there overnight. It occurred to me that he might be there to take delivery of more fissile material in the near future, and I thought I would take a night shift in our data logging room and at the same time keep an eye open. Farouk thought I was mad to stay up overnight but I persuaded him there was merit in doing some tests.

I installed myself with the lights off and kept watch. Klanski was up and about with two of the rig engineers standing on the top of the platform pacing up and down. Sure enough, a fast motor launch came up to the rig just after midnight from the offshore rather than the Baku direction. Two men came aboard with a steel container similar to the one I'd seen in the boat when we were chased. Klanski supervised its placement in the tool store that was locked up after them and the boat sped away again. There was no way I could get a better look since I didn't have access to the store and I crept back to bed.

There were further deliveries on the next two nights after which it was time for Farouk and me to return to shore. Farouk had watched one of these deliveries at my instigation - reluctantly - and said that the boats were from Kazakhstan. I managed to get a photo of the boat and the container.

This time our return to shore was a daytime journey with the steel containers on board and placed in the cabin. We had a much faster boat on this occasion and we were soon back on shore at the rig depot without being chased or shot at. The containers were personally escorted by one of the engineers who had been with Klanski and taken into the rig area that had been guarded by armed men previously. It was impossible for me to see more closely without raising suspicion and I relaxed and enjoyed the journey back to Baku.

Farouk had to return to his home and was very emphatic about the need for me to watch out for trouble. "Now you have a gun, don't be frightened to use it if you are threatened. The company will back you up if anyone gets hurt while you are defending yourself," was his parting message.

I called Colliston from the hotel room and arranged to meet him to pass on my findings, eventually joining up in the garden of the 26 Commissars that I'd visited on my first tour. As far as I could see nobody followed me and we spent only a short time in discussion. A large wedding group was there having its photos taken and we were not conspicuous. Now that we knew how the fissile material was delivered to Bakuoil he wanted to know how it was got out of the country and pressed me to spend time at the rig factory to see if I could see where the material was sent out.

As I left the memorial, Colliston melted away and I was just about to return to the hotel when I was startled by a voice.

"Hello Harry, you might have told me you were back in town." There was Anna again. "I've had quite a job finding you but Mr Colliston led me to you." A quick peck on my cheek and her beaming smile made the day for me.

"If you haven't anything better to do today we'll go out to the Everlasting Flame for a bit of sight seeing. Being an oil man you'll appreciate a natural gas well."

"Is this a social meeting or is there another reason?" I asked "I hope it's social; not that it matters, I'm glad to see you anytime."

"Harry, we hear definitely that the Mafia has you marked down as a nuclear expert here to supervise the transport of fissile material out of the country. We have tried to let it be known you're not but the bottom line is that they might try to kidnap you in any case as a way of putting pressure on Egliston's operation. I'm here to try and stop any attempt. I see you've got the shooter I gave you," she said, pointing out the bulge under my shoulder.

"Come on let's see this everlasting flame of yours. Let's enjoy the day," I said.

Anna was good company. She drove us out of the town in a Toyota 4X4 and inland past the ubiquitous oil wells into the never-ending undulating scrubland. Farouk and I had visited it just after my first arrival in Baku and I was glad to see it again, this time in female company.

Eventually, after a tooth-rattling journey, we arrived at what was now clearly a tourist attraction with coaches and plenty of people milling around. The eternal flame was a natural gas seepage that had been there for perhaps hundreds of years at the site and provided a focus for the old religious establishment built around it.

The time soon passed as we talked and looked at the buildings and as the number of visitors thinned we set out on the return journey. After we had been driving for ten minutes Anna noticed a car following us and making no attempt to pass although she had varied her speed.

"We should be able to lose them in this truck," she said and despite the bad road surface we got up to 140 km/h. The other car increased speed but gradually fell behind.

"If this thing holds together we should be OK. Anyway have you got your mobile handy? We should try and get through to Roscoff in case anything goes wrong," she said calmly.

"Tell him I'm going to turn off on the road towards the caves where there are the prehistoric carvings, we might be able to shake them off. There's a rough track we can take to get back to the main road near the airport. We should be safe then."

I phoned the number she gave me but all I got was his voice mail to which I quickly summarised our problem hoping he might get the message in time. With that she braked hard and spun the car into a side road I hadn't noticed, and accelerated up a steep incline into the hills. Eventually she pulled off the road into a small valley between rock cliffs and stopped the car.

"Climb up to that rock up there; you should be able to see whether we've been followed," she ordered, "I'm going to try to get on to Roscoff's mobile again and one or two other numbers."

I scrambled up about a hundred metres of rocky hillside coming out on a platform of rock that gave me views back where we had come. There was no sign of pursuit. The dust plume we had kicked up had subsided. With relief I went back to where Anna still hadn't managed to get through on her mobile.

"Let's keep moving. If we carry on this road for ten kilometres or so we should be OK, I don't want to take the risk of going back the way we came."

The road was rough and progress was slow as the sun went down and we had to rely on the headlights to avoid potholes on the twisting track. The airport was clearly getting nearer as one or two aircraft passed over at low altitude as they came in to land.

As we rounded a bend, the full beam headlights from a car in the middle of the road suddenly met us. Anna was clearly dazzled but did a handbrake turn and accelerated back in the direction we had come from. There was a rattle of gunfire and the rear tyres were shot out, sending us off the road and into the scrubland.

"Get out and run in the opposite direction to me, now!" she yelled as we stopped.

I didn't need telling and ran, falling and scrambling into the semi-arid scrub. I must have run several hundred yards when I slowed and took stock. Nobody seemed to be following me but there was activity in the direction Anna had taken. There was a pistol shot, a scream and then silence.

I had to find out what had happened and quietly made my way towards the direction of the scream now reinforced by voices shouting.

In the beam of the car headlight there was Anna being held by a man, while another was holding his arm that appeared to be bleeding. He had a pistol and as she struggled he hit her across the face knocking her to the ground.

The other rapped out a string of Russian that I didn't understand and then in loud, heavily accented English shouted.

"Dr Aldborough, if you do not come here in one minute exactly, your friend will be shot, and then we will come to find you and you also will be shot. If you come, I promise that you will not be harmed". With that he began to count the seconds. The one who was bleeding bent down and put his gun to her head.

Anna suddenly managed to kick him in the groin and scrambled up but unfortunately tripped and fell. Her assailant fired at her but missed and as she tried to get up he took careful aim. I had by this time taken out the pistol she had given me and brought her attacker in my sights.

I was lucky. He screamed as I loosed off another shot that stopped him before he could fire back. His companion ran behind the headlight beam and although I fired in his direction I missed.

There was silence as we all froze. Then a burst of automatic AK47 fire ripped through the scrub from his direction, the bullets whistling over my head. There was silence except for the moaning of the guy I'd hit, and nobody moved. Then in the distance I heard a car approaching.

We were either in great trouble if this was reinforcement for our attackers, but on the other hand it could be Roscoff. Anna seemed to have got clear. There was a scrambling from their direction: they seemed to be going back to their car, and from the sound of it the wounded man was being carried. There was the sound of slamming doors and then silence apart from that of the approaching car.

Anna's truck was still just off the roadway and the arriving car pulled up. To my horror it was not Roscoff. Two men got out and with the others fanned out, clearly hoping to hem us in. They turned off the car headlights – meaning they probably had night sights. I was against a rock about eight feet high and pressed myself against it. The sound of the stalkers disturbed the forbidding silence. They were getting nearer. I then suddenly saw a red spot move across my chest; someone had me in their sights. I leapt sideways as a shot rang out ricocheting off the rock. I came out in a sweat as I waited.

Then suddenly a loud oath came from a shadow six feet away and I fired my pistol at it. There was the sound of men running towards me when with a sudden clatter of its blades a helicopter swept up the hillside with a searchlight beam on. A flare was fired, illuminating the whole tableaux round me. The man I had shot was clutching his side as well as his foot. From the corner of my eye I saw a scorpion that was now scuttling into the scrub. It had bitten the wretch.

Several shots rang out, some from the AK47 that was then quickly silenced. Roscoff was shouting for Anna to keep low while they cleaned up. The cavalry had arrived. The shooting was over.

Apparently, he had picked up our message soon after we had called and immediately got the helicopter hoping to get to us before the opposition did. Three of the attackers had been killed, another gave himself up and the last, suffering from the scorpion bite and my gunshot in his leg was definitely out of commission.

Roscoff's men drove the attackers' and Anna's cars back while the rest of us, dead and alive, flew in the chopper. When we had landed at the airport and two ambulances had taken away our attackers he turned to me and in a very determined voice said,

"Harry, your presence here in Baku is making life a little too exciting. Now the Mafia has shown its hand clearly. One of their men has been injured and another three killed. Without doubt they will have you in their sights from now on. I suggest that you get out of Baku, tomorrow if you can. I cannot risk Anna further. Tell your Mr Colliston and your embassy that another attempt has been made on your life and you want to go and that I want you to go." With that he strode back to the Land Rover that was waiting for him at the airport.

Anna and I were driven ahead of Roscoff as we made our way into Baku. Anna had recovered from the blow she had been given apart from a graze but was, for her, a little quiet as we drove. Roscoff, as arranged turned off as we went through the city leaving Anna to drop me off at my apartment. As we stopped outside she leaned over and kissed my cheek "I think you should not go back to your room tonight, it is too risky. You will come back to my flat, which is secure. Anyway, it might be the last time I see you and we must make it a night we remember."

I had intended to persuade her to stay with me but this was a far better idea and I returned the kiss.

"I can't imagine a better way of saying 'au revoir', Anna." I murmured. We drove on.

Her flat was in one of the elegant pre-1917 buildings in the city, overlooking a park. It had been modernised and bore the imprint of her tastes, with Uzbek carpets on the floor and walls and Western style living conveniences. An American refrigerator took up a fair amount of the kitchen and contained a selection of wines. She chose one of the local sparkling varieties which I opened while she started cooking omelettes and mushrooms. I wandered round the flat inspecting her CDs and paintings, admiring her taste. To the strains of Tchaikovsky, and curled up on her large settee we ate and drank and went over the happenings of the day.

"Before we get down to pleasure let me sum up your position and you can ponder it at leisure," she said, going very serious. "Our Mafia friends seem to have decided that you are a good soft target to get back at the Egliston people. Whatever anybody else says they think you are an important figure brought in to oversee the smuggling of nuclear materials as well as being important to the oil operations."

"Also in this part of the world they have the honour killing tradition. When you add up the number of their men who have died in operations associated with you they will not rest until you are dead. I know you are working against Egliston and don't deserve all this lethal attention." She moved closer to me.

"You saved my life you know, Harry. I intend to show you how grateful I am. She sank into my ready arms and I carried her into the bedroom where there was a large four-poster bed. Our clothes seemed to melt off our bodies as we kissed passionately. We then both luxuriated in an extended foreplay that led inexorably to an even greater mutual orgasm.

We both fell asleep in a state of complete contentment, waking to the sound of the telephone. The clock said it was only six o'clock. It was Roscoff.

"Anna, tell Harry not to waste any time getting on to his consulate. I assume he is there with you. I've spoken to Colliston and said that you are safe in the arms of mother Russia but that our Mafia friends are likely to try again to abduct you now that you have shot and probably killed their men. I insist that you tell Harry to contact Colliston immediately and get the hell out of this country."

Anna assured him I was still in good health and very active.

"I think that Colliston can wait," I said pulling Anna back into bed. She didn't seem in a hurry to leave either and we again made love again in a way that recognised we might not meet again.

I rang Farouk to bring him up to date and to get him to pick me up and take me to Klanski. Then I got through to Colliston, who agreed that I should get out quickly. He advised me to make a booking on a regular flight out of Baku, as a diversion, as soon as I had decided with Klanski how and when to depart.

Anna and I embraced as Farouk announced himself at the door.

"We shall meet again, my English scientist," she said. "Keep safe."

I had fallen for her in a big way, but we both recognised that we would probably not meet again, at least while I was involved with the Egliston organisation. I resolved to try and return some day.

The fact that Anna and I had been rescued by the Russian unit under Roscoff had to be kept away from Klanski, as had Anna's role. Roscoff had been busy since the incident, fabricating a story that the Azeri authorities had been tipped off that a terrorist group was planning to take me hostage.

On receipt of Anna's phone call to her office a SWAT team had been scrambled to rescue us. Klanski seemed to accept this and was obviously anxious to get me out of the way now that the EROS work had been done. He knew that I knew about the smuggling but had been reassured by Campbell that I was able to keep it to myself. The Mafia attention was something he could do without and he was happy to agree to me going. In fact he had a transport flight leaving the following morning going back to the UK via Iran. He made arrangements for me to be signed on as one of the crew under a different name.

I needed to go back to the factory to wrap up arrangements and to see if I could pick up any further information on the fissile material and these arrangements would let me do just that. I would check out of my apartment and try and sleep at the workshop. It would be far safer there with Farouk and the security guards nearby.

Chapter 23. Egliston again

Harry wondered what Egliston was doing.

Egliston read the report from Klanski in Baku and scowled. As he looked through his picture window out over the English Channel the weather was blowing up for a storm with the heavy black clouds scudding across the sky. His mood changed to match that of the weather.

He had expected some opposition from one of the groups of Russian Mafia to his expansion of both legitimate and smuggling activities but he had hoped that Nicolas, his son, and Frobisher, would have been able to reach some sort of accommodation with them. The money they were getting from him was considerable and there was no excuse for this turn of events.

They would feel the full strength of his anger. The direct attack on one of Bakuoil's boats carrying uranium had been unexpected. Aldborough had unfortunately been on the boat but appeared to accept the event without doing anything stupid. He was now aware of Egliston's clandestine activities and knew about the smuggling of weapons grade uranium.

It seemed, however, as though his judgement on Aldborough's character had been correct, and that a mixture of carrot and stick should bring him into the organisation as a fully paid-up player.

The Russian Mafia had added one and two and made an erroneous four, identifying him as a key figure in Egliston's activities and that was something that had not been anticipated. It might be necessary to get him back to the UK for the time being until the furore had died down. Klanski had assured him that Harry had not been in contact with anyone other than technical people such as the girl he was with when he was ambushed. Even she appeared to be a fellow engineer with the Russian Oil company Sibneft and their relationship appeared to be sexual.

It really was time to bring Harry properly into the company's activities. He rang Campbell and told him to meet Harry off the plane and form his own opinion on his reliability and how best he might be used in the future.

His secretary placed a newspaper clipping on his desk as she brought him a cup of coffee.

"You might be interested to see this, Lord Egliston," she said. "It was in yesterday's edition of the Dorset Echo."

Egliston glanced at it and then picked it up, did a double take, and read it more closely. "Thank you Laura, that will be all," he snapped dismissively. It was indeed interesting, stirring up possibly worrying possibilities.

'WW2 unexploded bomb found in grounds of Corfe Manor!

Today the bomb disposal team from Bovington Army camp was called out to defuse a 1000lb high explosive bomb dating from WW2 that had been unearthed by workmen carrying out repairs at Norden Manor near Corfe Castle. It was successfully defused and the explosive melted out overnight. It is believed by locals to have been dropped during a night attack by a German bomber jettisoning its load after being hit by ack-ack fire during a raid on Poole. The plane was reported as having crashed into the sea off Swanage. Another bomb dropped at the same time killed a housekeeper employed at the Manor. Dr Charles MacLean the present owner of the property said "I'd heard rumours that there might be a bomb round here but never dreamt that it would be so close to the Manor itself. Thank God nobody has been hurt." His brother, the present Lord Egliston, the industrial tycoon, now serving as Lord Lieutenant of the County, owned the Manor during the war. Lord Egliston could not be contacted.'

Egliston had not given a thought to either Charles MacLean or Norden Manor for years. It felt as though someone had walked over his grave. The Manor still held evidence of his wartime spying activities buried under tons of earth. He had had no alternative at the time but to leave it and hope it would never be found.

The bomb that had caused the collapse of the tunnel in the vicinity of the house was one of a stick that had killed his mother and led to a turning point in his life. It was a coincidence however that an unexploded one had fallen so close to the first and it occurred to his suspicious mind that it might not be the whole story.

Although he had no real worries that his secret would ever be discovered, he decided that the Manor deserved a closer look. He could not personally investigate, as he did not want to meet MacLean, and told one of his security assistants to go and ask some questions under the guise of being a reporter.

In particular he wanted to know exactly where the bomb had fallen, whether there were any signs that anything else had been found, were the police involved and had anyone other than the disposal team been there? Perhaps it was time to make sure the evidence was irrevocably buried. He could not risk such a skeleton being found in his cupboard and resolved to do something about it.'

Chapter 24. Fissile Material in Baku

I didn't need, as it happened, to search for the fissile material when Farouk and I returned to the rig workshop. I had planned to pack up the calibration equipment that would be coming back with me and to check out two of the spare EROS tools for use if there was a failure offshore. To my surprise all the four spare tools had been taken from the locked store and were being prepared for loading on to a transporter. We could not contact Klanski and were not allowed by the security guards to go near to the tools as they were wrapped in plastic for transportation.

"Instructions have been received from London for these to be sent back to Britain" explained the workshop manager with a shrug. "They will be on a flight tomorrow morning on Klanski's order".

Presumably I would be travelling on the same plane. We were again unable to contact Klanski ourselves as he had gone to the Northern Caspian by helicopter.

Later in the day the security guards were sent away to deal with an alarm, which rang at the far end of the building. I decided to inspect the tools to see whether they had been tampered with and were secure for transportation.

To my surprise I found that in each one a section of the casing had been neatly machined out and a cover placed over the opening. While Farouk reluctantly kept watch I unwrapped a tool and screwed off the plate and found inside several black circular discs, of about six-centimetres diameter, mounted and sandwiched between other metal plates. I had seen uranium metal before at WTC and recognised the metallic plates immediately as uranium, presumably weapons grade. Each disc would probably weigh half a kilogram. The black plates between the metal plates would probably be loaded with boron to absorb neutrons so that there would be no possibility of a chain reaction. Farouk hissed that the building alarm seemed to be over and to get things covered up. I had everything returned and re-covered before the guards returned.

"We keep very quiet about this Harry. Remember that you are leaving and I have to work here and this is where my family lives." Farouk said earnestly. I promised him I would not involve him at all and that I would deal with it at the London end of the journey.

There were four tools being used to smuggle the uranium. If the uranium metal were weapons grade there would be in total about six kilos of U235, a good way towards the amount needed for an atomic bomb. It was a clever way of smuggling the material. Many oilfield tools contain radioactive sources and customs authorities were used to seeing them transported round the world. The uranium activity would not be detected in the background of other legitimate radioactivity. There was little I could do about it then. I dare not ring Colliston on my mobile in case the call was intercepted and certainly there was no landline connection that I could use at the workshop.

I learned that the tools were to be driven off during the evening to be loaded on the transport aircraft at the airport. Klanski had left instructions for me to be dressed as one of the technicians and to accompany the tools. Farouk was very worried about the future. He had been accustomed to ignoring activities that were no part of the normal run of things, a useful survival strategy. He looked on smuggling of drugs and caviar as semi-legitimate activities but this was in a different ball game. We shook hands, not expecting to meet again.

I arrived at the airport two hours later and drove directly to the apron where the plane was waiting. The Pakistani captain told me to go directly aboard and wait in the flight cabin. There were no customs or passport checks to my surprise; presumably money had changed hands. I had made a reservation on a commercial flight leaving during the morning as a decoy and prayed that the Mafia would be fooled. Colliston had made arrangements for a taxi to pick up one of his men from the hotel having checked out in my name. Eventually all loading was completed and the plane made a good take-off towards the rising sun. Was I glad to be leaving the country in one live piece! Fortunately I had brought some food with me and ate it in relief dropping off to sleep immediately afterwards.

I was woken it seemed almost immediately but must have been longer, by the engineer shaking my shoulder.

"We are about to land in Tehran; please fasten your belt". The crew, apart from the engineer, stayed in the cabin and I was told to stay with them because they wanted to make sure I came to no trouble from the Iranian authorities or anyone else. I was able to see that the tools were unloaded on to a carrier, which was driven off with armed guards in a following Land Rover.

After an hour we took off again, this time with the sun on our port side. The pilot turned to me and said, "Next stop, Hurn Airport in England." I hadn't given much thought as to what was going to happen when I got back to England, except that I wanted to speak to Rushton as soon as possible. Eventually we passed over the South Coast of Britain at Bournemouth outlined by the promenade lights and roads and came to a halt near a hangar at the edge of the airport.

There was a car waiting for me – there was no chance for me to contact Rushton - or even Charles. It was clear that I was headed for Egliston Hall, but for what sort of reception I was in for I had no idea. On arrival I was taken to a suite where I was told I could clean up as I would be seeing Campbell within the hour. He strode in just as I'd washed and shaved and offered me his hand to shake.

"Welcome back to Britain, Dr Aldborough. You've had an exciting time I hear. Come along and tell me all about it." He led me to a long wood-panelled room facing the lake outside and invited me to sit down. Coffee was waiting for which I was desperate, having not slept properly for the last leg of the journey.

"I have to tell you Harry," said Campbell seating himself opposite to me in a leather-upholstered chair, "that we have been very impressed by your work and the success you've had technically. We shall be taking up the technology in more of our fields. However, that's not why you are here. There have been some interesting things happening and I want to hear directly from you what you saw and what you intend to do. Start with your first visit. I want to hear about anything that might be relevant."

He sat back in the chair and fixed me with a penetrating stare. I was relieved that at least superficially I was not being suspected of my link with Rushton or even with Roscoff, and decided to play it that way. I started by clearing the position.

"There are clearly things going on that the company wishes to be kept secret. It was made clear to me at the start by Klanski that I should keep myself away from activities that I was not concerned with. Initially I assumed this was a purely commercial matter. It rapidly became clear that there was a hidden agenda. Lord Egliston implied that there would be other aspects to this job than that of oil recovery and that my salary reflected the need to recognise that I would accept these. I do accept this situation."

I went through the first visit, omitting the attempt on my life at the Maiden Tower. The episode when I was nearly shot by the guard at the rig factory I dealt with in full saying that I learned the hard way that I should keep a low profile about other activities going on in Baku. Clearly there was some smuggling of fissile material going on. I put in a good word for Farouk who had tried to keep me out of trouble. I summarised the results of the EROS work. Moving on to the second visit I had resolved to keep quiet about Roscoff and refer to Anna as a fellow engineer and social contact only.

As for the visit to see Colliston, of which Klanski was aware I stuck to my story about wanting to arrange technical seminars. The attempt on my life on returning with Anna from the visit to the eternal flame was a potential problem. The story I had concocted with Colliston was that the Azeri authorities had learned of the plan to kidnap me that day and had mounted the rescue with the helicopter after I had phoned Colliston.

Campbell said nothing, but continued to stare at me until I began to think I was about to be exposed as a fraud. Eventually he said,

"I'm glad you see it our way. Lord Egliston will be seeing you in due course. I think the time has come for you to involve yourself more in what I might call the strategic development of this company. Take a week to catch up with your data analysis and reports and then report to me at the Summerfield site on Tuesday next at 10am."

I was driven back to Wool Manor, where I decided to sleep off my weariness before I contacted anybody else.

Chapter 25. Lord Egliston - Split Personality – 1941

Flying Boat

Taylor went over to the picture window in his Egliston Hall office looking across the lake to the sea in the distance, with a smile playing across his otherwise hard face. He was beginning to enjoy himself in his assumed role of Lord Egliston and he allowed himself some self-congratulation on the way in which he was now being accepted by the community, the establishment and the military.

Later in the day he would be entertained at lunch at the Poole Harbour Sailing Club by the officer in charge of the take-off and landing facilities for the Clippers on the transatlantic run and Imperial Airways flying boats on the Empire routes, using Poole harbour as a base.

This building was used as the terminal for arrivals and departures and had a continual flow of VIPs.

To the outside world Taylor was Lord Egliston, an aristocrat, an army officer exempted from battlefield duties owing to his war injuries and a respected pillar of the community.

In reality he was now an active German spy in a position to acquire first class material for his masters in Berlin. The real Lord Egliston and his elder son, who had inflicted so much hurt on Taylor's family over the years, were both dead, and the other son had been sidelined. The plan thought up by his mother Nicole back in the late thirties was working superbly.

Indeed, six months after his eventful arrival in England, Taylor was beginning to believe he really was Lord Egliston, a necessary state of mind if the deception were to be a success. Nicole had coached him intensively in Major MacLean's mannerisms and speech and he had gone in detail through all the documentation in the Hall and manor on Egliston's private and public affairs, all the time feigning a shell-shocked personality to the outside world.

He refused medical help over this period, just as the real Major MacLean had fortunately done immediately after he had arrived home after escaping from Germany. He used the excuse of selective amnesia to cover his apparently hazy knowledge of his life before his injuries. Of the Major's time in Colditz Taylor had first hand knowledge as he had observed him there day by day and had given a very convincing account of the prison in his debriefing sessions with the security services.

Further back in time as a child he had been a jealous observer of Henry MacLean's privileges but now he was the owner of all that had been his property.

The real Major MacLean had had a detailed debriefing and medical examination in Switzerland before he was flown back to England via Spain. As a result of these he had been put on indefinite sick leave. Fortunately for Taylor he had been given copies of these reports and he was able to put on an appropriate act when a military doctor periodically examined him to assess his suitability for return to active service. Over a six month's period Taylor was able to convince the doctor that he would be unlikely to return to a field role for the foreseeable future but would be able to handle an administrative assignment locally. Eventually he felt confident enough to start meeting local people. He had made it known that his talents and position would make him suitable for a local military liaison role with the civilian local authorities.

Poole had become a hub for many wartime activities: BOAC flights to the British Empire, cross Atlantic Clipper flights, storage of military equipment, and defence forces. Local co-ordination of the civil and military activities had become an administrative nightmare and it was not long before he was assigned the liaison role he wanted. This gave him access to a lot of classified information.

He enjoyed seeing local dignitaries ingratiating themselves with him and telling him about how they were organising the war effort in Poole but his main problem was passing on the information he had gleaned to Germany. He had a radio transmitter but dare not use it except for urgent material and he mainly used an agent who took information from 'dead-letter boxes' around the area. His radio transmitter was installed in the priest's hole and tunnel he had used as a temporary hiding place for Major MacLean's body that he had rapidly disposed of after the shooting. Nicole, being part of the local community provided much more information. Local gossip let slip a wealth of information on local comings and goings of civil and service personnel billeted around the area.

He had cultivated a friendship with the officer in command of the Clipper terminal. Captain James Brown seemed honoured to be acquainted with a peer of the realm. Knowledge of the movement of dignitaries through the terminal was very useful to Taylor, indicating the links between Britain, its Empire and America. When he arrived at the sailing club for lunch he was introduced to a civilian, Mr A B Jones, who was to join them for lunch.

"You will see a lot of Mr Jones. He is responsible for the administration at the research station, near Renscombe farm on St Aldhelm's Head, developing the radar technology that is already being so useful to us. He will need a lot of help from the military in Poole and from the local authorities and will appreciate your collaboration," said Captain Brown.

Taylor already knew from local gossip and Nicole that something of the sort was in operation but had been unable to make any direct contacts there. By the end of the meal he had an invitation to visit the site with a view to meeting some of the staff and finding out how he could best assist Jones. This was a major breakthrough. On his first visit to the site he met several eminent scientists and engineers who had been drafted in on a crash programme.

Taylor knew that there was already a line of radar stations extending round the East coast of England as far as the Isle of Wight on the South coast and although rudimentary, had been very successful in detecting incoming bomber raids. He heard that Americans were involved. He was introduced to the young Jewish German, Dr Hans Reise, as a liaison at the working level and already identified by Nicole as a useful contact, who had fled from the Nazis in 1939. After graduating in physics and mathematics at Heidelberg University and feeling under threat from the Nazis, the young Reise left to do research at the Clarendon laboratory in Oxford under Professor Lindemann. From there he had been assigned to the new Dorset research site. With his knowledge of Germany and its language, Taylor was able rapidly to create a bond with the young scientist.

Taylor assiduously passed the information on to his handlers, requesting that they let him know of any information that would allow him to put pressure on Reise. When the reply came it was ideal for his purposes. Reise's father was an important banker in Heidelberg and had not been arrested, as many Jews had, because of his links to sources of finance for the Reich in Switzerland. Taylor got agreement from his handlers that the continued safety of Reise's parents should be used as a bargaining device to force him to pass on classified information.

****

Initially, Taylor cultivated Reise's friendship, inviting him to the manor for meals and reminiscing about his time in Heidelberg. Although Reise was very security conscious because of worries that he might come under suspicion owing to his background, he did give Taylor a lot of information, which in total formed a good overview of the research programme.

Detailed information about the microwave generators, magnetrons and klystrons being developed with the USA was however lacking in his discussions and the time was approaching when more pressure would be needed to reveal it. Taylor chose his timing carefully. Reise had been talking about his family and his fears. He was clearly homesick and Taylor decided to strike.

"You do realise that you have told me more than you should have about what is happening at the site?" he said casually. Reise was immediately on guard.

"Surely I'm authorised to say what I've told you as a liaison officer? Anyway you are not a security risk. I hope also that we have a friendship. You would be arrested immediately were I to hint that you might be a security risk."

"You are correct, I'm respected as a true blue Englishman," replied Taylor, laughing humourlessly, "The problem for you however, is that I'm not. I am, unfortunately for you, very close to the German government".

Reise stood up "I don't understand this."

Taylor barked at him to sit down, which he did, balanced on the edge of his chair.

"You must realise that your parents are still alive today only because they are of use to the Reich. It won't be long before that usefulness fades and they will go on a ride like thousands of other Jews to one of the German detention centres in Poland. In fact putting it bluntly, their future lies in your hands. Also your own future won't be very rosy if it is believed you have been a traitor to England."

Reise slumped back in his chair, the colour draining from his face.

Taylor went on. "You might think that you could denounce me to the authorities. I'm sure you won't, you've too much to lose. If I thought you would I'd shoot you myself here and now. Now pull yourself together - I'm going to tell you what I want. I am not asking you to steal documents and put yourself at risk. You are, however, going to pass all information I ask for verbally or written in your own hand to me. I want to know as much technical information as possible."

He wanted Reise to believe that the risk of his being found out was small, but that any reluctance to pass on information would lead to the loss of his parents. At a later stage he would tighten the noose when Reise had got used to the idea.

"Now, have a whisky and pull yourself together."

Reise walked out of the house like a zombie and feeling suicidal. Taylor, however, was a good judge of personality and had judged that he would not kill himself: He also judged that he would not sacrifice his family even if it meant betraying the country that had taken him in.

****

Over the next months the information Taylor got was first quality radar material. Unfortunately he wasn't to know that much of it would be ignored in Germany, whose scientists felt they had more promising technology. They had identified the ASV radar signals that were used by Coastal command to detect U-boats that had surfaced to charge batteries. The U-boats were able to continue with their success in sinking allied shipping. However; the intelligence that the Allies had developed centimetres wavelength radar went unheeded and many more U-boats were sunk in the following months as a result.

Taylor's link to the TRE establishment at Renscombe farm was cut in late 1942 by the transfer of all the scientists and engineers to Malvern, forming there what became the Royal Radar Establishment. Churchill had ordered the transfer because he feared that the Germans might carry out sneak commando type raids on TRE as reprisals for the raid on the German Bruneval radar in Normandy, in March 1942. Reise was also transferred and was unable to pass on information to Taylor.

Taylor had earlier warned his controller that the British had a team of commandos in training for hit and run attacks along the French coast and down towards Dakar. He gained this information after being dined at the Antelope Inn in Poole where the team had their meeting venue. The implications of this were not felt until the highly successful raid on St Nazaire and other exploits of the 'Cockleshell Heroes'. He did have successes, however. A decoy arrangement called Starfish had been set up on Brownsea Island in the harbour to divert the main thrust of bombing raids. After the leading German Pathfinder aircraft had dropped flares and incendiaries on the target area, Starfish would be activated with many decoy flares across the western half of the island. On the main occasion in May 1942, about 160 tons of bombs landed of which 150 tons were dropped on the island and only 9 tons on Poole itself. Taylor passed on this information to the Germans. Fortunately, errors in subsequent raids strongly decreased the effect of the bombing although considerable damage was still done. His main success was in alerting German e-boats to shipping that left the harbour and, passing on to the Luftwaffe, passenger aircraft schedules.

It was a blow to Taylor when the word came to him that Hitler had decided to cancel Operation Sealion, the planned invasion of Britain. He knew how weak the British defences were, especially if air attacks were concentrated on the fighter aerodromes. Then when Hitler instigated the Barbarossa invasion of the Soviet Union he almost wept at the folly. Nevertheless he continued reporting to his masters about the increasing defences and preparations for a future Allied invasion of continental Europe. 1943 came and he fortuitously met Lord Mountbatten returning from Quebec where he had agreed with Eisenhower the preparations for Operation

Overlord – the invasion of the continent. This provided the focus for his future spying activities.

Chapter 26. Check-up by Egliston

My first action in the morning, after my interview with Campbell was to contact Rushton and bring him up to date. He had received Colliston's account of happenings and had been trying to find out where I was. He seemed quite pleased with the intelligence I'd gathered despite my brush with death. After letting me go through my experiences again he encouraged me to dig myself ever deeper into the Egliston empire.

"I want you to stay close to Egliston now that it appears as though you have been accepted as reliable. Now we know he is using fissile material to get influence in countries desperate to get a nuclear capability it is vital we find out what has been delivered already, what is planned and where any stocks are. Presumably they are bringing some into the UK for temporary storage, rather than risking its loss elsewhere. It is most important that he doesn't get any inkling about your link to Charles and indeed to me. Whatever you do, don't let them see you with Charles MacLean."

I was desperate, however, to see Charles and Hans Reise and to find out where the 'time flashback' research was going, and rang the manor. Charles was thankful for my call as he had been trying to contact me in Baku without success.

He told me briefly about the latest developments and the way that Hans had buried himself away almost as a recluse after seeing some of the flashbacks in his house at Heidelberg. He was still very charged up about the discovery we made just before I went back to Baku that Henry had been a spy.

It wasn't surprising that Charles had been devastated by this revelation. Although he had long ago reconciled himself to being ignored and effectively being kept away from his family's past by his brother, he had respected him for his military service and had some sentimental memories of their childhood days. However, to be a traitor to one's country, to be untrue to the family name, despite the pressures placed on Henry as a PoW, was unforgivable. His first reaction had been to denounce him publicly and let events take their course, but I pressed him again to wait until Rushton agreed.

Rushton, without knowing about the flashback technology, had of course asked Charles and Julie not to do anything without his knowledge to avoid prejudicing his investigations into the Egliston Corporation.

Reluctantly, Charles had agreed to the cover plan of an unexploded bomb, as suggested by Rushton and he had worked out a detailed story for the press. The garden excavations had been re-covered and the house cleaned up so as to hide all evidence of the activities of the bomb disposal teams. Indeed a dummy bomb provided by Bovington had been driven away in an open lorry as a decoy.

Reporters had been and gone and the local excitement had died down.

Charles was therefore surprised to find a tall well-built man looking into his garden rather intently a few weeks later.

"Can I help you?" he asked the visitor, I'm the owner of this house."

"Yes, please. I'm a reporter from the Daily Express and I'm doing a feature on bombs and unexploded ordnance in this area left over from WW2 and, quite by accident, I heard about your problem of a few weeks ago.

Perhaps you'd be kind enough to give me some of your time and tell me about it," the man said, flourishing an 'Express' business card that appeared to back up his identity.

Charles invited him into the garden and showed him the site of the excavations and rolled out the story he had passed on to other reporters. The man quizzed him about how the bomb had been found and the history of the place, asking to be shown round some of the rooms as background material. Charles declined categorically to talk about his family and relationship to Lord Egliston although the reporter pressed him.

I arrived as the tour was taking place and was introduced as a friend of the family, without my name being mentioned. The man was, Charles noted later, particularly interested in hidden passages that might have been found, but Charles put him off by telling a general tale about priests' hide holes from centuries ago. Charles had asked that no photographs be taken on the grounds that he didn't want sightseers coming round.

"Are you thinking what I'm thinking?" I said after he eventually left, and decided to ring up the Express to check on the credentials of the visitor. I wasn't really surprised to find that the paper denied all knowledge of the man, only suggesting he might be a freelance hoping to get an article published.

"I suggest we tell Rushton right away," I said to Charles. "This could mean that Egliston is checking up on the story. I'd better make myself scarce because it would make things difficult for both of us if he finds out how well I know you."

****

The report from his security assistant was on Egliston's desk within hours of the visit. He was assured that Charles MacLean had shown no suspicion that he was anything but a reporter. There were also photographs, which a colleague had taken of the bombsite and of Charles, as well as a photograph of Harry taken from a parked car as he arrived. Egliston quizzed the security assistant intently, trying to convince himself that his secrets were intact. The assistant had done a good job, interviewing nearby residents and had convinced himself that the story of the unexploded bomb was genuine.

Egliston picked up the photograph of Harry. "I know this man. What was he doing there? What the hell is Aldborough doing at the Manor?" he growled. The security assistant was then given a strong tongue lashing for not finding out what Harry was doing there.

Having satisfied himself that his wartime secret was reasonably safe, Egliston now had a second problem. What business had Harry with Charles MacLean? Harry was heavily involved with the Bakuoil project and had appeared to keep quiet about the fissile material activities in his dealings in Baku despite the problems with the Mafia.

Although there was nothing in principle wrong with the two knowing each other, Charles's views on the Egliston Corporation might influence Harry's attitude. Alternatively there might be a hidden agenda. He would speak to Harry as soon as he could and in the meantime told Campbell to do some more digging into Harry's reports and if anything seemed suspicious to shake it out of him.

Chapter 27. Things begin to fall apart.

The call came through on my mobile while I was at WTC supervising the dismantling of the experimental equipment. Now that the EROS tools were being so successful in the field trials I no longer needed the Winfrith base and could rely on the Summerfield facilities. I had to supervise the work myself to make sure any commercially sensitive information didn't leak out. The first job was to get rid of the large block of oil-soaked limestone. Not an easy job. The only way was to break it up and bury the rubble in a lined pit that would stop any leakage into the groundwater. I had to get in some quarry workers with pneumatic drills and rock splitters to do that. The call was from Campbell. I had been expecting it but not relishing what it would entail.

"Harry, I want you to come to a conference on Long Island tomorrow. The first part is technical and Joe King will be there to make sure that the future production of your tools is put on a quality-controlled basis. "

"The second part is strategic and will be you and me with one or two others. I don't need to tell you that this is strictly need-to-know so tell nobody." He sounded a bit distant, but it appeared that I was still in their good books and nothing had come to light about my links with Charles or Rushton. As a precaution I sent an e-mail to Rushton to tell him about my call.

When I arrived on Long Island, having been met at Poole quay, Joe was already there with Bahir Farouk, the compound manager, and told me that Campbell would not be present at our meeting but would arrive later.

It was good to meet Joe again and he was anxious to hear about what had happened in Baku. It took two hours to finalise a production programme and specify the equipment and procedures that would be needed to provide tools for two other oilfields in the Caspian. Joe and Bahir decided to leave.

"Keep in touch," shouted Joe as their launch pulled away from the jetty.

My mobile rang as he waved. It was Rushton, sounding somewhat concerned.

"Harry, I have reason to believe that your cover might have been blown. Colliston has just contacted me to say that Klanski has been making more enquiries about you and he has discovered the true nature of your links to Roscoff and Anna. It is only a question of time before he knows about your link to Colliston. Go to ground and make sure that Egliston's people don't get hold of you. It's a bloody nuisance now that you had got their trust. I'll get protection for you but that will take a while."

"I think you are a bit late!" I shouted into the phone, waving and shouting towards the launch taking Joe away. I was too late. There was only one other boat at the jetty and that was being worked on and was clearly unseaworthy. I turned round to see the security guard strolling over.

"I've had Mr Campbell on the phone," he said. "He'll be here in half an hour and has asked me to make sure you are comfortable. Perhaps you would care to go to the conference room." Clearly he had been told to keep an eye on me.

"Sure," I said. "I'll get my laptop and start my report."

I walked over to the offices and went inside. The guard didn't follow me but positioned himself at the door.

I rapidly searched for a route out at the back but all doors were locked and I found myself shinning out on to the rear roof and then to the ground.

There did not appear to be anyone watching me and I ran down to the shoreline hoping there would be a motor or even a rowing boat that I could take. I wandered round the island and saw the tide was falling and that the mudflats were becoming exposed. It was only about two hundred metres to the high water mark at the harbour edge. Beyond that, the ground rose to a small headland that I remembered was a bird sanctuary.

Then I saw a line of posts starting to appear with the falling tide both on the shore and the island and realised that they probably marked an old causeway - maybe I could get across there on foot if the tide fell sufficiently. I decided to try it. The first fifty yards of the causeway had a reasonably hard surface and I was able to wade along at thigh height.

Suddenly there was no base to the causeway and I had to try swimming, but after a few yards I was in thick black mud that sucked me down. Almost in panic I managed to grasp one of the old stumps of timber marking the way. Clearly the causeway no longer existed as a viable route.

I hung there assessing the position. The stumps were about two metres apart. Perhaps I might be able to struggle from one to the other. Hopefully, I climbed up to stand on the stump and then leapt towards the next one. I managed two more posts this way but the next one broke off, flinging me into the black ooze into which I gradually sank. Unless I touched terra firma I would drown.

It seemed an eternity with no sound but that of seagulls round me. I dare not shout for help. At last, with the mud up to my chest my foot touched rock. The next half-hour was hell but I made gradual progress as I had clearly reached an intact section of the causeway.

I hauled myself out and staggered into the shelter of the trees. Surely I had been missed and they would soon be after me.

Looking back across to the island I saw a launch speeding towards the jetty on the island, probably Campbell. It was vital I got to civilisation for help. I reached a woodland track and made my way along it for about ten minutes without seeing signs of life.

Then I heard a car coming. Hiding behind a tree, I was overjoyed to see it was an RSPB van – Royal Society for the Protection of Birds. I leapt out and waved it down. The driver got out and walked towards me smiling. I can just remember saying,

"Thank God I found you" when his fist hit my jaw and everything went black.

Chapter 28. Heidelberg disclosures.

Hans Reise had been deeply affected by his discovery, through the flashbacks, that the Nazis had probably killed his parents soon after the beginning of the war. He had believed at the time that the assurances given to him by Egliston, as a spy, that the Nazis would spare his parents because of his father's contacts with Swiss banking organisations. He had co-operated with him in supplying information on radar as a further insurance for his parents' lives.

As late as 1945 he still believed, because of Egliston's assurances, that they were alive. Eventually, Egliston had told him, when the Allies were sweeping across Europe, that contact had been lost with the situation in Heidelberg and that he should prepare himself for the worst. It was now clear that Egliston had lied to secure his co-operation.

Reise wondered, now that he was confronted by the evidence, why he had believed Egliston. The man was completely amoral and ruthless as he well knew and he should have realised it all those years ago.

Now it was too late to do anything. He could not blow the whistle on Egliston without revealing his own dishonourable past in being a traitor to the country that had adopted him in his hour of need. Their business dealings since the war, although carried out to mutual benefit, had bound their lives together irrevocably and now he could do nothing against the monster. Egliston habitually treated him with ill-disguised disdain. At least he would now stop any further dealings with him.

Reise threw himself into thinking about the time 'Torch' and how it worked. He needed to improve the clarity of the images so that at least he could get someone to lip-read more of what was being said in those flashback scenes. He now had worked out a reasonable theory as to how the flashbacks worked and with better control over the time 'Torch' operation he would be able to home in more accurately on target past times, as well as getting clearer images.

He had managed to transfer the development funds he had secured from the Egliston Corporation into a personal account so that the additional development work would not appear on the accounts Egliston always insisted upon. Reise was reaching the conclusion that Egliston must not be allowed to know that the work had been successful.

Over the next month he made detailed changes to the 'Torch'. More accurate control over dimensions, a larger size and better frequency control were implemented and he settled down to a detailed flashback study of the goings on at his Heidelberg home during the war. He was able to home in on the early days of the war and to see his parents in their daily lives. With the help of his deaf, lip-reading housekeeper, he was able even to get snatches of conversation. It was clear that his parents were in day-to-day fear of their lives. All the servants had left the house and his father no longer went out to work.

The dreaded day came when he saw soldiers enter the room, after which he saw his parents no more. He actually narrowed the date down to 22nd December 1939. Egliston must have known, even when he first met him, that his parents had probably been transported to a death camp.

Anger came over him in waves as he went through these discoveries. There was no way he would ever work with Egliston again.

Like a man in a trance he kept up his viewing of the comings and goings in the house. It appeared to have been taken over by a high-ranking Nazi and his family. Meetings were held in the room, and occasionally he recognised some visitors. One was Albert Speer, the munitions minister, whom he knew had lived in another house on the Schlosswolfsbrennenweg.

Obsessed, he scanned each passing year all day long, fascinated by the comings and goings. Hans's housekeeper sat in on many of the sessions relating the results of lip-reading, but never discovered any references to Reise's parents. One day, there began what appeared to be a routine meeting, between a civilian and a group of German officers. Three others he had not seen before then joined them.

Then his heart almost stopped. One of the arrivals turned full face to him. There was the face he had seen and dreaded so many times during the war. What the hell was Egliston doing in German uniform in a meeting with the Germans in the middle of the war?

Most of the conversation could not be deciphered by lip-reading as they were speaking with their heads close together, but he was able to gather from snatches that they were discussing a plot against Hitler.

Eventually the meeting ended and Egliston was left, with the one German in civilian clothes. Again, they were not being able clearly to see their lips, which frustrated any attempt to understand the conversation. Egliston's final remarks were however clear as they shook hands before leaving.

"We have an agreement. We shall survive this war and prosper, 'auf wiedersehen'," Reise went over the sightings time and time again but became no wiser.

His mind was in turmoil. He knew Egliston was a spy, but surely not important enough to risk coming to Germany while the war was still being waged. What did his final words to the German mean? Was Egliston part of the plot to kill the Fuhrer, and did his certainty that he was going to survive have any significance?

What was clear was that Egliston not only knew that his parents were dead but his presence at the house at that time surely meant he was involved in their deaths.

****

Reise sat at his desk and wrote a report to Egliston. The cover note read,

For the eyes of Lord Egliston alone:
Time Flashback Project.

I enclose a report on this project that has now proved to be a failure. The original crude sightings are now known to be an artefact of the apparatus that was being used. Although my theoretical studies have shown that the ability to see some flashbacks in time past is possible the power that would be needed to induce them would be completely impractical. I have therefore stopped work on the project. I shall continue with some theoretical work but I fear that I am not optimistic of success. I shall submit the accounts and a report for the record in due course.

Hans Reise

Chapter 29. Reise's Revenge 2001

Hans Reise had an easy-going constitution and projected the avuncular image of a benign scientist but right now he was not a happy man. In fact, he built up a burning desire for revenge against Egliston. The hours spent obsessively viewing time-flashbacks at his Heidelberg home were beginning to eat into his soul as he saw how he had been duped over a very long time. He could not believe how gullible he had been. If he had had a gun and Egliston in front of him at that instant he would have killed him.

He recalled how their relationship had never been personal after the first months and that even in that period it was illusory. The relationship was now that of business associates with a shared guilty secret.

Immediately after the war he had provided technical and scientific input to Egliston's enterprise in a marriage of convenience in building up businesses based on electronics and radar. It was highly profitable and Reise had swallowed his reservations.

As a fairly rich man he went back after a few years into academia and had an arms length relationship with Egliston in which Reise would recommend bright graduates he encountered in his university work to him as well as passing on promising research ideas, receiving in return substantial commissions and a handsome retainer. All this he had agreed to, despite a general antipathy towards Egliston.

The flashbacks had now revealed a deeper level of deceit that made him despise himself for being seduced by the financial return. Not only did Egliston know his parents had been sent away to death camps early in the war but he had actually visited the confiscated the Reise home in Heidelberg, where he had met dissident Nazis as part of a German espionage conspiracy against Hitler. That plot had clearly failed but Egliston had somehow managed to avoid the consequences of its obvious failure and had survived and prospered.

Reise was now driven with his single-minded obsession to continue his search into the past. What had happened to the art treasures in the house after the Germans had left? Who had been there?

Every day he settled down in darkness with the equipment, eating his meals brought to him by Katrina while he watched the phosphorescent glow of images from the past. He did not have long to wait to find out from his flashback searches of the time in 1945 when he knew the Allied forces had swept across the town. The first troops he saw in the house were American GIs who used the house as a place for rest and relaxation which seemed to involve drinking the cellar dry and making love to women brought up from the town. There was no systematic attempt to loot the contents however.

The Holy Grail, so to speak, of Reise's search materialised a month or so after the GIs arrived. British troops appeared in their stead who were clearly there as a part of a well-organised operation to strip the place of any valuables. An officer supervised the intensive operation directing the packing of the paintings and objets d'art. As he watched him Reise thought his movements were familiar. Then the officer took off his hat and walked across the room towards Reise's vantage point.

It was Egliston! He watched in disbelief as the operation continued. He knew of course that Egliston with his fluent German had been sent to Germany after the war ostensibly to interview captured Germans, but he had never mentioned being in Heidelberg.

This was the last straw for Reise. Egliston himself had stolen his family's property. How Egliston must have laughed behind his back! Hans almost cried with rage.

He resolved that he would search back further into the man's history. There must be other revelations and somewhere, somehow he would find a way to bring the man down without inflicting personal damage to himself.

He would go to the Norden Manor where Egliston had lived during the war to do a detailed flashback scan. It would mean he would have to confess his wartime role to Charles and reveal Egliston's treachery, but he would have to risk the consequences. Charles, he knew, hated his brother, but would certainly not wish to know he had been a traitor.

Nevertheless, he would have to take the chance. There was a strong possibility that Charles had independently found out about Egliston, but his flashback equipment was inferior to Reise's and anyway Charles would surely have said something about such a discovery.

Having decided on a course of action he rang Charles to ask if he could visit and update his equipment. Charles readily agreed. Reise worked another week searching for more flashback information before packing up and securing the equipment in a storeroom at his Heidelberg home.

Charles had, like Reise, been using his flashback equipment extensively and welcomed him into the Manor in the expectation that they would be discussing technical developments. Reise bided his time to reveal his past as a spy and to tell Charles what he had discovered.

They worked during the first week on tuning and upgrading the 'Torch' with the developments Reise had made over the last month and Charles was filled with enthusiasm, as he had only been unable to scan limited cameos of the past with his prototype equipment.

During one evening they had done justice to Gladys's cooking and Hans judged the time was ripe for his speech of confession and supplication.

"Charles, I've some very bad news. It will shock you and you may, probably, wish to go to the police. I'm placing myself in your hands and I'll understand if you do decide to have nothing more to do with me. I hope sincerely however that you will agree to continue our working together."

Charles stopped with his glass of wine halfway to his lips.

"Go on," he said tersely.

Reise went through his well-rehearsed confession starting with his wartime introduction to Egliston, his recruitment as a spy and their joint spying activities. Charles let him go on for a full half-hour without interruption. Before lapsing into silence Reise looked him earnestly in the face and said,

"I will leave now if you wish. I know you have not wished to talk about your brother for reasons I understand but you must believe me. He was a German spy."

The room fell silent for a full further minute while Charles stared at Reise and eventually spoke with a deep sigh.

"I know Henry was a spy. I know because of this damned flashback device. I suspected you knew as well. He was probably brainwashed when he was a prisoner in Germany. The truth will come out, I'm sure. I understand, but I can't forgive, what you did; nevertheless I shall not tell anyone about what you have said. Henry will eventually produce enough rope to hang himself. When that time comes your secret might come out as well. I shall not reveal it before then you can be assured. In your case there were reasons for your actions but I don't suppose that will have any effect on the authorities." He paused. "Why are you telling me this? You presumably have a reason."

"Quite right, I have. Over the past month I've been going over wartime events that occurred in my Heidelberg home. The developments to the flashback 'Torch' I've made enable me to tune in on any time I wish over that period and believe me, I now have a good idea of what happened and how your brother fits in to my story."

He then described his discoveries in detail, being listened to in silence. He ended by saying:

"The outstanding questions as to what Egliston was doing in his visits to Germany during and then after the war and how they fitted into his role as a spy are still unclear, but I believe this manor holds to the key to understanding this."

Under this unhappy truce, they worked systematically over the next week with the flashback equipment, viewing scenes onwards from the time Charles's grandfather was known to live at the Manor. Charles was astounded by the clarity of the flashbacks now that the improvements were built in to the equipment. Nicole, the housekeeper, was the most frequent person to be seen as she went about her duties. They saw the arrival of Henry in 1941 after his escape from Colditz. He was clearly suffering from shell shock and would sit for hours crying and pacing to and fro.

Charles was deeply affected by this and said he could now understand the reasons for his brother's behaviour.

Nicole bore the indignities he piled on her with a stoic resignation. Then one day they saw there was a sudden change in Henry.

He became a vigorous figure, who appeared to eat well   and   to spend a lot of the time working at the desk. He also showed great affection for Nicole, whereas before he had ignored or been brusque to her.

"When I met Egliston at the Manor during the early part of the war his attitude to Nicole was formal but courteous," remarked Reise. "In these flashbacks they seem to behave like mother and son."

Charles looked at him with the light of understanding beginning to dawn on him.

"I want to go through that period just before this change of character minute by minute if necessary," he muttered, slowly and thoughtfully. That is what they did, all night and all day until all had become clear in one dramatic scene.

They had watched Henry sitting with his head in his hands in front of a fire before he suddenly looked up, staggered to his feet and lurched towards the watchers with what appeared to be horror on his face. The absence of sound made the whole thing appear like a pre-war movie.

A few seconds later a bullet wound appeared in his chest, blood splashed out and he crumpled backwards to the floor as a second figure walked towards him and bent down over the still body. The figure holding a Luger then turned placed it on the desk and laughed.

The fearful thing was that the second man was also Henry. It was like a nightmare to Charles. Nicole then came on the scene and the two of them wrapped the body in a blanket, with Nicole then cleaning up what must have been a bloody mess on the floor and desk.

Charles and Reise replayed the scene and sat in silence before Charles spoke. "When you mentioned mother and son, the thought came to me out of the blue who our spy really was. He was not Henry. He was an impostor." Charles' face became dark. He continued.

"Nicole had a son, Peter Taylor, who left to go to Germany several years before the war. He had the same build as Henry but had slightly different facial features. I was only about seven years old at the time and I had forgotten all about him. The story was that he had quarrelled with his mother and gone to live with German relatives. I had forgotten until now that she was originally German, as had most others round here. Her loyalty was never questioned in all the years I knew her. Taylor had obviously had his appearance changed somehow, in Germany, and dyed his hair black to alter his features. Seems incredible but plastic surgery is the only thing it could be. It is clear to me that the present Lord Egliston is not Henry. Henry died in 1942. It explains everything!"

"What happened to the body, I wonder?" mused Reise.

"That is something I am going to find out," returned Charles angrily.

Chapter 30. 1944 - Egliston's changing loyalties

Today, Studland beach on a summer's day is full of people, nudists in their allotted section of the beach providing light and passing entertainment for the masses of tourists, 'twitchers' watching for Dartford Warblers, and people messing about in boats.

If you walk away from the nudists, as most people do, along the three-kilometre long beach, towards the chalk downs rearing out of the sea and ending in the chalk stack known as Old Harry, you will come across a relic of WW2, Fort Henry. It is a concrete bunker about thirty metres long facing out across the expanse of the beach, originally built by Canadian troops, and now restored by the English National Trust and looking much as it might have done in its heyday in 1944.

Taylor nearly met his Maker there at that time, and the experience helped to change the direction of his life. In 1944 the beaches, resembling some of the French Normandy beaches, were being used for Operation Smash, a rehearsal using live ammunition and a landing by tanks and troop carriers in preparation for the Operation Overlord D-Day landings. It was a dangerous place to wander about in.

In 1944, Taylor was fully aware of these military activities and had passed on the information to his controller. Fortunately for the Allies, he was convinced that the preparations were for an assault across the

Channel near Calais, rather than the Normandy beaches. In June 1944 he received notice from the War Office, as liaison officer, that several top military leaders and government ministers were planning to observe the trial landings from Fort Henry and that he was expected to make sure facilities were available for them in the nearby Studland Manor. Eisenhower himself would probably also be flown in to join the group.

Taylor immediately recognised the potential for a mass assassination, when security might be stretched at the height of the live ammunition operations and it was that to which he bent his plans. His controller told him that the opportunity was such that a suicide mission would be in order and that he should sacrifice his life, if that was necessary to kill the Allied leaders.

The idea of self-sacrifice did not appeal to him. How could the task be executed leaving him alive at the end? Although still a committed Nazi he now had serious doubts about Hitler and the Third Reich's prospects. He rapidly came to the conclusion that an expendable agent, not he, must be found to do the job. His controllers were easily persuaded of the logic and brought in an Irish Republican Army 'sleeper' from London who would be very happy to kill high-ranking British Officers.

Under cover of darkness, Sean Murphy, a long-standing member of the IRA who had been placed in London at the outbreak of the war made his way to the Manor. His deformed leg, the result of a gunfight in Belfast, had fuelled further his bitter hatred of all things British and had also kept him out of the forces.

In a simple disguise with forged papers as an injured soldier returning from leave he reached Wareham station and caught the small train on the branch line that passed through Corfe Castle. There he melted into the shadows, walking to Norden Manor under cover of darkness. He was taken aback when Taylor in British officer's uniform met him at the door and was drawing his revolver, thinking he had been set up, when Taylor stopped him with a curt order to enter quickly.

"You nearly died there," growled Murphy. "Khaki makes me see red if you see what I mean. Have you got some whiskey to calm me down?"

"You'll have whiskey when I'm ready and we've established a few ground rules," replied Taylor. "First, this isn't a chance for you to settle personal scores with the English. You will do exactly what I say or this project is as good as dead, and so are we. You do not go out of this house until I give the order. The operation will be planned in detail and we will go over it time and time again until I'm satisfied that we are ready. We have two weeks. As yet I don't know how we will carry out the job, that's why I need to use your experience from Ireland."

Murphy seemed to accept the ultimatum and melted into the Manor, not to be seen outside in daylight from then on.

Fort Henry was only a hundred yards or so from Studland Manor, from which the VIPs would walk, having been transferred from Poole town by car. They would of course be strongly guarded during the journey and during the time they were in the Manor. The two venues for attack would be first, the road to Studland where a bomb would be exploded as the car was passing or, secondly, in the bunker itself during the beach assault. The two men rapidly ruled out the former as decoy cars might be used, the difficulty in getting sufficient explosive and in escaping afterwards.

During the Operation Smash assault however, during the live ammunition assault, the group would be inside the bunker and their guards would either be inside the bunker with them or well away from it near to the Studland Manor house.

Turner had reconnoitred Fort Henry and realised that it would be possible for an attacker to get right up to it to and to push grenades through the slotted viewing aperture without being seen by guards in the Manor house. The effect of explosions inside would be devastating. During the assault there would be so much noise that the attack might not even be noticed at the Manor until it was too late and the attacker could escape. Taylor himself would make sure he personally was in the Manor at the time after having made sure the agent was in place.

The next week was not an easy time for either of them. Murphy got hold of the whisky one evening while Taylor was out. He became belligerent when Taylor returned, demanding to know more about him, why an English 'toff' was working for the Germans. Taylor felled him with one blow and held a revolver to his head.

"Listen carefully you scum. I hate the British as much as you do, but I hate weakness as well. Any more of this and you are dead. Do you understand?"

Murphy nodded, his face a picture of hatred, but he backed off.

Taylor had drawn up detailed drawings and had even risked taking photographs to train Murphy. He had secured grenades and a machine gun for his use. It was so easy for him. As liaison officer, he was briefed by the War Office on the detailed plans; how many cars, the security and the timings.

The day came and it was announced that Montgomery and Eisenhower would be attending together with other high-ranking officers. As expected,

Taylor was ordered to meet the group at the Manor and give a briefing before the Operation Smash.

All was going to plan. Taylor was well known by guards assigned to security in the Studland area and planned to smuggle the agent in his car boot through the road checkpoints and drop him off near to Studland village itself after the area had been given the security sweep by troops. It was arranged that the agent would attack when the live ammunition assault had been underway for thirty minutes. Taylor had hidden a bicycle in the gorse and scrub near to the harbour for Murphy to get back to Norden and then to lie low. There were plenty of tracks along the south edge of the harbour, used during daylight by quarrymen, and it would be very unlikely that he would meet anyone. If he did, it would be too bad for that person.

The assault began on time, with all the VIPs transferred to the bunker. Guards were placed in its end sections.

At fifteen minutes into the attack Taylor showed himself at the front door of the Manor with field glasses, this being the signal for a further fifteen-minute countdown by the agent. The assassination attack was now irrevocable. Taylor settled himself with other officers behind the blast protection in front of the Manor windows and waited, fascinated by the lethal firework display outside. The assault was spectacular with a shelling of the beach from an offshore armada and dropping of bombs from planes coming in low over the Manor. Taylor had never experienced realistic attack.

With five minutes to go to the planned attack by the agent a message from Prime Minister Churchill came over the communication equipment in the Manor, which had to be passed on to Montgomery for instant reply.

The telephone inside the bunker was found to be dead, having been disabled previously by Murphy.

"Sorry, old man," the colonel in charge said turning to Taylor "Take this down to the bunker, the password for the guard to open the door is 'Marlene'. Take a man with you."

Taylor was in now in a quandary, as well as danger from stray bullets. By the time he got there the agent might be attacking the bunker, but there was no way he could delay. Hopefully he could get there before the attack and with luck the agent might realise the need to wait. On the other hand he might open fire.

Heart pounding, he and a squaddie ran towards the bunker with the noise and flashes of the landing assault ahead of them. To Taylor's relief there was no sign of his agent as they came up behind the bunker towards the entrance. Taylor to a quick look round the front facing the beach and was horrified to see Murphy putting the first grenade through the slot.

Murphy obviously saw Taylor out of the corner of his eye and whirled round, opening up with his machine gun without asking questions. Taylor had fallen to the ground but took a graze from a bullet across his shoulder. The squaddie wasn't so lucky and was knocked back by the burst. Taylor realised he could take the next burst and rolled sideways down the slope to the beach, drawing his revolver and loosing off three shots, one of which found its mark. Quickly Taylor ran across, putting two more shots into Murphy. He then realised that he hadn't heard the grenade explode.

Looking down he pushed Murphy over and saw three on the ground. If he was quick he could still put them in. He picked them up and immediately realised that they had not been primed. The reason was clear.

There was a smell of whisky. He thought that if he was quick he might be able to get the primers out of Murphy's pocket and do the deed himself. He had just got one out when Murphy, with blood coming from his mouth, shouted a last cry of rage.

It was too late; the occupants of the bunker would have heard. He shot Murphy full in the face, shouted the password and that the danger was over. The door was flung open, the guards rushed out and Montgomery himself appeared with his revolver drawn. "You seem to have made a good job of that," he said, looking down at Murphy before he and the VIPs were rushed back to the Manor surrounded by the guards.

Taylor was livid at the turn of events. Although he had survived and in practice was praised for dealing with the attacker, he had failed in his mission and would be blamed by his German controllers. The irony was that the British would probably decorate him for his actions. He was safe: there was no way in which the agent could be linked to him.

****

1944 was the year in which the direction of Taylor's life changed irrevocably from dedicated support of the German cause to dedication to building his own future, even if this meant discarding his past hates and prejudices. In fact the timing of the conversion can be tied down to one particular day. The Luftwaffe had made many raids on the Poole area because of its strategic importance as a port and as a military staging post. In the early war years the night raids were not very successful owing to the effectiveness of a decoy strategy. In this, flares and fires were deliberately started on the wooded

Brownsea Island in the centre of the large harbour to divert the main attacks away from the town and docks a mile away.

Later, the air raids had more success partly because of the intelligence Taylor sent. Sporadic raids continued and on the 24th of April a few planes came in a night attack on the large ammunition factory near Wareham. One such raid, having missed the target and being damaged by ack-ack fire, jettisoned its bombs over Corfe village in a desperate attempt to gain height and to escape.

Taylor's mother Nicole had been visiting a friend in the village and instead of taking shelter ran towards the Manor to be with her son. A large bomb landed in the rear garden and another exploded nearby just as she was taking a short cut through the garden. She was killed instantly, although it was not until the next day that her remains were found. Taylor did not appreciate the irony that his spying actions were indirectly responsible. He was devastated, being lost in grief for weeks afterwards. She was the only person in his life whom he had loved.

In his troubled mind it was the British who were to blame and in the next few weeks he took considerable risks in gathering intelligence and passing it on to his masters in Germany.

Unfortunately the bomb had also collapsed the tunnel from the Manor in which his transmitter notes and code books were located. He had been unable to recover the material, first because of the dangers of discovery involved and, secondly, he had been in the habit of booby-trapping the area with a grenade in his absence. He had no idea whether this was still live.

There was no option but to leave the roof fall undisturbed and hope that nobody would find the tunnel in the future. In particular he cut off the wooden catch that would open the door to the tunnel and filled in the cracks with beeswax. He had then to make more use of dead letter boxes to pass on the information, a much more cumbersome method, until he could replace the lost equipment.

Nicole had provided the impetus for his hatred of the British and was the catalyst that kept it going. With her absence his resolve began to fade.

Chapter 31 1945 - Egliston to Germany

When D-Day came on June 6th it took Egliston by surprise. Although it was clear that an invasion was imminent, he had not believed it would go ahead in such bad weather. He was wrong as well in his forecast that it would be aimed further east than Normandy where it was in fact directed.

He continued to send data on the volume and type of forces and equipment sailing out of Poole but gradually as the Allies made strong progress he began to have doubts as to whether Germany could win the war.

There were so many factors against the Fatherland. The U-boat campaign in the Atlantic was no longer effective. Radar developments, which allowed submarines to be detected and destroyed by patrolling planes, had effectively stopped the campaign. The Americans were pouring vast resources into the war, Stalingrad had been lost, the Axis army in Tunisia had surrendered and then the Fascist regime in Italy collapsed.

He realised his position could rapidly become untenable and decided he would no longer be prepared to give his life for the Nazi regime. Once Germany was beaten he would without doubt be exposed as a spy unless he took steps to prevent disclosure.

Now that Nicole was no longer there to stiffen his resolve, he began to consider his future. He had access to large amounts of money from the Egliston estate and assets and provided he made proper advance provision he could escape to South America where he would be financially and physically secure.

On the other hand if he could find a way of maintaining his deception as Lord Egliston his future could be very rosy indeed. The information he had gathered on the technology of radar had convinced him that, post war, a lot of money could be made. The key question became how he could destroy the evidence in Germany about his past.

As a first step he cut back on the amount of intelligence he passed on. The absence of a transmitter was a good excuse. Then the chance he had been waiting for came as a bolt from the blue.

He was summoned to travel to the War Department in London. He was ushered into a room in the bomb hardened command area complex under Horse Guards Parade after a wait of some hours. To his astonishment there was General Allen Brooke, Churchill's confidante, and the deputy Prime Minister, Clement Attlee, together with several others whom he did not recognise.

The General, without introducing him to the others there, began to question him about his knowledge of German and his experiences in Colditz and, also, before the war at Heidelberg University. After some time he turned to a civilian seated against him and said,

"I think Egliston is the perfect man for the task, as you suggested. Give him and the others a briefing. I expect you to get things moving as soon as possible."

With that, he and Attlee left.

"I should introduce myself," said the person to whom Allen Brooke had spoken, "I am John Carswell, Deputy Secretary at the War Ministry. Let me tell you what all this is about. We have received through our embassy in Madrid an approach from certain elements in the German army to discuss a possible peace deal. They are planning a coup against Hitler and his key people.

They want to meet a small delegation from the Allies to get our response and to give us more information. "

"You, a Brigadier and I will travel under cover to Heidelberg to meet the conspirators. It clearly involves a considerable risk both to them and to you but a face to face meeting is the only way we can make progress. Ultimately it might not be in our interest to agree to a deal that falls short of unconditional surrender but first it is up to us to get the best out of it. You are a key person, you know Heidelberg, you speak German fluently, and importantly, one of the people you will meet allegedly knows you from the past."

"Who is that, may I ask?" said Taylor, his heart in his mouth. If it were one of the real Henry MacLean's acquaintances it could be very tricky.

"Reinhart Klein. Where did you meet him?" was the reply.

Taylor received the information with a mixture of relief and apprehension. Klein had been one of his fellow students at Heidelberg. It was clear that he knew Taylor's true identity and was going along with the deception.

"At Heidelberg University, he was reading law. We were not close friends, but he used me to get experience with his English. I am not surprised that he would get involved with this sort of thing. He was not a Nazi when I knew him," Taylor replied without expression.

Taylor needed to think about this. Did Klein wish to sabotage the talks or was he a committed conspirator? Taylor realised he would have to go along with whatever Klein wanted.

The meeting went on for an hour. It was clear he was being given no option but to go. Many briefings and preparation would be necessary giving him time to plan ahead. He was worried about Klein. When he knew him he was not a fanatical Nazi, and although strongly nationalistic, he had tended to view the Hitler regime with a hint of cynicism. It was not surprising that he was part of the plot. Why had he asked for Taylor, specifically knowing that he was a spy? There was clearly another agenda afoot. Ever an opportunist, Taylor prepared himself well to take advantage personally of whatever arose.

A month later, under extreme security the three-man team, Brigadier Alwyn Jones, the civil servant John Carswell and Taylor boarded a Dakota plane for Madrid. On arrival they were whisked away to a private room at the airport. After dark they were taken to another plane for Zurich, where they landed in the early hours. Another clandestine car journey took them to a house near the German border where they were told to catch up on sleep and wait.

At about mid-day Klein appeared. He greeted Taylor as Lord Egliston and was very formal. Egliston felt a wave of relief over the unfolding charade and knew he could play events to his benefit.

"This is the plan," Klein started. "My papers show you gentlemen are on the staff of General Schausenhof and they are for all practical purposes genuine, having been signed by him. You and I are officially in Switzerland for discussions with agents who operate in Spain. I would have preferred to meet you here and not to go to Heidelberg, but the General must stay closely in touch with developments in Germany. Tomorrow we shall cross into Germany and drive to Heidelberg directly to the General's home." He paused briefly. "In the meantime I shall brief you thoroughly on the cover and your supposed identities. I do not need to stress too much the risk that we are all taking. I know you all speak German fluently, but avoid if possible speaking to anyone on the journey. I shall do any speaking necessary. Once in Heidelberg we shall go to the house on the Schlosswolfsbrennenweg, which, you might be interested to know, is near to the home of Albert Speer, Hitler's industry minister. I expect the discussions to go on for two days."

The rest of the day was spent in familiarising themselves with the papers. Klein refused to talk about the subject of the discussions saying that the General wished to do that himself.

Klein himself drove the Mercedes staff car. They were passed through the checkpoint going into Germany without being required to get out of the car and were soon making good progress. There was very little conversation and that was just between the British seeking to polish up their German. Twenty kilometres from Heidelberg Klein stopped the car and used a public telephone.

When he came back he was looking a little worried. "A change of route will be necessary. Apparently the Reichsfuhrer is in Heidelberg and roadblocks have been set up on the main routes into the city. I shall go cross-country, but we still must get there before nightfall to avoid any air raid curfew."

After a quick look at the maps he set off again. They were soon in the thick woods round the Neckar valley and progress slowed. Taylor recognised one or two of the villages that he had hiked through as a student just before the war. Eventually the car passed through residential suburbs and came to the river, passing over the Alte Brucke that had armed guards at each end. Their route to them past the castle overlooking the town and past the large houses along the Schlosswolfsbrennenweg. The car turned into one, guarded by soldiers with guns at the ready. Klein led while one of the servants followed with luggage. Speaking in German, he said,

"Your rooms are in the annexe where there is a small conference room for your purposes. It is proposed that you take your meals there. There is an attendant on duty that can be trusted. The meetings with the General and others will be held in the main house. It is not uncommon for him to hold conferences with small groups of his staff in private and your presence will not excite any curiosity from the servants. The first meeting at which we shall put our ideas forward will be at 9am tomorrow. I am at your disposal at any time. Call me on the internal telephone. Good night, gentlemen."

The Brigadier suggested that they met briefly in the conference room before retiring. "Bear in mind before you say anything that the rooms will be bugged. When you do, speak in German. I want to go over briefly our initial statement."

An hour later, after a meal which was brought in by a servant who said nothing, the team retired. Taylor had a large room with a second door at one end, which was locked. As he half expected it was opened shortly after he had locked his main door and there was Klein.

"Nice to see you again, Franz," said he using the name Taylor had used in Germany during his time as a student. "You make a very convincing Lord Egliston, even I would be fooled. When I heard you were being prepared for the role I never thought you would be successful. For your information I work in a Ministry and read your reports on a regular basis. I have begun to think that your ardour for the Fatherland's cause has cooled off a bit in the recent months, no? Perhaps you

246

were wondering what my position, and more specifically yours is in this set up?"

"It is of interest to me, putting it mildly," said Taylor. "When we were at Heidelberg we weren't particularly close, so you didn't suggest me for old time's sake I'm damned sure. Bringing me over here puts both of us at risk, so why?"

Reinhardt sat down in one of the leather-backed chairs and quietly went through his story. "My German friends think of you as Lord Egliston. They have never heard of Frank Schneider or your role as a spy. They know of the escape from Colditz and of your role as a liaison officer in Poole. You are the genuine article, my friend, as far as they are concerned. As part of my role in the Reichsministry I see your intelligence reports and very good they have been. However, I note that they have been of poorer quality recently, which makes me think there is something we can discuss. Perhaps you are losing confidence in our Fuhrer to win this war?"

Taylor looked directly into Klein's black eyes and saw a hint of amusement there.

"You know my dedication to the Nazi cause when I was here," he replied.

"Indeed, and it doesn't fit with what I see at the moment," said Klein. "Let me put it to you. You quite like this charade as Lord Egliston. You see the Nazi cause getting weaker month by month. You are beginning to think what will happen to you if the British, Americans and the Russians get to Berlin?" He sat there with a smile playing round his lips.

"Perhaps you had better tell me the full story," said Taylor "I don't like guessing games."

Klein eased back in his chair.

"Let me boil it down to the essentials. Firstly, why you? The General three years ago wanted a new headquarters and a home near here. He wanted it near Speer's house because the two are close - maybe he sees him as a future ally against Hitler. Anyway here was a house, this one, once occupied by a Jewish banker who had been transferred elsewhere, Auschwitz to be precise. His access to funds and influence in Switzerland had delayed his departure. The banker fell out of luck, his house was taken over and he took the trip East. His name was Reise, the father of your scientist friend Dr Hans Reise. I suddenly thought of you and how useful you would be both to my friends and to my own interests."

Taylor burst out,

"I've been using the security of Reise's family as a lever to get radar data. If he knows they have been disposed of heaven only knows what he will do!"

"He will do nothing, he would effectively hang himself," said Klein.

"He might do that and denounce me as well beforehand!" exploded Taylor.

"No he won't, when he gets over the shock his self-interests will take over. Anyway, back to my story. I and a few others involved in this little plot we are all here to discuss, believe it would be prudent to start contingency planning. I have in mind escape strategies to friendly parts of the world, and money. We wish to get gold, diamonds and art out of the country into safe places. We also need a guarantee of a warm welcome somewhere and the opportunity to share in various business activities post war. You are in an ideal position to help with all these. You might ask what's in it for you. In fact I guess that's your first question. Let me suggest that I can ensure that all records relating to Franz Schneider will be accidentally lost. There will be nobody except me who can show that Lord Egliston is an impostor. Secondly, I've no doubt that you will find ways of profiting from our misfortune."

Taylor paused for a minute.

"I'll tell you what I think when these next two days are over. Then perhaps we can talk again," With that, he stood up.

"Goodnight," he said, turning away. He knew this was the chance he had been waiting for.

The next few days were fascinating. There was a well-advanced plot to kill Hitler and key figures in the Nazi party. One of Hitler's ministers who was not identified would join the Wehrmacht conspirators in a coup to take over the government. The Allied team assumed it would be Speer but could not be sure. The conspirators would declare a cease-fire after which they would sue for peace. However, they said they would be quite prepared to continue with the war if appropriate assurances and peace conditions were not forthcoming. The two days were spent clarifying details of their proposal. The British team was encouraging but made clear the need to bring their Allies, specifically the Russians, on board. This was a stumbling block with the Germans, as they had no confidence that the Russians would co-operate, but the British, acting on their brief, encouraged the plotters in their plans.

On the last night Klein again visited Taylor to get his response to their private proposal. Taylor had thought deeply about it and saw it gave him everything he wanted. He and Reinhardt worked out how they would proceed. They agreed that Taylor would cease his spying work. He would destroy his equipment and records and consolidate his position. He should wait to be contacted by an agent who would be dedicated to the task of implementing a post war survival plan for Taylor, Klein and his friends.

The next thing they considered was whether their position would be improved if the Wehrmacht conspirators' plot failed or succeeded. Klein's view was that the plot would fail or be abandoned and that their plans should be based on this assumption. Certainly, Klein was making sure he would be distancing himself from them. Taylor read between the lines and came to the conclusion that he would make sure it failed.

The return to Switzerland and back to Britain was uneventful. They carried no paperwork or any records of the meetings in case they were searched or arrested. Once back in London the team underwent a detailed debriefing followed by meetings with political leaders. The planning of the conspirators had impressed Taylor's colleagues who felt that there was a high probability that the plot to kill Hitler would succeed and that a new leadership would be able and prepared to sue for peace. Taylor himself had his doubts on this conclusion based on his talk with Klein but went along with the general view, although covering himself by voicing some doubts about the Wehrmacht side of the plot.

It was clear that there was a strong divergence of views amongst the British government representatives on the course of action to be taken and Taylor was told to return to Dorset. There was no time to be lost in preparing for his future: events could move very rapidly.

Taylor had decided to cease his spying activities and set about the process of eliminating any evidence that might link him to his real identity. Now was the time to become once and for all, the real Lord Egliston. The first action was to destroy all evidence of his spying activities.

There was a difficulty. The bomb at Norden had buried the key evidence of transmitter and code books and there was no way he could recover them. There was no option but to leave them and hope that nobody would find the tunnel in the future. All the rest of the evidence against him was still in Germany and he had to hope that Klein would keep his side of the bargain and systematically remove all records.

The other issue to be faced was how he handled Reise. He had maintained sporadic contact with the scientist following his move to Malvern, ensuring a steady flow of information on radar developments. They met each time Reise travelled south to the operating radar station at Langton Matravers. Reise's cooperation had been obtained by the threat that his parents would be killed if he did not continue to provide data. He considered what Reise's reaction would be when he was told they had been killed. He could not denounce Taylor without incriminating himself as a spy. His only alternative would be to commit suicide and turn in Taylor. Taylor guessed that, despite his hate of the Nazis, Reise would probably continue to spy as before.

If, however, Taylor put it to him that he was ceasing his spying because of his growing antipathy towards Germany and wished to offer Reise the chance to make his fortune in a post war industrial venture funded by him, his cooperation might be assured. He could see the advantages in using the unique knowledge Reise had in radar technology.

Taylor was not told what the British government had decided in relation to the German plot presumably because of its political sensitivity. He was certainly not asked to take any further part. He suspected that while not sabotaging the planned coup, the view would be taken that the unconditional surrender of the Reich after a full defeat would be more useful and that Hitler's growing irrational behaviour would speed that defeat.

A month later he received a long message from Klein through an intermediary. Some dissension had arisen amongst the conspirators and he was making sure he would not be implicated were their plan to go wrong. In the meantime he was using the cellars of the General's house as a store for valuable art and gold stolen from Jewish families. After any defeat it would be Taylor's task to organise its removal from the country. The most important part of the message from Taylor's point of view was that his German records were now alleged to show that he had died in 1940 from diphtheria and that all subsequent records had been destroyed. Taylor suspected nevertheless that Klein had kept some evidence for use if ever he, Taylor, ratted on the deal.

Taylor began his planning in earnest. Now that he had a contact in Whitehall, Brigadier Alwyn Jones, he suggested to him that he would be an ideal person to undertake interrogation of Nazis in Germany after an Allied victory. With a small command he would also be able to follow up any fugitives and seek out stolen art. At home he decided that Egliston Hall would be an ideal repository for anything he might be able to spirit out of the country.

Next he turned his attention to Reise. Taylor had never revealed his true identity to Reise, who had no reason to suppose that he was anyone but Lord Egliston, a person who was a traitor to his country. He had no intention of correcting this belief, at least at this stage, and neither did he intend to tell him that his parents were dead and that the Wehrmacht had commandeered the family home. The first step was to secure his co-operation in planning for the future by offering him a technical directorship in a future company for the exploitation of electronic equipment.

Taylor engineered a meeting with Reise, who travelled down from Malvern. Despite his obvious hate and disdain for Taylor he agreed with Taylor's proposals. Klein's analysis proved correct. Reise realised he was trapped and had better secure his own longer-term future.

Chapter 32 - 2000 - Showdown with Egliston

Hans Reise and Charles, each with their own obsession with finding out about the past, spent long periods either flashback scanning for further clues or just sitting in the dark panelled rooms of the Manor thinking and occasionally talking.

They did not talk much, each buried in their own thoughts. It was clear that neither would be able to carry on their daily lives until they had resolved and agreed what to do.

Charles went through phases of seething anger over Taylor's, as he must now start calling him, crimes of murder and theft of his family's heritage. He was at other times both relieved and saddened. His family would not now have the stigma of having produced a spy, but the thought that this monster of a man had killed his brother, disposed of his body and robbed him of his companionship for the last fifty years filled him with remorse. The thought that he should have been and would be Lord Egliston did not at that time worry him unduly.

He would have to tell Rushton as soon as possible, who would also have to be told of Harry's invention. Harry himself was still out in Baku and had been very much against telling Rushton about the flashbacks, fearing that a security blanket would be put on the invention. He would have to be persuaded.

Finally there was Julie, who knew about the spying but not the invention or Harry's work for Rushton. She and Harry had broken up their blossoming love affair over Harry's apparent absorption into Egliston's business. What a mess!

Hans Reise had finally come to the end of the road as far as Egliston was concerned. The man was, to him, evil. He had destroyed all those things most dear to him and should be made to suffer.

Reise had for too long compromised any principles he had once held. All those years ago when the war had finally come to an end he had had the chance to shake off his connection with Egliston.

They had had a no-holds-barred quarrel in which Egliston had made it clear that neither of them would be able to blow the whistle on the other without bringing both down. Egliston was a persuasive advocate and Reise had decided to swallow his reservations.

He could have refused to have anything more to do with him, gone into academic research, as he did later, and forge a career for himself.

He had taken the precaution of depositing in his bank a full account of his dealings with Egliston as an insurance against the possibility that the man might decide to silence him forever.

However, Egliston had come to him with the proposal that he could become technical director of a company that Egliston would finance to develop radar technology for military and civil applications.

It was a Mephistophelean contract that had made him a rich man but he had thereby forfeited any right to criticise Egliston.

The flashbacks had now changed everything.

The thoughts twisted his ability to think clearly and he made the fateful decision to have a confrontation with the man.

He would not reveal anything about the flashbacks but would say he had uncovered evidence that Egliston had lied. At the very least he would want to know where Egliston had disposed of the Reise family heirlooms.

Chapter 33. Egliston turns the screws on Harry and Hans.

My head felt as though it was bursting when I came to and I thought for a moment I'd gone blind, but flashes of light synchronised with the pain spasms disabused me. I gradually worked out, there being no windows, that I'd been locked in the cellar of the house on Long Island and I lay there in the complete darkness feeling the worse for wear.

I recalled gradually that they had thrown me into the cellar without a word. After a while my eyes acclimatised, my head cleared somewhat and I could find my way round by the faint light leaking in under the door. I worked my way round the room and it was some time later I realised there was a working light switch near the door and I was able to turn it on and look around. There was no obvious way out. It would not be possible to jump on anyone coming in as there were two steps leading directly up to the door putting me in a two-down position.

All I could do was to sit on a sack of potatoes and contemplate what had happened.

By now Egliston would have been told of the recent events and my career with his company would be at an end - in fact my whole future, if any, could be in doubt. I had plenty of time to think about it, because I was left there for hours. My watch had been removed and I had no idea of the time. I must have eventually fallen asleep because I was woken with a start as the door crashed open and the thug who had jumped me came in. He hit me in the mouth as I started to get up.

"That's a taste of the future, you bastard," he spat, dragging me up, twisting my arm behind my back and pushing me up the steps. "You're going with me on a little boat trip."

It was dark by now and there was little chance of anyone on the mainland seeing what was happening. I was pushed aboard a motor launch, tied to a seat in the cabin and tape was put over my mouth. The boat made its way up the southern side of the harbour, keeping to speed limits but well away from most of the traffic, and passed out into the open sea past the clanking chain ferry. The throttle was opened and we headed directly south into the choppy English Channel and round St Aldhelm's Head towards the cove Julie and I had visited in happier times. A Land Rover was waiting for us at Chapman's Pool and I was driven up to the Egliston Manor and locked in a stone building against the Estate farmhouse.

After what seemed hours, I was taken into the main house and put in a windowless musty room with a bed, a toilet pan and a sink. It looked and probably was built to be a prison cell. I was again beginning to ache and feel nauseous and just lay there hoping to feel better.

Nobody came to interrupt my thoughts and I decided to try and clean up and get some sleep.

I awoke what must have been some hours later, feeling somewhat better and ready for some food. What did Egliston know about me? There was no reason why he should know about the flashback discoveries. He might have linked me to Charles but that would not be anything to be bothered about. Rushton's call while I was on Long Island had told me my Baku cover was blown. All he would know was that I had found out about the smuggling. Unless he had some use for me my time would be limited once he had found out how much I knew and whether I had passed on any information. I had to play for time and hope that Rushton might follow up where I was.

I was getting very hungry when eventually the door was unlocked and I was given some meagre bread and water and left again. Eventually I was taken through corridors and to a room at the front of the house where I was sat upon a chair with the two thugs behind me. Five minutes later in walked Egliston himself and sat at his desk facing me.

"Well Harry, I thought I could trust you to keep your nose out of things that didn't concern you and to keep quiet. You did well with your enhanced oil project and it will make our operation out there quite a bit of money. You also seemed to take the little incidents with the Mafia out in Baku in your stride, and in fact I was planning to bring you a bit closer into the core business. Now, we find you were poking your nose into our uranium sales and talking to the British authorities in Baku. You've also been close to that wretched brother of mine. We do have a lot at stake and I can't take the risk that you can keep your mouth shut. However, I need your co-operation before we say goodbye and I'm sure you'll give it. Bring that old fool in."

My heavy friend turned and returned a minute or two later: my heart missed a beat, as he pushed Hans Reise on to a couch alongside the desk.

****

Hans Reise had reached his decision. He would confront Egliston, without telling Charles, and demand the truth as far as the war years were concerned. There was the risk that Egliston might decide to have him killed but he had made sure that his disclosures would be made public through his solicitors if he died in suspicious circumstances. Egliston would not risk that. Reise established that he was in residence at the Hall and rang demanding an immediate interview. Egliston at first refused to see him but after Hans had indicated he wanted to talk about their wartime collaboration and that it would be in his interest to listen he was granted a meeting. A car picked him up at Wareham station, where he had been taken by Charles in the belief that he was returning to London, and drove him into the depths of the Purbecks and down into the deep valley of the Egliston estate. He was not taken to Egliston's office but into a small meeting room in a side wing. Eventually Egliston entered and sat down.

"I don't appreciate people demanding meetings with me at short notice. You of all people know that. What do you want? I can give you half an hour." Egliston's words were delivered in his most arrogant tone.

"You'll give me all the time I need," said Reise in an uncharacteristically assertive voice, making Egliston's attitude even more dismissive. "You rat. I've discovered that you lied to me all through the war and afterwards about my family. I kept quiet about your spying activities because of my involvement and because I believed you." Reise's anger was getting out of control.

"I now know my parents were taken away from their Heidelberg house early in the war probably to die in one of the German concentration camps. You knew because you were there in person in the house in 1944 and again after the Allies passed through in 1945. I shall not tell you how I know. What I do now want to know is what became of my parents and what happened to the treasures you looted. I am quite prepared to make your wartime spying activities public if I don't get what I want."

"You know about my visits to Germany do you? Believe me, I'll find out how you discovered that shortly. However, you will find that the British sanctioned both visits that are ironically both still covered by the Official Secrets Acts. You will find that the first was an official delegation sent in secretly to see if dissident elements were prepared to conclude a peace over Hitler's head. It is obvious that came to nothing. My second visit was as part of an official attempt to recover art looted by the Nazis and to make sure other works were secured. Unfortunately the art I collected from your house was burnt in an accidental fire at a collection point. You can try and verify this with the Ministry of Defence if you wish."

"I don't believe you," shouted Reise "What happened to my parents?"

"Frankly, I don't know," replied Egliston, "I did recommend that they were kept alive, but my influence as a spy was limited. I admit I kept up the fiction to keep you sweet. The short notes you received from them were forged. What are you going to do about it?"

Reise had gone silent, the wind taken out of his sails.

Egliston went on the offensive.

"I need to know how you found out about my visits to Heidelberg. You will tell me if you want to leave this house alive, there is too much at stake for this to get out. No, don't tell me again about the affidavits you left with the bank and solicitor. I know all about them and can get access to them if I really want". He sat there thinking and then a grim smile spread across his face.

"One thing now occurs to me. That letter you sent me about that flashback project saying it had failed. It did work didn't it? You've been looking at flashbacks in that dammed Heidelberg house." He walked over to his desk, rummaged in a file, and then waved the letter Reise had sent to him. "I'm going to find out all about it and you're going to tell me."

Reise put his head in his hands and went silent.

"I think you are going to be a guest of mine for as long as it takes. I also think I'll get someone to have a look round that Heidelberg house and bring back anything they might find." So saying he pressed a bell on the desk and a security guard came in. Egliston succinctly gave him

Instructions and he departed.

"I shall know everything within a week," he smiled cruelly. "In the meantime you must make yourself comfortable. I might even show you my art collection."

****

I was as surprised to see Hans as he was to see me. He appeared a really old man, as though all the stuffing had been knocked out of him.

He looked at me plaintively and said, "Egliston knows about the flashback equipment in Heidelberg and he's going to bring it back here."

So Egliston didn't know about our discoveries at the Manor, I realised. He would not necessarily know about Rushton either. For the time being Charles was safe though it would only be a short time before Egliston did find out and took action.

"I'm going to keep you for a time and then when I've had a chance to think we'll meet again," said Egliston with a satisfied smile.

Hans and I were taken away and locked in rooms next to one another but weren't able to talk.

****

After dropping Reise off at the station Charles decided he needed to talk to someone before he spoke to Rushton. He thought I was still in Baku and the only person he could trust was Julie.

Unfortunately she was out of the country on business and he left her a message to contact him as soon as she returned. In the meantime he decided to do nothing. He was reluctant to contact Rushton, as he would have to reveal the existence of the flashback 'Torch' and needed to discuss it first with me.

It was several days later when Julie rang him and hearing her father's agitated state decided to come down to Dorset immediately. She arrived late on the Friday evening and Charles was able to tell her all that had happened. They decided to get Rushton involved but before they were able to do this other things intervened

Chapter 34. Tyneham gold

Egliston's men moved quickly and the flashback kit from Heidelberg was brought to the Hall two days later. Hans had been forced to telephone his housekeeper with instructions to open up the house and give assistance to the men. Egliston had rapidly realised its strategic and personal importance and moved heaven and earth to get it brought over and installed. I pleaded ignorance as to how to work it, which Egliston believed, as he knew I had been in Baku for the last month. Hans was subjected to some rough treatment, which reduced his resolve not to co-operate, and he agreed to demonstrate it to Egliston. I was allowed to watch, but in the company of the thug who had taken great delight in kicking me earlier.

It didn't take long to get it working in the main meeting room in the Hall and the images produced were of excellent quality. Despite his resolve, Hans was getting interested. He had made great improvements since those we had seen in the Manor months ago and the blurring similar to camera-shake was absent.

"Make damn sure you learn how to use this," growled Egliston, glaring at me. "Your life depends on using this out in the field. What a pity you didn't play straight with me, you could have made a fortune." It needed skill and an appreciation of how the equipment worked, as Egliston fully realised. It was not the sort of job he could delegate to one of his thugs, and Hans would be too frail. .

"I want you to tune this thing on to the time before the war when I lived here. I used to come in here to do fetching and carrying jobs for the MacLeans. My mother would also be here." Hans tried to explain that the settings depended on the location of the equipment as well as the time elapsed since the event. "Get moving then," he snapped, "do what you have to do, I don't have all day to waste."

Eventually Hans succeeded in tuning into the year 1936. There were plenty of images of the old Lord Egliston and his sons. The servants came in and out and eventually Taylor's mother appeared. Egliston, despite his hard personality, was moved momentarily by the images of the only person he had really loved. "That's enough for today," he eventually growled, and walked out of the room. Hans and I were taken back to our cells. Now that Egliston was getting his way we were treated more humanely, with decent food and books.

Next day Egliston had me brought in to his office where two of his men were waiting. "You are going to have a little trip into the Dorset countryside," he announced. "Years ago just after the war some troops under my command buried some cases of value to me for safe keeping. They were placed in the grounds of Tyneham House, which was part of my estate at the time."

"Unfortunately, the War Department took over the land in 1943 and to this day it has not been returned to me. The cases were buried near the Manor. Until now there has been no way I could get in there and carry out the necessary lengthy and public search. The Manor itself was destroyed during live firing exercises after the war and the location of the cache has been lost. Your little toy could find it. The whole of the Tyneham village and surroundings are in a prohibited area used for army exercises so you will just have to keep your eyes open for any unexploded ordinance."

I tried to explain that because the Hall itself had been destroyed, the physics of the flashback process were such that chances of success were small unless the cache was in a heavy stone building or cellar, but he brushed my objections aside.

It wasn't just bluff on my part, I really didn't think we would be successful. The power requirements for the kit had been substantially reduced since our first trials and a small petrol-driven generator provided enough power. The equipment, my two minders and I drove in a large van as soon as night fell, to the remote deserted village of Tyneham.

The once populated valley is bleak during the day as it is filled with deserted buildings and long-gone villages. At night it is eerie with the right atmosphere for ghost-hunting. During the day either the army would have been carrying out live round exercises in the vicinity or it might have been one of the public access days and we would have been seen.

We drove on the metalled road to the village and then veered off towards a clearing in some trees and bumped over the rough ground in the moonlight towards the site of the house, now just a ruin, surrounded by tall trees.

The minders had been told that the cache would be found in a cellar within a fifty metre square area in what had been the gardens of the house.

The equipment mounted in the van was driven slowly back and forwards scanning over the area. To my surprise some flashbacks of stone garden furniture appeared although of poor quality as I focussed on the time Egliston had said the cache was hidden.

The minders kept a close eye on me but were obviously intrigued by what they saw. Eventually I had to pause to relieve myself, also hoping I might be able to race off into the darkness, and I walked away from the operation closely followed by a minder.

Suddenly, after walking about ten yards there was an explosion that threw me to the ground sending me temporarily unconscious. When I recovered, the truck was on fire with the other minder in the driver's seat. Shrapnel from the explosion had hit the guy who had followed me and he was unconscious and bleeding but not badly. I then tried to get the driver out but the heat was overwhelming and I had to drop back. There was a second explosion and he and the van disappeared in a ball of fire. There was no hope of saving him. We must have detonated an unexploded shell left over from the military exercises and which we hadn't seen in the poor light.

The second minder was still unconscious but breathing and his bleeding had almost stopped. I decided the time was right to make my escape. I ran up the long deserted road, along which we had come an hour ago and kept running for a mile or so until I reached a telephone box from where I phoned Charles, reversing the charges as I had no money and asked him to come and pick me up urgently.

"Thank God you are there," he exclaimed before I had chance to say anything. "Julie'ss here and we were worried because we hadn't heard from you since you returned from Baku." I was relieved to find he was there and able to come immediately. He said he would drop everything and come to pick me up. I hid in the darkness, anxiously waiting. I really should have tied up my minder while he was unconscious. I also realised he would have a mobile phone and kicked myself for not taking it. He would get in touch with Egliston as soon as he came to.

Half an hour later Charles's old Bristol car appeared. I leapt in and told him to drive like the devil.

As we drove back along the narrow winding road to Corfe we passed through the small village of Church Knoll where an oncoming car almost hit us head on but Charles managed to swerve. Clearly my assailants had raised the alarm. "We've got to get to the Manor before Egliston's men, Julie is in great danger," I shouted. The front door of the Manor was wide open with the house lights full on when we arrived.

"That's strange; surely Julie would have shut it. Come on in before you are seen," said Charles. I had expected Julie to be somewhat cool but she did not even appear when we went in.

"My god, look at this, she's been kidnapped," shouted Charles, thrusting a sheet of paper into my hand. It was an A4 sheet that had been pinned to the study door. The message was brutal and to the point.

'Charles MacLean, your daughter is safe but you must make no attempt to find her or contact the police.

She will be released when you have persuaded Dr Aldborough to return to the Hall. He will probably see you shortly and I am sure that you will respond as quickly as you can. If he has not returned to Egliston Hall before mid-day tomorrow she will suffer. You can assure him he will not be harmed. - Henry MacLean.'

"This is my entire fault, Charles," I said ruefully. "The guy I left at the scene of the explosion must have come to just after I left and got through on a mobile to Egliston. In my haste I forgot to look for one on him rather than running all that way to a phone box. Egliston must have moved very fast, realising that I would contact you fairly quickly. He knows that Julie is an excellent bargaining chip. You realise that Egliston will not let any of us live once he has the flashback equipment working and access to the technology."

Charles nodded agreement and I went on.

"The explosion destroyed Reise's flashback 'Torch' in the van at Tyneham and fortunately Egliston thinks that was the only one in existence. Now he has seen what it is capable of he might keep us alive long enough to pass on the design information. However, ultimately by getting rid of Hans Reise and the three of us he believes that he can put his spying genie back in the bottle. The time has come to get help from Rushton. Even if I hand myself over to Egliston, Julie will not be safe. The only way to get her back safely is to hope that Rushton can organise a rapid assault on the Hall before Egliston can harm her. Lock that door and I'll get on to Rushton straight away."

****

Egliston was an obsessive planner and especially now. Events could rapidly go out of control unless he kept a tight grip. As he sat in his study waiting for a report from his men who had gone to Tyneham he concentrated on how he should proceed.

His discovery that Aldborough knew about the smuggling and, worse, had been in contact with the consulate was worrying. Was he working alone? Who else knew? What other activities had he engaged in while in Baku? Particularly, who was the girl Klanski had told him he had spent considerable time with? All had to be resolved before he decided what to do with Harry.

Then there was Reise, safely locked up in the Hall. Whom had he told apart from perhaps Harry about his flashback discoveries of his dealings in Germany? Unless they had had a duplicate of Reise's equipment at the Norden Manor it was unlikely that anybody would know his true identity.

The flashback discovery was mind-blowing. His active mind flashed across dozens of potential applications. If he could establish that nobody else but Reise and Aldborough knew about aspects of his past, the flashback apparatus itself and the stocks of uranium, he could safely get rid of them. If there were any other people involved they would have to be dealt with. There was no way that after all this time he would let his true identity come out. He, his organisation and his son would be destroyed if it did.

Perhaps he should deal with Charles MacLean after all these years. Aldborough had obviously got to know him through Charles's daughter, Julie, but his spies had reported that they had not met for some time and had apparently ceased their brief affair. However, he decided to make provisional arrangements for his escape if all went wrong. He might have to leave behind the art collection and that cache of gold from the concentration camps still buried out at Tyneham since the 1940's as well.

It was a stupid action, he thought in retrospect, to allow Aldborough away from the Hall to try and locate the gold hoard; it had lain there for sixty years and it was sheer greed and the need to prove that the equipment worked that had disturbed his better judgement. At that moment the phone rang. It was one of his men at Tyneham who gave him the news that his man had been blown up together with the 'Torch' and that Harry had escaped.

Things were getting out of control. Whatever the reason for the explosion it was vital that no evidence linking him to the event was left. He knew that it was unlikely that the army people would be anywhere near at that time, and that only locals might investigate. He rapidly sent two of his men dressed in army uniforms he had acquired from his dealings with Bovington army camp together with a lorry to go to Tyneham and salvage as much as possible and remove any evidence linking it to himself. They would keep any locals away.

An hour later they reported back that they had convinced the local farmer that all was under control. The explosion and subsequent fire had been so severe that it would be unlikely that there would be sufficient evidence left for the police to trace things back to him. Most importantly they had recovered the remnants of the flashback equipment. It was a pity about his man who had been killed in the fire, but he had no family in the UK and his disappearance could be covered up.

In the meantime he had decided what else to do. It was likely that Harry would try and contact MacLean rather than the police. He decided to go to the Norden manor with one of the minders who had dealt with Harry.

Egliston already had long-standing emergency arrangements to fly out from the local Hurn airport in his private jet and also had an ocean-going cruiser based in Ireland. From there he could go to his residence in Uruguay where he knew he would be safe from extradition. While driving to Norden he put his jet on standby. He then managed to get his son Nicolas on the mobile and alerted him to his plans.

On arrival at the Manor he and his man burst in when Julie answered the door. Before they could stop her, however, she had set off the alarm. Rapidly they gagged her and forced her into their car before anybody arrived to investigate the alarm. On the spur of the moment he wrote out a hostage message to leave for Charles to find.

It was possible that the hostage threat would work. He knew MacLean would never risk anyone hurting his daughter; the danger was that Aldborough would go directly to the police. It was time to arrange for a speedy departure and to cover his tracks with a hostage. When they got back to the Hall he put Julie in the underground art gallery, which had a small lounge and living quarters, firmly locking the complex that also housed his uranium store. He sent his man back to the Manor to look out for Aldborough.

The underground complex was well hidden and was protected by a thick reinforced concrete door. If all went wrong and he was on the run he would say Julie was with him as a hostage for his safe passage and they would never know differently. He went back to his office to gather together vital documents he would have to take with him. He also gave orders to his men at the oil terminal to load the remaining down-hole tools that contained plutonium on to his cruiser and to make it ready to go to sea. All he had to do now was to wait until Aldborough contacted him, after which he could button up the whole messy episode.

Chapter 35. The assault on Egliston Hall

Rushton moved fast after I'd told him about the latest events. With my finding of fissile material and its method of transport from Azerbeijan using the logging tools as a cover, coupled with the happenings at the Hall he at last had a good chance of nailing Egliston. It was also clear that Egliston had made deliveries of U235 to Iran and also possibly Turkey.

Rushton arranged to travel by helicopter directly to the Special Boat Squadron unit at Hamworthy in Poole and told us to meet him there, making sure that any possible Egliston watchers outside the Manor did not see me getting into Charles's car. He also wanted any information available on the layout of the Hall and estate.

Charles pulled out drawings and photographs of the Hall that had been left at the Manor when Egliston moved out fifty years ago but he had nothing more recent. It was certain that the hall had been changed considerably over the years.

It was dark by the time we left for Poole and Charles got in his car alone and picked me up in the village where I had made my way via the garden wall. As far as I could tell there were no watchers and there was no-one following us as we joined the main road out of Purbeck.

"We're going to have to come clean with Rushton about the flashback equipment and also the fact that Egliston is not your brother," I warned Charles as we drove quickly into Poole. "He'll hit the roof when he knows." Charles was more concerned that if Rushton decided to make an assault on the Hall it could result in Julie being hurt or worse, and had gone very quiet.

We were admitted quickly to the SBS unit after showing our passports as Rushton had specified. He had clearly started the wheels moving. A gnarled-looking individual with a Zapata moustache introduced himself as Captain Sinclair and led us into a windowless room that was obviously used as their control room with a mass of communication equipment and local maps spread around.

Charles passed over the information on the Hall geography that he had brought, as six other equally hard-looking men came in. I told them as succinctly as I could the background to the emergency whilst Sinclair interrogated Charles about the Hall and estate layout. Rushton arrived in the middle of this and took Charles and me aside.

"I was wondering where you had got to. I knew you had left Baku but the trail went cold. Don't explain now, we have more important things to deal with. I want you to be under no illusions about this. Egliston will have made arrangements for his escape should the Hall come under attack even though he hopefully knows nothing about your links with me. He won't be expecting an SBS assault at this stage so the element of surprise is with us."

"Now I want to know about the Hall and how we can best get in and later I'll hear about what you found in the Summerfield compound - and what the hell was going on in the MoD land at Tyneham that I've just heard about?"

The SBS men had worked out an initial attack plan in the meantime involving coming up to the house from the sea but they were bothered about their lack of knowledge of any alarm and CCTV cameras. It was then that Charles said he knew of a way into the estate that would put the attackers right outside the main buildings. He described a tunnel that had been constructed in the nineteenth century to bring water from hilltop reservoirs to the lakes outside the Hall. Starting near a farm on the hill outside the estate the tunnel had been driven through the hillside and was large enough for men to walk down. He had explored it as a child and thought it unlikely that it would be guarded. It probably had not been accessed for decades.

It was decided that a five-man team would go in and head directly for the rooms I had been locked in, hoping that that would be where Julie and Reise were held. Once the Hall was secured we would drive in on the main road from Kingston village with Rushton and one of the SBS men as soon as the call came from the team.

The operation started shortly after midnight with Charles taking the men to the heavily overgrown entrance to the tunnel. The lock refused to budge being rusted heavily, but cutting equipment from the SBS truck soon dealt with it. His men, dressed in black and their faces also greased black, started down the tunnel armed with stun grenades and Uzi weapons.

Rushton then drove us through the Kingston village and we parked in the wood outside the estate to wait. He had a communicator to receive progress reports from his team but the depth of the tunnel was too great for the signal to get through. The suspense was terrible for Charles and me, but Rushton sat impassively in the darkness. I began to tell him about the flashback technology and all had we had learned. He wasn't at all pleased and was a little incredulous.

"I'll want to know all about that later when we've put the screws on this bogus Egliston and this time no keeping bloody secrets from me!"

After half an hour there came a crackle from the communicator and a report that the team was outside the main building without having been detected and were about to enter the main house. There was no report for another fifteen minutes when the message came through that they had rounded up Egliston's security men, one of whom had been wounded. Reise had been found but had suffered a heart attack and was in a bad way. There was no sign of Julie or Egliston.

Rushton drove down into the valley with the wheels screeching at the corners of the deeply dipping sinuous road. We went directly to Reise who was unconscious on the floor in the main study. He had been covered with blankets and a doctor had been sent for. They had established that Egliston had, fortuitously for him, been in the estate farm and had disappeared when the first shots were fired. The gates to the estate were immediately secured and an alert sent out to airports and the harbour authorities.

I sat with Hans in the hope that he might recover sufficiently to tell us where Julie was. The security staff members were rounded up, and formally arrested by the police who arrived after being given the all clear. Rushton was browsing through the office records and files, obviously finding very useful information. Charles was pacing to and fro getting more and more disturbed. It was in this atmosphere that the telephone rang. Rushton answered and stiffened, beckoning me to pick up the secretary's phone. The grating voice was unmistakable.

"Listen, and listen well. You do not know where Miss MacLean is and you will not find her. Do not interrupt. You will lift all surveillance at airports and ports, which I assume you have already put in place. If I am arrested I shall not reveal where she is until she is dead. I don't know whether she will suffocate or starve first. When I am out of the country I undertake to let you know where she is before it is too late." Charles pulled the phone from my hand and shouted into the handset, "You bastard, you killed my brother and now you have my daughter: I'll not rest until I see you dead!" He dropped the receiver and collapsed.

Rushton picked it up in a calm clear voice "We understand, ring me at this number when you are willing to talk. It will be manned continuously".

The phone went dead.

It was then that Hans stirred "… Julie - art gallery, hidden, fuel store building, use flash…." His voice faded away. "What the hell's he mean?" said Rushton, kneeling to catch any further words. Hans was again unconscious and we weren't going to get much more from him as the ambulance arrived and he was driven off to Poole hospital. The prospects for his recovery were decidedly poor.

"I don't know," I admitted. Then I had an idea.

"When Julie and I walked along the coast here back in April we trespassed into the Hall grounds to have a quick look at the place. We saw a delivery of some goods to a building near the farmhouse. They were from a boat that had landed at Chapman's Pool. The building had heavy concrete doors and a stark white interior similar to the fissile stores I saw once at the Winfrith site. That could be the fuel store he mentioned, though it's only now I realise what it could be. Hans was telling us to use the flashback to see what happened there and how to get in. I'll get the equipment from the Manor and we'll try it. From what I saw it would be very difficult to gain access unless we see how it's done.

Rushton assigned one of his men as a bodyguard to go with Charles and me and we drove away in one of the

MoD vehicles to the Manor. The equipment was in the study where I'd first seen a flashback during the storm last April and had been very much modified since I last saw it. It took some time to make sure we didn't damage anything or to change any settings as we got it in the MOD truck. I just hoped Charles knew how to set it up.

Three hours later we were back and trying to set up the 'Torch' near to the building where I'd seen a door open to reveal a laboratory. The army had run a power cable from the hall and it wasn't long before Charles, now recovered and working feverishly, detected a flashback. We had no idea as to what time the flashback showed. There were several of the security guards milling about the entrance in the flashback. This time it appeared that material was being taken out of the store and loaded into a truck. The doors appeared to be closed remotely.

Rushton had the security guards brought out from the cellar where I'd been incarcerated.

"I want to know how to get into that building," he snarled at them. There is a girl in there and if she dies I'll make damn sure you take the rap."

There was no response apart from one of them spitting on the ground. "Take them away and work on them," said Rushton, "Don't be too worried about the methods you use."

Charles in the meantime was still scanning with the machine and it was clear that we would be lucky if we managed at this stage to get anything useful from it. It took another three hours before we got a clear view of someone coming out of the building and holding what seemed like a remote control. It was clearly one of men we had arrested.

"Get that man out here, now!" shouted Rushton. He was brought out.

"Kneel down," ordered Rushton, drawing his gun and placing it at the man's head. "I promise you that I shall blow out your brains in one minute if you do not tell me how to open that door."

The seconds went by and the man looked at Rushton impassively and it was only with five seconds to go he spoke.

" You will find the control unit in a safe in the farmhouse. The key word to open it is azeri3. It won't help you though. If Egliston put the girl in his so called art gallery it will need Egliston himself to get in. The lock for that is inside and is operated biometrically."

Within two minutes, one of Rushton's men came back with the control unit. My heart sank as I saw it had been smashed. "The safe door was open and the unit was on the floor," he said.

"Get a locksmith – now!" said Rushton turning to one of the SBS men who spoke on a mobile phone to their control room.

Charles was feverishly scanning through time to get any clues as to whether Julie had been put into the building. It was a further two hours before he got a positive result. There it was. It was possible clearly to see Julie being dragged handcuffed into the entrance and some five minutes later the door was closed with Julie still inside. Our problem was now how to get in there.

The SBS had managed to get a locks expert who set about testing the controller and the lock itself with an armoury of electronic test gear. It took him an hour but eventually he turned to us and said, "Eureka!" pushing the heavy concrete doors aside. Within a few minutes we were in there but all we could see was a sterile array of racks used for the fuel storage. There was no sign of Julie and Charles was getting desperate.

"Where is this art gallery Hans mentioned? Look for another door!" he shouted. There were two corridors leading off the storeroom and, rushing down one we were confronted by a steel door with an access pad at the side.

"We shall be lucky to get past that," said Rushton. "It's operated by iris and fingerprint recognition technology. Presumably it's set only to respond to Egliston's prints and he's unlikely to help us unless we do as he says. I'll get the experts in. Don't worry, Charles, I'm sure it won't take long."

It did. Lock experts weren't able to bypass the electronics and the door stubbornly stayed locked. They were reluctant to smash the device in case the whole thing became jammed. Rushton put a call through to some expert at Bovington who might have been able to get Egliston's prints from items in the office and somehow use them to make a dummy fingerprint. That was a long shot but worth trying.

The only other way to get through would be to burn through the reinforced concrete and we had no idea how thick it was. Thermal lances were brought in and the long process started in parallel with the work on the lock. I was worried about the air supply inside the art gallery. By my reckoning she had been in there at least six hours and there seemed to be no way of checking whether there was any ventilation on.

Eventually after a full day of burning, a hole about six inches diameter was made but we couldn't see anything inside. When the aperture was about a foot diameter and the concrete round it had been cooled enough to crawl through I went in, followed by a paramedic. The place was in darkness and was extremely stuffy. It was indeed an art gallery with large paintings on the walls but no immediate sign of Julie.

In increasing desperation we worked our way systematically along the walls until we found her tied to a chair with a plaster across her mouth. She was unconscious and the paramedic gave her oxygen after we'd released her bonds. She responded immediately, murmuring incoherently. In double quick time we had her outside and in an ambulance for hospital with Charles and me in tow.

The medics sedated her after giving her a thorough medical examination and an intravenous drip. We were left to wait until she woke twelve hours later. Considering what she had gone through, she was recovering well physically but the ordeal of being tied up in complete darkness would no doubt leave mental scars for a long time. It was clear that when Egliston knew the attack was on he had tied her up and deliberately turned off the lights and ventilation in anger at the way events had turned out, knowing she would die within a few days if we did not do business with him.

Had it not been for Hans and the 'Torch's' help she would have died. Hans himself was still in a critical condition and would have to have surgery if strong enough. Julie was discharged after a few days and taken back to the Manor to recover. Rushton mounted a 24hr security cover on the Manor on the assumption that Egliston was still in the country and might try to get at one of us.

****

He was still in the country. A phone call was made to the Hall the day after Julie was brought home, while Rushton and his men were in the thick of going through the files found in the office. I was examining those relating to the Bakuoil Company, when the unmistakable voice came on the phone. Rushton signalled me to get on the extension.

"I shall ring off in thirty seconds, don't interrupt," ordered Egliston. Miss MacLean is probably dead now unless by a miracle you found her. You did not remove the checks at the ports and airports. I am going to give you one and only one more warning. You might have found the uranium in the store at Egliston Hall but you have not found the plutonium and the rest of the material. Poole Harbour and much of the town will be contaminated with plutonium if I am arrested. An associate will detonate explosions that will release the material and might even cause a dirty nuclear explosion if I do not report in to him on a daily basis over the next month. You are unlikely to find the explosives. Even if you do you will find they are set to go off if disturbed. One more time, take away the port and airport surveillance. Goodbye." The phone went dead.

"I am not going to take any notice of his threats," declared Rushton, "I do not believe there is any plutonium out there. He would surely have all the material available under lock and key here. Nevertheless I'll get a thorough search going on the Bakuoil base on Long Island".

We all hoped his optimism was justified.

****

After this episode I had a good look at the gallery. It was sophisticated, with temperature and humidity control. More surprising was the amount and value of the paintings and sculptures. Many items had clearly been looted from Europe at the end of the war but there were many more, some of stolen art, which had been added over a period of many years. Egliston had made good use of his time in Germany following in the wake of the advancing Allied armies. Rushton brought in experts who estimated the total value to be over half a billion pounds on the open market and identified several old masters that had been assumed to be lost. Some of them would have been those belonging to Hans's family.

Hans was still in hospital as the heart attack had sapped much of his strength, which was at low ebb as a result of his treatment at Egliston's hands. Nevertheless he was looking forward to getting out and working on the flashback technology. More than anything he wanted to see the art that had been looted from his parents. At the first opportunity we brought him out to the Hall and in a wheelchair took him round Egliston's gallery. After an hour or so he was physically and mentally drained and had to be taken into the Hall to rest.

Somewhat later he called me over and there were tears in his eyes.

"Harry, I don't think I shall survive much longer, the last few weeks have taken their toll."

"Nonsense Hans." I said. "You are as strong as a horse. We are going to make our names with the flashback. Egliston's career is finished and he will soon be arrested. You know what happened to your parents and can put all that behind you. You have a lot to do and we can't afford to lose you."

Hans smiled wanly and said in a weak voice, "You know, and I know, that my chances are slim, Harry, and I could go at any time. I want to tell you about the arrangements I've made. More than anything else I want to thank you for your part in getting rid of Egliston. But I want to give you some advice. Don't let power go to your head or you risk becoming a monster like Egliston. I'm putting my trust in you, and have made you and my colleague Professor Burton, executors of my estate. That estate's proceeds will be devoted to scientific research. I have specified how." His eyes were drooping at this stage and the doctor told us to leave him to recover. He didn't. A few hours later he had passed away.

In his will he had in fact named me as an executor, with the Deutsche Bank as another trustee of the fund, to be used for research. Everything he owned was bequeathed to the trust, as he had no relations. The purpose of the trust was to provide bursaries for scientists and grants for scientific research. Hans clearly wished to atone for his collaboration with Egliston over his life and for his treachery during WW2.

Chapter 36. Back at Norden Manor

A week later the search of Egliston Hall was reaching a conclusion and the press had stopped pestering us. Julie was out of hospital and I'd taken her out for a run in the car for a blow of fresh air. She wanted just to sit and look out over the sea, relax and talk.

While driving across the ridge of the Purbeck hills I pulled into the car park that gave a view across the green but desolate Tyneham Valley with the deserted village below us where I'd had my brush with death a week or two ago. There was a slight haze and we could just make out the sea and the ghostly outline of the Isle of Portland in the far distance. It was the first full chance to talk since our parting in London two months ago. At that time she had made it quite clear that our growing romance had foundered on the rocks of my employment by Egliston's organisation. I would at that moment have liked to think that we could have restarted our relationship: she was so bright, beautiful and vulnerable I would have agreed to anything.

"Harry, I've got to rethink my life. The whole of my world has changed. Before Baku reared its ugly head I was in love with you, really in love. Now I don't know. You showed a side of your character I'd not seen before when you told me about your decision to go in with

Egliston's organisation and it nearly broke my heart. I know now that Rushton had put pressure on you to go through with it. Now I don't know how much of what I saw was real or not."

"Then my career started to go sour. I'm going to throw in my job with the bank - I'd decided to do it before all this happened. It was getting more and more frenetic, and I couldn't see where it was all going. I even thought that if we got together we could make a good business team developing your oil recovery invention and exploiting it."

"Now there's this flashback invention. I don't know how it will affect you because it has the potential to make you quite powerful and you could well become another Egliston. Dad needs help, you don't. I know there's a pile of legal nonsense to get through but Dad could well turn out to own everything that's in the Egliston name. He will certainly get the estate and the title and I shall help him with that work. I think you and I have drifted apart and we should give ourselves time. I certainly need space to see what I want."

I hadn't expected this, mainly because I'm poor at the psychology of the female mind. I was still in love with her and thought that we would start again like a house on fire. I knew we could make a marvellous team and told her so. She gave me a long kiss and said that she knew I would understand that for the moment we should keep apart. We talked for a long time about how things might turn out but I must admit it was my turn to be emotionally shattered.

We had arranged to meet Charles at Norden Manor for dinner when he had finished at Egliston Hall where we were staying. We had watched the sun go down over the silhouette of Portland and the Manor was in darkness when we arrived: clearly Charles had not yet returned.

Rushton was still keeping a security check on the place and the armed guard told us to lock the door behind us, assuring us that someone would be patrolling outside whenever we were there. We made our way to the lounge to have a well-earned drink before we started to think about dinner. Gladys had left an open fire burning in the hearth and a cold meal for us all in the kitchen to eat whenever we wished.

"Let's have a drink to happier tomes when all this is behind us, while we're waiting for dad," said Julie echoing my thoughts about the drink. The lounge exuded warmth and we sank into the leather upholstery of the settee opposite the cracking log fire to enjoy the homely atmosphere. This disappeared immediately.

"I'm sorry to upset this scene of domestic bliss," came a familiar grating voice from the shadows behind us. Egliston emerged from the shadows, holding a gun that was pointing directly at me. Julie stifled a scream and I instinctively held her to me.

"You despicable shit," I shouted starting to get up. "I'm going to get you for what you and your miserable son did to Julie if it's the last thing I do."

Julie was trembling almost uncontrollably.

"Sit down or it will be your last action," he snapped taking off the safety catch and raising the gun.

I felt it better to do what he said and sank back into the leather, holding her to me.

"I let myself in," he went on in a more relaxed manner, standing with his back to the fire. "Charles really should have changed the locks when he moved in all those years ago. It was quite easy to slip past Major Rushton's guards to get in one of the less used doors to this place. This is quite like old times. Now you can sit there while we wait for him to return."

Egliston was looking his age now; he was unkempt and the arrogant air he had when I last met him had gone, to be replaced by a somewhat hunted look. I kept quiet to try and make him less trigger-happy than he appeared to be.

After a minute he gradually lowered his gun and eased himself into a high-backed chair at the side of the blazing fire.

"I for once made a mistake in employing you, Aldborough, and another mistake in not dealing finally with Charles and this young lady, years ago. I didn't know you knew each other when we met in London. I thought you were ambitious enough to cut a few ethical corners. I also thought you would see that it would be very profitable working for me. That's water under the bridge now. Now I want to know more about this flashback toy of yours and what you've seen here in this manor. I never thought it would be so successful. Our friend Hans seems to have shut me off from the project since he got it working in Heidelberg."

" Oh, you probably didn't realise I was putting up money to Hans to support your project." He grimaced in a satisfied way when he saw the surprise on my face. "He seems to think I misled him about his wretched parents' fate during the war when he saw a flashback of me with some Nazis at their old place in Heidelberg. He even accused me of being a spy. He was quite mortified to think he might have been fooled into passing information to the Germans in WW2. He's gone to his Jewish heaven, I understand?"

"Now, what flashbacks have you seen here? I might have to shoot your girlfriend's knees off if I don't hear the truth."

He had us over a barrel, so to speak, and I'd decided he probably intended to shoot us anyway before he'd finished. He presumably wanted to know what proof we had of his spying activities, but more importantly whether we knew he was an impostor and who else knew.

While there was any hope of his switch with the real Henry staying a secret his own son could lo forward to inheriting the peerage even though he might be in prison. If Charles and Julie were disposed of there would be no other potential heir to contend with.

He was a very shrewd character and would be able to spot a lie from me a mile away. The best approach would be to play for time and hope that Rushton would call in as he'd promised and before Charles came and give us the chance to escape. Perhaps he might even be persuaded to say when he had killed Henry and how he had disposed of the body. I decided to go in at the metaphorical deep end.

"It's a long story and yes we have seen your activities here" I started, and then went as slowly as I could through our developments from the first accidental sighting in the study on my first night here.

He suddenly said, "You must have been surprised at my sudden recovery from shell shock."

"We know of course that you are not Charles's brother, you are in fact Frank Taylor." I replied.

"Of course!" He burst out with an ugly laugh. "Henry led me a merry dance. Colditz was the original plan. He was taken there specially to let me watch him and get his mannerisms correct. I intended to kill him when the time was right. It seemed a marvellous opportunity. My mother, Nicole, put up the idea when she heard he was a prisoner. I underwent minor plastic surgery to make myself look like him. I already had roughly the same colouring and build as he did. I'd grown up seeing him every day in my childhood and I could easily pass myself off as him after a few months of practice. Any other small differences could easily be explained as physical and mental war damage. Unfortunately he escaped just before we were ready to make the switch and got back to England.

"My mother was able to help us implement an alternative plan. The prize was valuable. We could place a German spy in the middle of the British establishment and be in a position to sabotage and observe military defences in the south of England. When our German armies had landed he would be a key person in the new administration. I was landed from a U-boat just below Egliston Hall and made my way to the Manor early in 1940. The very first thing I did was to shoot Henry. I'd hated him since we were children. He was arrogant and treated me like dirt. I always knew I'd get my revenge. Nicole looked after all the possible problems over here."

"The main thing she did was to get rid of Henry's father by pushing him over the St Aldhelm cliffs. He was a frail man and used to go up there to brood. It was well known that he suffered from depression and it was passed off as suicide. After that it was easy. The supposed shell shock gave me time to get used to my new life and Nicole covered up any other problems."

"What did you do with Henry's body? You obviously couldn't risk it being found," I chipped in hoping his momentum would carry him on.

"A stroke of good fortune. As you say I couldn't risk throwing it over the cliffs or even burying it in the garden because of it being identified. By great good fortune there was an air raid in the village the following night and two villagers were killed. I gave permission for the coffins to rest in the Manor until they were buried. Nicole and I put Henry's body in one just before it was taken away. A detachment of soldiers lifted the coffins out for the funeral and nobody noted the heavier weight.

"After Henry and his father had been disposed of there was nobody left who posed any real threat to me except Charles, and I dealt with that by keeping him well at arms' length. In retrospect I should have got rid of him then I probably wouldn't have the problems I have today."

Taylor, as I suppose I should start calling him, didn't seem in any hurry. I knew that he was waiting for Charles to arrive and he would then kill us all. How could I warn Charles? I was sweating somewhat now because I couldn't think what to do except keep him talking. Julie clung to me with her eyes closed.

"Why were you in Heidelberg while the war was still going on?" I said.

"What a marvellous and ironic chance." He shook with laughter. "The British thought they had an ideal person in me to try and negotiate a peace deal behind Hitler's back. I speak fluent German, I was part of your aristocracy and I was an officer. We met in Heidelberg at the Reise family house. It was a charade. The German side obviously knew the British negotiating position at the start of each day and the whole thing collapsed, as I planned. It was clear to me and many others that Hitler was finished but of course I didn't want the war to end at that time. I managed to get my records in the German ministry relating to the switch with Henry, lost. We also managed to get a lot of gold, foreign currency and art treasures out of the country in the closing stages of the war. I made a particular point of getting the art collection that had belonged to Reise's family. Ironic, don't you think?

"Of course Miss MacLean had plenty of time to admire my treasures when she was locked in." He laughed again. "With my local position it was easy to arrange army transport to bring the items to Egliston Hall. Unfortunately most of the gold is still there at Tyneham, as you know".

While he was speaking I suddenly momentarily noticed Rushton's face at a gap between the shutters. Taylor couldn't see it from where he was sitting and Julie had her eyes shut. Unbelievably Rushton held up a message, which said 'when lights go out, move fast'. He then vanished.

"What are you going to do now," I ventured, wanting to keep Egliston talking and to cover up any noises off stage.

"I shall probably get rid of you three and then I shall disappear, sail away. I've obviously had contingency plans for a long time, although I must say I didn't believe they would ever be necessary. My son will have to face the music but I suppose he will be Lord Egliston in the fullness of time. Nobody will have sufficient proof to deny him and there won't be any male members of Charles's family to inherit. I shall be sailing from England to-morrow."

At that point the lights went out and I threw Julie to the floor with myself on. There was a burst of automatic pistol fire from the window and shots, presumably from Taylor. I felt one shot brush my ear; there was a few seconds of chaos. I lay on the floor not daring to move, before the lights came on. A black clothed soldier came in shouting to keep down and not to move. Then Rushton appeared.

"He got away damn him!" he shouted. Then he saw the blood pouring from my ear and dripping on to Julie. He rapidly found my wound was more spectacular than harmful and that Julie was unharmed. Charles appeared and embraced Julie.

It seemed that Charles had arrived back at the Manor and had seen Taylor through a crack in the shutters. He had got through to Rushton, who had organised the rescue. Julie and I had unfortunately arrived while Charles was at a neighbouring house telephoning, having forgotten his mobile.

A more highly visible armed guard was placed on the house for our protection to supplement the low level surveillance that had failed us, until Egliston was caught. Clearly he would kill Julie, Charles and me if he possibly could.

We soon found how Egliston had got away. He had been wounded during the melee and spots of blood led through the hall into the kitchen. They ceased abruptly at the panelled wall. It was clear he had used another hidden passageway that we had not discovered. It was some time before we found how to open the wall panel that led in. The passageway led under the road outside to a house opposite of the same vintage as the Manor. Another hidden panel there had let him escape and presumably drive away.

Rushton arranged for the watch placed on all airports and ports to be intensified. I had recalled Egliston saying, just before Rushton had stormed into the Manor, that he would be sailing the next day. It was quite late before we locked the house, with the armed guards reinforcing our safety. To my surprise Julie led me to her bedroom. I thought we were supposed to be going our separate ways. We lay naked in the four-poster bed and she held me tightly a long time before we made love, slowly. I don't think she let go her embrace all night. In the morning her catharsis was complete and she seemed in control of herself. Looking at me with those greenish brown eyes that made me miss many a heart beat she whispered, "Last night doesn't change what I said, Harry. You've given me the strength to get myself sorted out and I shall always be grateful but I think we must run our individual lives, until, and if we are sure we want each other for always. Thank you, Harry." She turned away from me and I slowly, sadly left her room.

The most likely exit place for Egliston to get out of the country would of course be Poole itself and every boat leaving the harbour was scanned. Nothing suspicious was seen over the next week. The breakthrough came one morning. One of the large Sunseeker gin palaces approached the mouth of the harbour. At first sight it appeared to be innocent but a sharp-eyed customs officer recognised the boat's skipper as one of the Summerfield employees who should have no real business being in charge of such a boat. It was hailed and told to heave-to and allow boarding, whereupon it accelerated away.

Unfortunately the chain ferry which links the two havens at the 200 yards wide mouth of Poole Harbour was half way across at the time and the boat crashed into it, the helmsman misjudging speed and distance. The boat sank quickly, leaving no sign of Egliston, although his man was saved.

It was eventually assumed he had been washed out to sea on the strong ebb tide. In a sense we had a cautious sense of relief that Egliston had gone for good.

Such men leave their evil at work, however, and I had a call from one of Egliston's men.

"Egliston's gone, but you had better know that he had a cache of U235 on board." came the voice, "From what I know of the stuff it could cause a big bang and contaminate most of Poole at the same time." The call ended there. I passed on the message to the police and to Rushton's office and before very long all shipping had been stopped and people were asked to stay indoors until advised it was safe.

The next few hours were tense as SBS men were sent down to locate the wreck and to see whether there was any evidence of U235 release. Fortunately for Poole no radioactivity could be detected. The uranium had been put into watertight containers and was recovered safely.

****

We now knew how to trace the remains of Charles's brother Henry from what Egliston had said. He was in a grave somewhere in the Purbecks with someone else's name on the head stone. All we had to do in principle was to look through the parish records of local villages for the villagers killed in an air raid on the area in April 1940. In the event, it to several days to search the records but we eventually found two likely graves in a nearby village churchyard, at Kingston Matravers. Charles was determined to get the bodies exhumed to allow a positive identification and a reburial with proper dignity. A DNA test would be necessary to clearly identify the remains.

We weren't able to trace any living members of the families of the two people whose names were on the headstones and we were able to obtain an order for exhumation. The first coffin reached proved to be the resting place of two skeletons. The search was at an end. To make absolutely sure Charles provided a DNA specimen that proved conclusively that the larger of the two skeletons was the earthly remains of his brother. Henry would be allowed the dignity Charles felt he deserved. The funeral took place in the small churchyard of Steeple village a week later on a cold and miserable morning; a sad end to a sad story.

Chapter 37. Egliston's Legacy

The media storm broke with the death of Egliston in the speedboat crash in Poole Harbour. The Financial Times had 'Collapse of the Egliston Empire'. The Sun had 'Nazi Bogus Lord Dead'.

Rushton would have liked more time to question employees of the Egliston companies he had been monitoring. He moved rapidly to organise swoops with the Russian and Azeri authorities on company operatives in Baku and Moscow.

Egliston's son, Nicolas, had disappeared with other key men, but only small quantities of fissile material were impounded in Baku.

In the UK the government's Department of Trade and Industry had the private companies owned by Egliston and his son placed into administration. The Egliston conglomerate companies quoted on the London and New York Stock Exchanges had dealings in their shares suspended until their directors had secured their companies' trading positions.

It would be open season for the legal profession for years.

Charles's position was far from clear. He would assume the peerage that had been criminally appropriated by Taylor as well as the family estate. The extent to which he would own the personal fortune that had been held by Taylor in his Lord Egliston persona appeared to be a legal black hole. Taylor had used Egliston family resources to create his wealth but had also used funds obtained from illegal activities as well as WW2 booty.

There would be claims from many who believed Taylor had wronged them. Egliston Hall held the art that had been plundered from Germany and, also, bought on the black market. It also held a considerable amount of uranium: enough to make three U235 atomic bombs.

My position was unclear. I was still on the books of Bakuoil as an employee: the company held an exclusive right to use my invention for two years and all the development tools and equipment were impounded by the government. The existence of the flashback invention was firmly suppressed by the UK government and made subject to the Official Secrets Act. It would only be a question of time, however, before someone else discovered the technique and I pressed hard and futilely with civil servants from the Ministry of Defence to be allowed to continue work. Eventually I reconciled myself to a long wait while government committees pondered what to do.

The administrator of the Bakuoil and Summerfield companies brought me in for discussions with managers and directors who had been part of the legitimate side of the businesses. Egliston had fortunately been very careful to ensure that the illegal operatives were in segregated business sections that naturally melted away as soon as the news broke.

I was able to give a clean bill of health to Farouk who was made operations manager in Baku and told to get production restarted. I decided to return to Baku to make sure that my project was set up properly. My income for the foreseeable future would depend on it.

Now that my relationship with Julie appeared to be on ice it would be a great opportunity to resume a friendship with Anna. However, there were a few things to be sorted out in Dorset. Julie threw herself into helping Charles sort out the chaos surrounding the estate and asked me to stay and lend a hand although I thought it would be better if Julie and I made a complete break. Charles, however, was very insistent as he was still worried about her health and didn't have anyone else he could turn to. I stayed.

Scientists had been brought in from Aldermaston, the UK nuclear weapons establishment, to remove all the uranium and to decontaminate the building. Fortunately for Charles and for all of us the design of the uranium store had been professionally carried out and the whole operation was completed within a week, enabling the heavy security to be removed.

The fabulous collection of paintings was still there and a security company was brought in by Charles to guard it. Our frantic attempt to rescue Julie had left the main entrance to the art gallery with a one foot diameter hole that would take some time to repair if indeed the store were to be used at all.

An assessor from the National Gallery was sent down by the police to make an inventory of all the art works and where possible to identify them. It really was an Aladdin's cave. The expert, a diminutive avuncular, very intense man walked around as though he had won the lottery. He could hardly believe his eyes. A quick survey revealed several Old Masters, which had disappeared during the war as well as some that had been stolen over the last sixty years.

Charles certainly hoped that the whole situation could be resolved quickly, as he had to pay for the security. Taylor had purchased many of the paintings quite legitimately but it was unclear whether they now belonged to Charles, to Egliston's son who had disappeared, to the state or to others. I suggested to Charles that he should ask the National Gallery to take them all until the legalities could be resolved. That would save him quite a lot of money. The offer was accepted quickly and we were shortly able to lock up the complex and forget about it for the time being.

The administration of the Egliston estate was a nightmare. Under Taylor, the estate had been well maintained but several of the management staff had disappeared. They had been brought in from Eastern Europe and the Middle East and none of the other staff were part of the local community, presumably because of Taylor's insistence on tight security. Julie took over this management and recruitment and Charles and I were interested to see how she coped. We needn't have had doubts because the administration was soon operating smoothly.

Rushton had put the flashback equipment under lock and key and neither Charles nor I were allowed to touch it until some government committee had decided what to do. However, the question of what Taylor, as I shall now call him, had been trying to find at the Tyneham House ruin within the controlled military area intrigued me. Rushton was reluctant to let us, without clearance by the ministry; use the flashback to see whether I could find the treasure Egliston had talked about.

However, there was increasing pressure from the Culture Ministry to investigate where Egliston's art works had come from and they also were intrigued by the hint I dropped that there would be more works of art to be found. He eventually agreed, reluctantly, and arranged for the local area at Tyneham to be swept for unexploded ordnance and for the flashback 'Torch' to be recommissioned.

Under the command of one of Rushton's men together with a team from the Bovington barracks with picks and shovels we made our way to the site where there was a blackened area at one end but no other evidence of the massive explosion and fire I had witnessed. The whole area was as sombre as it was on my previous visit and the old Manor that the army had wrecked, as part of their exercises over the years, brooded over us. The tall trees put the whole area under a green canopy.

We waited until dusk so as to be able to see the flashback images more clearly. This time I planned the exercise systematically, unlike last time when I was more concerned with escape.

According to drawings of Tyneham House that Charles had obtained from Egliston Hall it seemed likely that there was a cellar and tunnel linking it to the house roofed by stone slabs the length of the garden. The treasure could well be down there. It took a little time before we had focussed in on the war time period that Taylor had specified.

Eventually a flashback 'Torch' image appeared of a mobile crane lifting a slab of concrete about ten feet long and four feet wide. A large number of ammunition and other steel boxes were then lowered in and eventually the block replaced. The soldiers would probably not have realised they were burying treasure, assuming it to be obsolete ammunition.

On today's viewpoint, from the surface, the area appeared just like another part of the overgrown garden. Our present day soldiers were set to work with their picks and shovels and before long the concrete slab we had seen in the images was there before us. The army organised a crane from the nearby Lulworth camp and eventually, after finding the lifting bars on the concrete, the space below was revealed.

The ammunition boxes were very rusty and it was with great care each one was lifted out. We didn't want to find obsolete munitions.

It really was treasure. There were large quantities of gold rings, jewellery and macabre gold fragments that had been gold dental fillings as well as ornaments of gold. It was painfully clear that most of the contents had come from the extermination camps of the Third Reich and had been taken from the victims.

There was no wonder Taylor had hidden the hoard until he could dispose of it without arousing suspicion. The take-over of the Tyneham estate by the army had foiled his plan and he had lost all records of where the material had been hidden. Rushton impounded the whole lot and that was the last we saw of it. It was also the last we saw of the flashback apparatus for a long time.

Chapter 38. Flashback

I was raring to get my hands back on the flashback project as soon as I could, but the government men in grey suits and military in khaki uniforms had put a complete blanket on its use and classified it as secret - just as Hans Reise had warned me they would. Rushton had locked it back in the Hall cellar.

There was no doubt a scientific committee somewhere in the government offices in London's Whitehall contemplating its collective navel until someone decided what to do with the invention. To be fair, in their position I wouldn't have known either. An argument for keeping it highly classified was that it would let them use it for eavesdropping on secret meetings long after the events had taken place, with no fear of detection. It would be a boon for the solving of crimes; the perpetrators could be seen and identified in many cases.

The trouble is that these scientific genies tend to come out of their bottles in the course of time. I wanted to patent it, even if I were liberal with its licensing, before someone else discovered the technique, as they surely would.

The scientific aspects were very important. Astronomers have been trying to detect gravity waves from cosmic explosions such as supernovae for a long time. A small modification would allow my time 'Torch' to act as an amplifier of gravity waves just as a MASER is used to amplify radio waves. The time 'Torch' would open up history and astronomy as though events were in the here and now.

Eventually, after many sessions in which I made myself thoroughly objectionable, I persuaded Rushton that it would be in his interests to let me use it within the confines of the estate. It would be useful to him to see who had visited Egliston both recently and also all those years ago after he to the Hall back from military use. He pulled some bureaucratic strings and Charles and I were given limited clearance after a solemn lecture on what sections 1 and 2 of the Official Secrets Act would do to us if we told anybody.

In the course of its use I would be able to do some research on the technique – what, for example were the limits on how long ago we could see flashbacks. There was no prospect of theoretical developments. Hans had had some promising ideas but I didn't have the skills to develop them further. My interest was in instrument development. As far as Rushton was concerned our use of the equipment paid off handsomely. Charles and I set it up in the main meeting room of the Hall as well as in Egliston's study.

We were able to look in on meetings of what appeared to be Egliston's inner cabinet of managers, some of whom we knew were concerned with the smuggling, and their visitors. At least three more names were added to Rushton's list for investigation.

Charles for his part wanted to find out more about his family as well as Taylor's life in the closing stage of the war, in particular how he came into possession of the gold hoard and who else, if anybody, was involved.

There was nothing in the records at the Hall to cast light on this. Rushton, mollified by the intelligence pay off from the flashback, gave us free rein for its use as long as it stayed on the estate or near to it.

Charles dearly wanted to try and see if we could detect the murder of his grandfather on the cliff top of St Aldhelm's Head. Although I didn't think it a very good idea, because of the psychological effect it might have on him, I went along with the hunt.

For once we failed miserably. Although we scanned with flashback along a half-mile stretch of the cliff edge for hours, nothing from that time could be detected, probably because erosion of the edge over sixty years had moved it back several feet. It wasn't the best place for detailed work because of the strong winds and danger especially at night.

As Charles was bitterly disappointed I suggested as a way of cheering him up: a long shot testing of one of his ghost theories. When we first met he was telling me about his theories and he mentioned the Roman soldiers seen in the vicinity of Chapman's Pool by more than one observer in the past. Could we repeat this with the flashback? He leapt at the proposal.

The rocky outcrop where he had been told the sightings had taken place was still there and we set up the equipment hoping for the best. So far we had only probed back about sixty years and we knew the efficiency of the equipment probing as far as Roman times would be very low, in particular the frequency of the ultrasound needed could be multiplied by a factor of about a thousand.

Charles was like a small boy with his enthusiasm but this faded after an hour or two when we detected nothing further than about seventy years ago. I then had an idea. Hans had said that it was likely that in radiation space some past times, for example a hundred years ago, could be beyond the reach of flashback. There would however be other times in the more distant past that would be actually nearer in radiation space and amenable to flashback.

I tried the idea by trying ultrasound settings half, a quarter and so on times what we had used normally. In the fading light of the day we soon found images that included animals and people dressed as they would in the early days of the first millennium. Hans had been right. If we searched long enough we would surely have seen the Romans. Night had fallen, however, and it was getting bitterly cold.

We had established that the usefulness of the equipment could be extended to times long ago and could cast light on distant history. Charles had forgotten all his disappointment about not seeing a flashback of his grandfather's death and was ecstatic.

"We can rewrite the history of Purbeck!" he enthused.

"Let's keep Rushton happy first," I said, pouring cold water on his enthusiasm.

Rushton insisted on our continuing our search of Taylor's past and his visitors. The most memorable flashback we obtained was from 1945. Three people were seen in the study with an ammunition box of the type we had found in Tyneham. I did not recognise Taylor's two companions and Charles didn't either although they stirred something in his memory.

Rushton was brought in to inspect what we were seeing and immediately recognised the weasel-faced one. "He really did keep some vile company! Believe it or not that's Adolf Eichmann, the man responsible for implementing the solution to the Nazi's 'Jewish problem'. The Mossad found him in Argentina and spirited him back to Israel in 1960 for trial and punishment.

This is definite proof that Taylor acted as a conduit for the escape of Nazi war criminals and their money. I don't recognise the other man but if you can get a photograph of your flashback I'll find someone who does." Taking the photo wasn't easy. The light levels were low and we had to 'freeze frame' the flashback by slowly decreasing the ultrasound frequency to compensate for the passage of time.

It wasn't until several months later Rushton told us what happened with the information we provided.

"Our mystery man was still alive and living in luxury in the Home Counties. He was a member of the House of Lords, had served in government and was a respected Member of the establishment.

By the time I found him he had cancer, and he is now dead. He confessed almost on his deathbed when he knew we had proof he was a Nazi collaborator who had made it easy for some Nazis to escape.

He had been well paid for his work. He was persuaded by us to leave all his estate to a Holocaust charity and we agreed to keep his murky past secret, as I'm sure you will."

Chapter 39. Back to Baku

Russian Influence

After the excitement of the unmasking and death of Taylor and the sorting out of the Egliston estate, boredom set in and the wheels seemed to come off my future. Julie had seemingly written me off. I could not develop the flashback whilst the security ban on it continued.

My enhanced oil recovery development was intimately tied up with the future of Bakuoil and Summerfield, which had for the time being at least stopped using my equipment and could well be bought by another but unsympathetic oil company. Financial support from them and from the government to go on with the research and development at WTC had been frozen and there was no way I could join up with another sponsor. All this was highly frustrating because the results from the Caspian Sea offshore tests were excellent.

My immediate financial position was distinctly sick. Charles, now that he was likely to benefit handsomely from becoming the new Lord Egliston, offered to help with the cash flow and by providing food and lodging, which I accepted gratefully in the short term.

Rushton was struggling to get to the bottom of the illegal activities of the Egliston Corporation and had asked me to make myself available when required. It was with some relief and anticipation on my part when Rushton summoned me to a meeting with his security and other officials at the Department of Trade and Industry in its large glass-fronted emporium on Victoria Road in London.

"You're going to be very useful to us in Baku" he had said with one of his half smiles. I didn't like the sound of that one little bit.

It appeared that in Baku itself Klanski and about six other Bakuoil operatives had disappeared without leaving a forwarding address after the news of Egliston's exposure and death were made public. They left so quickly that they neglected to destroy or take much of the company records, which contained a fair amount of incriminating evidence.

The factory, on the other hand was bare, having been raided, presumably by the Mafia while looking for fissile material, drugs or any thing else of interest or value. Thankfully for Bakuoil and my project the field engineers, including Farouk, who were not part of the clandestine operations, had shut down the oilfield and had secured the platform in anticipation of an extended shutdown. A group manager had been sent from London to Baku by the company administrators to hold the fort until decisions had been made as to the future of the company. The Sandline military assistance operation apparently vanished into thin air but was probably operating behind the scenes in Abkhazia.

Inside the Department of Trade and Industry, I was escorted into an airy room overlooking Westminster Abbey where an assorted group of individuals ranging from a suave Armani clad senior civil servant to a colonel in uniform, were seated round an oak table. They had clearly been there some time judging by the used plastic coffee cups and paperwork strewn round the table.

I was treated like an exhibit at the zoo, presumably because I'd been the subject of their discussion. Rushton led the meeting. I was subjected again to a detailed cross examination by the Armani suit about what I'd seen of the more questionable aspects of Bakuoil's operations and of the personalities involved, particularly those involved with Sandline.

Apparently there was evidence emerging that the smuggling, military and other operations based in Baku had not fallen apart, but were being pulled together by Taylor's son Nicolas in a new operation in the Caucasus region now involving the local Mafia, with whom Egliston's people had begun to cooperate.

Rushton had already made most of the decisions as to my role, aided and abetted by his friends round the table. I was being set up to return to Baku to work with Colliston and local security people to identify some of the personalities in the old operations. As before, I would ostensibly be sent as an employee of Bakuoil to assist with the restarting of operations under new management and to look after my enhanced oil production project on the oil field. I reminded them, with some understatement, that my safety might be somewhat at risk, bearing in mind I'd been shot at twice and escaped being pushed off a high building and I might be reluctant to help them out.

"You don't really have any alternative, old boy" smiled Rushton "All your eggs are in this basket and they will probably all get broken if you find it difficult to help us. Rest assured you are much more use to us alive than dead and I promise that your security will be high on our list. The local Baku people including Miss Kaplinski will be working with you and I know you've successfully worked with her in the past."

He really is a hard bastard, but on that occasion and in that company it didn't seem right to remind him of the fact and I contented myself with saying with some feeling that I would enjoy working with him again.

Another of the grey suits at the meeting then spoke.

"My interests are more mundane than the cloak and dagger activities of Colonel Rushton," he said with a nod towards him. "My department is anxious to ensure that Bakuoil and Summerfield are both brought back into operation. Being potentially very profitable British companies it is in our interests to make sure they come out of administration as soon as possible.

It will take time to get the legalities of the new Lord Egliston's equity resolved and therefore I have placed the equity owned by the ex-lord Egliston and his son in a trust. One of my staff has been appointed Trustee and will look after those interests and is now, together with others, getting the company operating. You will work with the group manager in Baku and have the opportunity to secure your own project's welfare when you are there. You will of course continue as an employee of the company for the present until a new contract is worked out."

That was essentially the end of the meeting and Rushton escorted me out. In the next few days I had several meetings with security people and directors of the Egliston companies. The army at Bovington gave me more instruction on self-defence including the use of firearms, which seemed to be a wise precaution after my last experiences in Baku. I was very happy to hear that Anna would be one of those affecting my welfare; perhaps the happiest thing I had heard since the whole trip was sprung on me. Julie had made it abundantly clear that for the foreseeable future our relationship would be platonic and I persuaded myself my conscience was clear. When, a day or two later, the Aeroflot plane from Moscow circled round the Baku peninsular before landing out of a clear blue sky I looked forward, but with some apprehension to the next few weeks.

Farouk met me at the airport and embraced me.

"Hi Harry, meet the new operations manager of the field operation. I was formally appointed today. Welcome back to Baku!" He guided me out of the terminal chattering wildly and obviously very happy about the turn of events, taking my luggage and leading me to his car. Hovering in the background like the angel of death was Colliston, who shook my hand and greeted me much less effusively. In the car he turned to me.

"Welcome back Harry, I hope your stay will be less eventful than before. It is of course part of my job to make sure that it is successful. The other part is to make sure the ex-Egliston operations are closed down". He handed me a pistol, an action that tended to belie his words on my safety.

"You are mainly at danger from reprisals from individuals in the Mafia for the events of your last visit. You will be in more danger if they realise you are still working with us as well as your overt engineering role with Bakuoil. For the present I have a minder who will be unobtrusively with you as well as Anna, who has been loaned to the operation by the Russians. She might be a welcome addition to your security," he smiled wanly, for the first time. He arranged to meet me for a full briefing on the security operation after I had sorted out my work programme with Farouk.

This time, an apartment in the centre of the town fairly near to where Anna lived, had been assigned to me for the stay so that I could be guarded more easily than in a hotel. Farouk left me there to settle in, telling me to meet him after my security meeting with Colliston the next day.

There had been a six hour delay in getting through Moscow and I was feeling somewhat drained after the rather bumpy four hour flight to Baku.

After an hour's sleep I had just had a shower, dried and slipped a dressing gown on when there was a knock at the door. Feeling like a poor man's James Bond I retrieved the pistol Colliston had given me and stood beside the door while unlocking it and shouting,

"Enter". The door opened slowly and there was Anna.

"Well, well Harry, quite the professional, but I'd better give you some professional instruction before you try that again. Slip off the safety catch for example."

She put her arms round my neck and we kissed just as I'd remembered vividly. She then stepped back with the gun, put it on the settee and then moved forward to undo the belt to the dressing gown.

An hour later when my welcome back to Baku had been consummated and we lay perspiring in the large double bed I told her what had happened since I left Baku in a hurry. "And what has happened to Miss MacLean? I notice you didn't have much to say about her," said Anna.

"I'm sure you know all there is to know," was my somewhat peevish reply.

"Of course," she replied, "you are having a very British platonic affair. I just like to see you squirm. I'm not the jealous type - and anyway it doesn't mesh with my job."

"What is your job, Anna?" I asked, "Now we know each other better I ought to know."

She looked at me without blinking. "Before I get on to that Harry, we're fine as we are. Don't get any romantic ideas; I'm not going to tie myself down. You're the nearest I will get to a permanent lover, and I won't mind if you decide to settle down in an English cottage with the wife of your dreams. Now, you asked about my job. I'm sorry to spoil your illusions but I'm definitely not a secret agent. I work for the Russian Industry Ministry in the corporate fraud department."

"Unfortunately in Russia there is a lot more corruption in industry than in the West and the Mafia is involved in so many cases. That means a lot of violence and I have had to learn how to protect myself. That's another reason I don't want a deep relationship."

She then gave me a full briefing on how my minders would work. She would accompany me for much of the time and at others when I was not offshore, there would be someone watching my back. At my apartment, a neighbouring room would be a base for a minder who would be able to monitor the corridor and my apartment itself.

"I shall be at your meeting with Mr Colliston tomorrow and we'll leave that part to then." she concluded. "There isn't a minder next door there at the moment by the way," she added. Never being slow to take a hint I carried her across to the dishevelled bed - might as well keep up the momentum!

****

The residual equipment at the factory had been well and truly damaged by the Mafia in their raid and it was clear that it would take some time to get it functional. Farouk had two technicians assigned to me and we set about the detailed job of repairing the spare EROS tools for use offshore. We then went offshore to check over the installed equipment and found that we would have very little to do to get it going again.

In contrast to the last time I was there, the sun was shining, the sea was calm and the sinister aspect of the place had disappeared. For a time I forgot the intrigue and danger and enjoyed being an engineering scientist again. It wouldn't last.

The meeting with Colliston the next day involved me slipping into the consulate by the back door so to speak because it was important that it was perceived that I was there in a purely technical role rather than as a cog in the machine investigating the Egliston organisation.

Anna had assured me that a minder would cover my journey but I didn't notice anybody following me, which I should have taken as a reassuring sign that I was in the hands of professionals; on the other hand there might not have been anybody there at all. Colliston, Anna and two others were there already. One of the two strangers was British and introduced as a security adviser on the region who had been brought in by the embassy, mainly to follow up the Sandline questions. The other was an anonymous-looking Azeri representative from the government security services. The Brit by contrast had a very alert and dominating presence, was about forty years old and looked an archetypal officer with matching accent and mannerisms. He clearly had a good grasp of the political and industrial nuances of the region. He was introduced as Colonel George Cavil.

The meeting had obviously been going on for some time.

"Harry," began Colliston, "during your last two visits to Baku and also in England you met directly and indirectly a large number of people in or associated with the company. I know that you have given as much information as you could to Rushton but you might have forgotten some and also not realised who were good guys and who were not. Your memory might be stirred further over the next few weeks as you see more and more people. We have good evidence that elements of Egliston's old empire under Nicolas, his son, are regrouping in the Caspian region and we want to identify who and where. This whole area is ripe for such people to prosper, with civil unrest, guerrilla operations, pipelines and corruption. You think of it, and it's there. George here knows where the opposition are likely to meet. There are also various industry meetings and exhibitions and so on, as long shots that we shall have to cover as well."

"We want you to accompany Anna, or George, as appropriate and help our surveillance. We have some places bugged or under close observation where the targets might meet. You will not be seen I hope but there are times when your face will be exposed to view. You will be accompanied occasionally by one of the new managers of Bakuoil who will legitimise the reason for your presence. All you have to do is finger for us possible suspects and we will do the rest. First, however, I'd like you to go through an album of people we believe were part of the set up. Some you will know already. Then we will go through your schedule."

I identified some mug shots of people I'd seen and forgotten but Colliston already knew them and the overall exercise drew a blank.

The visits for the next three weeks were to include a petroleum seminar in Georgia, and others in and around Baku. One of the dangers I would face would be that possible suspects would recognise me, and Colliston suggested that a small amount of disguise would be appropriate. As a result I found myself growing a beard – ridiculous!

Baku had a lively Petroleum Engineers Society with regular seminars and meetings. Most of the professional engineers were in the habit of attending and I made the point of going as well for both personal and surveillance reasons, as I would have every reason to be there with my credentials as an engineer. It was surprising how many engineers I had met before.

There were a lot of small independents in the region that had recruited far and wide, some of them from BP, my old oil company. I enjoyed myself enormously, almost forgetting why I was there and even gave a seminar to the Petroleum Institute on enhanced oil recovery. There were several whom Bakuoil and Summerfield had employed, and I passed on their names but I suspect none would have been involved in smuggling. All the bad guys appeared to have gone to ground.

The most boring parts of the job involved sitting in small rooms that had a CCTV screen viewing people entering and leaving oil and other company buildings. Talk about looking for needles in a haystack!

Anna spent some time keeping me company and we talked a lot about our past. She had usually changed the subject of her past when I raised it, but hours spent in the watching eventually dragged it out.

She had trained and qualified as an engineer in Moscow ten years ago but had been selected by the Russian security services for training as an agent to gather industrial espionage from Western companies, spending some time in both the USA and Britain. She wouldn't say which companies were her targets. She said was very good at the job, but had tired of it. She hinted that an affair with one of the people she had been spying on had gone wrong and her role had been exposed. She had to return to Russia and she had been transferred to the Industry Ministry.

Her current job looking for corruption gave her much more freedom and more money and with the constant travelling and danger stopped her getting emotional entanglements.

My history sounded humdrum by comparison. She must have been sadly let down in her love life because it had clearly left its mark emotionally. She could be rather cold at times.

After a week of watching I succeeded in pointing out at least three people who had probably been in on Egliston's scams because they had been at the London office in Nicolas Egliston's presence.

Chapter 40. Problems in Tbilisi

Part of the continuing penance being paid by Charles to Rushton for the privilege of using the flashback equipment was to spend regular periods most days making flashbacks in the meeting room and study of the Hall to monitor whom Egliston had been meeting.

It had paid off handsomely in establishing links between him and possible criminal activities, but there was an awful lot of dross there: routine meetings with staff and with others in connection with his many activities. Charles had been getting a little rebellious and was thinking of telling Rushton where he could put his requests. His technique was continually to call in Rushton to see what he had found even though the scene in the flashback was obviously trivial. Even Rushton was getting short-tempered.

On this occasion Rushton had been called in for the fifth time in an hour and was determined to put a stop to Charles's technique.

"What the bloody hell have you got now? Why can't you use a bit of judgement?"

He looked at the scene in the flashback. There was Egliston, his son and a group of four smartly dressed individuals round the conference table. One of the four was standing, pointing at what seemed to be a map. Rushton suddenly froze.

"My God! He's one of the opposition!"

He dashed out of the room and Charles could hear him issuing orders over the telephone and when he returned he stood looking at the flashback.

"Harry is in for a much rougher time than I thought," he murmured.

****

Colliston had decided that I should pay a visit accompanied by Cavil to Tbilisi in Georgia, where there was a conference on industrial developments in the Bakuoil region. He thought it was probable that some of our targets would be there to make contacts and do deals; maybe Nicolas Egliston himself would appear.

Anna insisted on coming along although Cavil argued against it on the grounds that too many watchers would increase the chance of us being spotted. Tbilisi itself could be dangerous for visitors bearing in mind the guerrilla activities in the country and the malign influence of Russia.

Colliston over-ruled him, but declared nevertheless that Cavil would be in charge. We flew by Aeroflot in one of their older planes and installed ourselves in the Vere Hotel the day before the conference started.

"The next few days could be interesting," said Cavil after we had gathered in the hotel bar before eating on the first evening. "Oilmen are interested in Georgia because of its own oil reserves but mainly because of the Baku –Tbilisi – Ceyan pipeline that will be used to ship large quantities, probably a million barrels a day, of Caspian Oil to the Mediterranean sea. The Abkhazian region is in the throes of civil unrest and separatists will try and use the oil as a lever to hit at the central government.

Cavil speculated that's where Sandline operatives might come in, either to help the Georgian government or the separatists if they pay more.

"I'm sure that we won't see much in the conference itself but in the side meetings, hospitality sessions and the hotels. I shall be wandering round mainly digging for signs of Sandline. You two and Hank should cover the hotels and maybe the seminar itself." Hank was the Canadian field engineer sent in by Bakuoil to manage the main offshore operation.

George gave Anna a list of the conference hotels and which of the attendees would be staying where.

"We will meet at ten each evening here to compare notes," he concluded.

Hank, as a director of Bakuoil, actually wanted to meet several people from the Georgian government and local people and was happy to leave the wandering about to us as well as the boring part of watching certain buildings where companies associated with the industry had offices.

On the second day I struck gold. I was watching the offices of a pipeline company from a car we had hired when none other than Nicolas Egliston got out of a Mercedes and quickly went in. He emerged an hour later, got in the car and drove away but not before I'd taken a photo of him and three others with him.

I decided to follow in my hire car, which wasn't easy in the narrow streets of the old town and I thought I'd lost him once or twice. Once in the suburbs it was easier to see the large car at a distance and I had no fear that they would notice my somewhat decrepit car. Eventually they turned into a villa with steel gates and a guard who opened them up as soon as the car approached. I drove past along the road, which wound around the hill behind the villa to a point where I could see down at the building behind the high walls. There was a helicopter pad in the extensive grounds. With the binoculars it would be possible to see identify anyone who walked outside the main building but as nothing seemed to be happening I decided to report back to Cavil and drove back to our hotel.

There was no sign of Anna; she was presumably still staking out various offices in the city. Cavil soon arrived, marching in with his military air.

"Finished early, Harry?" he said with a half sarcastic air, "I'd have thought that this would be the most promising time of day to see people now the sessions are ending at the conference."

I ignored his snide remarks.

"We've struck gold," I replied. "Egliston junior is in town."

Cavil span round and for once he gave me his full attention. "You're sure?" he snapped. "We've got to be 100%."

I went through what I'd seen, the office building they had visited, his three companions and the villa outside Tbilisi and the vantage point I had found.

"Right, I want to see this place. I'm going to collect my camera and some binoculars and you can drive me out there straight away. There's no need to leave a note for the others, I've a mobile and I'll contact them when we I've decided what to do. Stay there," he snapped rushing up to his room.

I took the chip from my camera and left it with the desk for prints to be made. I also left a note for Ann. Cavil would contact her through the hotel later on. I gulped down a beer just before Cavil returned to the lobby.

"Come on, let's go" he said striding out to the car.

It took quite a time to get out to the villa in the heavy undisciplined traffic but eventually we arrived at the vantage point about two hundred metres above the villa. Threading our way to the edge of the rocky outcrop we could clearly see below us a group in the garden of the villa with drinks. Egliston junior was there, clearly recognisable, with his group that I had seen earlier.

"Well there they are, what do you want to do now?" I said still looking through my binoculars.

"We are going to pay them a visit," came the reply. I turned round to see Cavil standing three metres away with a gun pointing at my chest. "You weren't supposed to see Egliston," he said, glaring at me venomously. "He was a fool to go into Tbilisi when he knew you were there. You weren't supposed to be watching that building anyway.

"What the Hell is going on?" I shouted.

"Shut up or I might be tempted to kill you here and now," spat Cavil taking out his mobile phone, stamping in a number and saying, "We are up here above the villa. Aldborough is with me. Come and collect him."

Ten minutes later I was inside the villa, locked in a small windowless room. Cavil had gone, returning to the city. I seemed to be making a habit of being locked in small rooms!

****

Hank and Anna had installed themselves in the bar at the hotel when Cavil marched in, ordering a whisky for himself. He seemed to have lost some of his usual confident air and growled, "I've had a disappointing day. None of the Sandline people appear to be in town and nobody seems to have seen them either. I propose to return to Baku as soon as I can get a flight, there are other, more profitable things I can be doing than this. I'll square it with Colliston when I get to my room. You two and Aldborough can stay as long as you like. Where is Aldborough by the way?"

Anna had been about to tell Cavil about the message left by Harry earlier in the day about prints, but her intuition told her to keep quiet and she simply said that their paths hadn't crossed and she assumed he would be back shortly. Finishing off the double whisky, he went.

"That seemed very odd to me," said Anna turning to Hank. "Only this morning he was pushing us to cover more ground. Anyway, I would have expected Harry to be back now. I'm going to see if those prints are ready. It might throw some light on where he's gone."

She returned an hour later with the prints and spread them out on the bar for them both to see. "My God, that's Nicolas Egliston!" she gasped. "He must be following them. I'm going to get Cavil back here."

"I wouldn't do that if I were you," a familiar voice said from behind them. Turning round they saw a slightly dishevelled Colliston.

"Colliston, what the devil are you doing here," Hank said, standing up.

"Where's Cavil? I want an urgent word with you and Harry before he appears," snapped Colliston. "Is Harry here?"

"Come up to my room, we can talk there. Cavil just left us saying he wanted to phone you. He's intending to leave here because he thinks it's a waste of time. Harry is in trouble, we were expecting him some time ago," Hank said.

"Cavil would say that" said Colliston with irony. "I hope I'm not too late."

When they were gathered in Hank's room Colliston dropped the bombshell.

"Cavil is probably in the pay of Egliston. Rushton contacted me this morning. Somehow they found out that he has been at meetings with the Egliston duo a year or so ago. I've known him for only about a year and he seemed to be very good. The people in the MoD in London also thought so and recommended him to us. It isn't surprising that we've not found any of the big fish in Sandline or other Egliston ventures out here with Cavil tipping them off!"

"Harry could be in deep trouble," said Anna. "Look at these photos he left for me. There's Egliston junior and a group of others. It must have been taken earlier today. There's a photo of a villa, presumably in the hills around the city."

"I think we've got to assume that Cavil is leaving town because he knows that Harry has seen Egliston. I also assume Egliston has snatched Harry before he can tell anyone. Unless we can find him quickly I don't rate his chance of surviving much longer," Colliston said doubtfully. "I'm going to confront the bastard. Show me his room."

Anna led the way but when they arrived, the door was ajar. Colliston had his pistol out and kicked it open, ready to fire if necessary. Cavil had gone. They raced downstairs to a surprised concierge who told them Cavil had checked out and had taken a cab to the airport.

"I've no power to arrest him or to get the Georgian police to stop him at the airport if that's where he's going. Hank, will you go there and if you see him watch which flight he's going on. If its Baku, ring my office and tell them to make arrangements for the Azeris to arrest him on arrival," said Colliston. "Anna, you come with me."

They to a taxi to the British consulate while Colliston phoned ahead to his colleague there. While on the way he looked again at the photos. "With a bit of luck my colleague Alan Whitcombe might know where this place is. My bet is that it's where Egliston is right now".

Whitcombe, a cynical old hand, did know.

"That's where one of the nouveau riche Georgian businessmen lives. That means he's probably one of the Mafia and the place will be like a fortress. You'll find it almost impossible to get in there. The local police won't help because he's a powerful guy and though I could go to someone in government that could take a long time. I will try, but I can't promise anything."

****

This was the second time one of the Egliston family members had kidnapped me and locked me up in a windowless room and it occurred to me that I might not be so lucky in getting away this time. I assumed that he and Cavil were betting that nobody knew where I had disappeared. In that case, all Nicolas had to do was to keep out of sight until the furore had subsided and make sure I was never seen again.

Thank God I'd taken those photos. It would hopefully only be a question of time before Anna and Hank found this place, but by then I might have been made part of a motorway or something equally permanent. My thoughts were then interrupted by the sound of a key in the lock and the door being flung open. There was Nicolas with a thickset thug alongside, one of his companions I'd seen early in the day.

"You are a nuisance, Aldborough," spat Nicolas. "What a pity for you that you went to Cavil first or we would have had to get rid of your friends as well. You weren't supposed to be in that part of town, according to Cavil's plan. Anyway, all's well that ends well. My colleagues can make sure you are the victim of a hit and run auto accident. As you know, the driving round here is appalling," he smiled with a sardonic smile.

"Too bad, my colleagues know where I am. I managed to phone Anna while I was waiting for Cavil," I tried to sound convincing.

Nicolas laughed. "Pull the other one, Aldborough. You told Cavil you hadn't had time to tell anyone. Anyway she didn't have a mobile phone with her according to Cavil. I shall get great pleasure from killing you. You were the one whom I blame for my father's death. He recruited you against my advice."

Turning to his men he snapped:

"Get him out of there and handcuff him. When I know Aldborough's become a road statistic I'll be going back to Baku. Tell the pilot I wish to start in two hours' time"

As I walked past him he lashed out with his fist hitting me full in the face, knocking me to the ground. I dimly and painfully remember being kicked repeatedly in the back and the groin before I passed out.

****

Anna and Colliston, together with a security guard from the consulate, had decided to drive out to the villa to try and bluff their way into Egliston's hideout as a long shot and delaying tactic while Whitcomb went off to try and get some help from his contacts in government security.

Night was beginning to fall as they approached the villa along the winding road and passed the house where they had seen Egliston junior.

"We will try at the main gate. I'll use my diplomatic status to try and get in on the pretext that I heard that Harry intended to visit there, and had disappeared. It might be enough to keep Harry alive for the time being," said Colliston.

As they drove down the hill to the villa the front gates opened and a Land Rover swept out followed by a Mercedes.

"There's Harry in the Land Rover!" shouted Anna.

Colliston allowed the distance from the two cars to increase to avoid suspicion and trailed them as they headed in the darkness towards town. As they got into the urban area they were able to get closer, mingling in with other traffic. The Land Rover was going down a feeder road to a large hotel when it suddenly stopped in the middle of the road and a body was pushed out. Colliston had stopped at the entrance to the road.

The Land Rover sped away and the Mercedes drove about a hundred yards towards the hotel before doing a U –turn and driving towards Harry, who was presumably the person in the road. At that moment Harry started to get up, stopping as he saw the headlights racing towards him.

Colliston had by now realised what was happening and accelerated directly towards the car with Harry in between. The Mercedes swerved away at the last moment, Harry fortunately rolled in the opposite direction and Colliston braked violently stopping a few inches away from the now prostrate Harry. Anna let off three shots towards the Mercedes, which sped away.

Within a minute they had Harry in the car, had done a U-turn in the road and were driving into the town before the people coming from the hotel, having heard the shooting, were able to see them.

"I'm going to the Consulate!" shouted Colliston. "It's the safest place until we can sort out what to do."

Harry was unconscious by now but it seemed to Anna, who was nursing him in the rear of the car, that he was otherwise not seriously harmed. When they lifted him out and got him inside he was beginning to come round and bruises on his face were starting to make him quite colourful.

Chapter 41. Endgame

Nicolas watched the Land Rover and Mercedes shoot out of the entrance to the villa into the fading light, smiled to himself, and then strode back inside where Joseph, the owner of the villa and head of the local mafia was helping himself to a drink at the bar.

"I don't like this sort of mistake," he said, "Your man was supposed to keep these British snoopers away. I've got too much money involved in this pipeline deal to risk any problems with the government. So far they are happy to keep out of my business affairs as long as they don't get political pressure from the Russians or the foreign oil companies."

"Don't worry, my men will make sure it looks as though Aldborough was killed in a traffic accident. If we had just killed him and lost him in the mountains the police might have started asking questions. Cavil will make quite sure the trail is stopped," replied Nicolas. "My people will be leaving Tbilisi today anyway. We've set up the military security in Abkhazia and I need to get back to Baku to get the nuclear materials moving again. Now I want to make sure our financial arrangements are in order."

The Mafioso's money-man, who reminded Nicolas of a gnome, was called in and the two settled down to business. The meeting was interrupted by Nicolas's mobile ringing. Joseph scowled at him. Nicolas ignored him.

"This had better be important," he snapped to his caller. After listening intently for a minute he said, "Listen carefully, I don't want you back here. Get that car lost in the mountains and then go to ground. You're a crowd of incompetent fools. I'll see you back in Baku."

"Aldborough's been rescued and Cavil has taken a flight back to Baku. I'm going now. I'm afraid you're going to get your friends in the police to hush this up," With that he ran out, shouting for the helicopter to be got ready.

Within fifteen minutes he was away.

****

I seemed to have been hit by a train judging by the way that my body was reacting. I vaguely remember seeing Nicolas's fist coming towards me at some time in the past but after that there was nothing except for a brief period when I came round to see car headlights racing towards me. I remember rolling over automatically but then everything went black again.

"Wake up, Harry!" a voice called out from the shooting lights in front of my eyes. Gradually I saw what I took to be an angelic figure, that solidified into the much more earthly (or heavenly, depending how one was feeling) form of Anna. I was in a hospital bed and my body seemed to be complaining bitterly in every part.

"I suppose I should say 'where am I'" I said, "Though it seems obvious."

"You're in a private clinic in Tbilisi," she said. "We wanted to make sure there are no broken bones and that your vital parts are OK. I can assure you that you a still a fully functioning male. Except for a broken kneecap, that is. Unfortunately you are going to be out of action for a month or two. We want to return to Baku and get you attended to in a private clinic. We must in your absence pick up the trail again. Egliston junior has got away and Cavil managed to give us the slip when he flew to Baku. You are staying here overnight to make sure you aren't concussed then if you are OK we will be catching an early morning flight."

Anna stayed at the clinic until I was pronounced fit to travel, spread across three aeroplane seats, and we duly caught the flight late morning. We drove directly to the clinic, where I was deposited. The others went on to the consulate in Baku where Colliston was holding a council of war on what to do next.

Anna brought me up to date two days later after I'd had surgery and was splinted up.

"We have intelligence that Nicolas Egliston has gone to ground in Kazakhstan together with Cavil and the Sandline people. I'm assuming that they have gone to reorganise the smuggling operation now that the Bakuoil route has been stopped. They have also had to abandon the Georgian operations at least for the time being, thanks to our intervention." He grinned. "Welcome to the exciting side of diplomacy Harry, you look decidedly colourful."

During the next two days I was able to check up with Farouk on the oilfield work and make arrangements for the continuation of the EOR applications. Other companies had heard about the success and were anxious to carry out feasibility studies on their fields. I also was anxious to get back to the work but that would have to go on the back burner for a while.

Anna brought me up to date a week later after her visit to Kazakhstan. This was one of the largest republics in the old Soviet Union and had a leading role in nuclear weapons research and testing. Since the break-up of the USSR most of the weapons had been returned to Russia.

The USA was involved in enterprises, such as the Cooperative Threat Reduction Programme, that transforms the various weapons sites to peaceful applications.

The nuclear experts have in many cases gone to Russia and other countries but it is likely that some have been involved in diverting materials to the highest bidder. Anna met leading figures at the Institute of Nuclear Energy whom they hoped might be able to help our investigations. There was some evidence that the fissile material that had been smuggled by Egliston had come from the Ulba nuclear sites and had reached the Caspian Sea through the port of Aqtau.

They found that the trail was dead. There had been no sign of the Egliston operation for two months although it was clear that much of the U235 must have come from weapon material that had been stolen. The quantities were potentially very large – enough for five U235 and five plutonium bombs. The problem now was, although we had found and accounted for the U235 - where had the plutonium gone?

Chapter 42. Return to the Purbecks

With a broken kneecap, a sprained forearm and my head swathed in bandages I was a sorry sight and could not do much for myself. I wanted to get away from the hospital and from Baku; there were too many sad memories.

The hospital facilities weren't bad, in fact they were good since they catered for the expat oilmen. Colliston couldn't find an early scheduled flight back to the UK that could accommodate me easily with my leg projecting out in front of me, and took great pleasure in saying he had fixed a berth for me in a transport plane carrying oilfield equipment to Moscow. From there a BA jumbo would take me in the first class section where I could stretch out my immobilised leg in comfort.

The journey to Moscow was hell, with a very bumpy flight and in freezing temperatures, so that when I was finally rolled up the aisle into the nose of the BA jet in Moscow it was like heaven. The stewardesses fussed over me as someone had passed on the word I was a high-ranking government employee who had been injured in the fight against international terrorism.

An ambulance met the plane on the arrival apron and I was lowered to the ground on the lift normally used for food transfers. Bakuoil had arranged for me to go to a private hospital in Poole for medical checks before I was released into the world again and it was there that Julie appeared the next day.

"Well, well, you didn't come out of that fight very well did you!" she said giving me a peck on the nose which was about all of me that could be touched. "Welcome home. I think you had better come back to Egliston Hall when they've finished with you here and until the world has got ready to see you again. Dad will no doubt keep you company when he isn't playing with your flashback equipment. Your friend Rushton still spends a lot of time there and I suppose he will want to debrief you. I might pop in from time to time as well if you're good."

I didn't know how much she knew about Anna but decided I should make a clean breast of our relationship. The reaction to all that had happened to me was beginning to set in and I wanted to talk to someone about it anyway.

"Julie, I need to talk out what has happened. I know it's selfish but will you listen?" I said.

"Florence Nightingale's my middle name," she said and sat down across the room.

It really helped me sort out my thoughts which had been tumbling about in my head for some days. She said very little, for which I was grateful. When she left, she gave me another touch on the nose.

"I'm not going to talk about our relationship. It can wait," she said as she left. "See you in the Purbecks."

A week later I was discharged from hospital but not until Rushton had been in to trawl over what had happened.

"I shall need your help to wrap up this episode, then I'll be with you and Charles to sort out some more of Egliston's history with that equipment of yours," he promised.

I was glad to arrive at the Hall because I was keen to get to the equipment myself and to start planning for the next stage of my career. I'd seen enough of the oil work and was hoping to sell out of my EOR developments. Further research into the flashback idea would pay handsome dividends. I was also anxious to see whether there was any future with Julie or whether I should make a complete break

Charles and Julie were there to meet the limo. He pushed me in on the wheel chair and installed me in a self-contained apartment within the Hall with an outlook across the lake in front of the house. The place still had security guards at the gates but there was a more relaxed atmosphere within than there had been when I had left. I felt at home and was able to relax.

Chapter 43.   Last Gasp

It was like the anticlimax after Christmas when all the visitors have gone home, the excitement has faded away and the humdrum jobs have to be sorted out.

For me there was also the unwelcome prospect of having to do some work again. Rushton's men had finally left, having gone through everything with a fine-toothed comb and got as much evidence as possible on Nicolas and on the Egliston activities, legal and illegal. Egliston's son Nicolas had disappeared off the radar so to speak and was probably operating somewhere in the Caucasus.

I didn't see much of Julie. Much of her time was spent with meetings in the City sorting out the legal and financial complexities of her father's interests. When she was at the Hall we did not spend much time together. She was clearly giving both of us time to acclimatise to the new situation.

I really began to like the place. It wasn't large by the standards of the landed aristocracy and most of it was on one level, a great advantage for me on temporary arm crutch. Egliston had clearly spent a lot of money over the years renovating everything in sight as well as installing every modern convenience and electronic gadget. Despite being a cultural philistine he had retained the atmosphere of the last century and the paintings displayed around the house enhanced the atmosphere and were obviously worth a mint.

Outside, the garden and lake were in first class condition and several estate workers from the village had been hired to keep it that way. I enjoyed browsing around the grounds. Charles had settled in as Lord of the Manor and was busy going through all the books and objects around the place he had known as a child. For a period of recuperation it was just what I wanted: I needed to plan the rest of my life.

I had decided that I would, at the right price, sell the rights to my EROS invention and I was making some tentative enquiries with oil and service companies with that in mind. The prospects seemed bright and I would be certainly be able to retire if I wanted to but the trouble was I didn't want to.

I'd decided that I would concentrate on developing the flashback technology in the short term and look out for something interesting to turn up. The fly in the ointment was Rushton and his government mates who still couldn't decide whether to keep the flashback under wraps or not. The equipment was still there under lock and key at the Hall.

After a month of this inaction I was walking again and exploring the Purbecks, looking at the churches, prehistoric sites and tasting the delights of the pubs. This blissful existence had to come to an end, and one night it did. I was woken up in the early hours by being thrown on to the floor of my bedroom.

A bright torch dazzled me and I was finally horrified to see Nicolas himself with a couple of black-clad companions standing over me. I was frogmarched into the main sitting room and tied to a chair and gagged. Five minutes later Julie and Charles were brought in and similarly dealt with. At least they had been allowed to put dressing gowns on. All this time nobody had spoken.

"What a pretty sight!" Nicolas snarled. "You perhaps thought you had seen the last of me. Think again. You will stay alive for the time being: later I might think of doing a better job of eliminating you than those fools in Georgia did. I had intended to say good riddance to the UK but there are three things I want. First, I've still got a legal claim to the Egliston assets, or so my lawyers tell me. You three are obstacles to that claim. Secondly, it appears that your government friends didn't find the plutonium cache that is here. All you took was the weapons grade U235. You seem surprised, but I assure it is still there."

He paused, savouring the moment.

"Finally my father told me about your flashback technology. I shall have it, and you Aldborough, will tell me all about it now that that fool Reise was inconsiderate enough to die."

He turned to his men and gave them orders to search through Charles's office.

"I have a little problem with the plutonium though, and you Aldborough will help me. My expert has been delayed and I have to keep moving. You know enough about handling nuclear materials with working at that Winfrith site. We shall be here for as long as it takes. You," he said turning to Julie and Charles, "will be supervised and you will turn away any callers and field any telephone calls. Any problems and you will all die. Aldborough, if you don't collaborate, you will all die."

We were left there trussed up. An hour later he returned.

"We are ready. You, Aldborough will come with me. You two will get dressed and be ready later," he snapped.

I was thrown a pair of white overalls and led to the fissile store that still appeared empty, as it did after Rushton's men had finished. They walked over to a large steel cupboard that was screwed to the wall and pulled it aside revealing a close-fitting steel door with a biometric pad at the side. Nicolas put his fingertips on the pad and with a rumbling sound the door swung open. There was the noise of a fan starting up and I was pushed inside. There were about thirty safes of the sort I had seen at Winfrith on well-spaced racks.

Nicolas turned to me. "I'm told that there is at least ten kilos of plutonium in here. That, as you know, will make a few bombs. It will also make a blue flash and we shall all be dead if it isn't handled properly. I have these flasks. It is up to you to make sure it is properly loaded."

"I don't have any experience in this, "I protested, "All I've seen are racks like these."

"We'll have to do our best; I can't wait for my man to get here. Get started!" he shouted.

All I knew was that about half a kilo of plutonium is enough, if mixed with water, to go critical if it is not well spaced from other plutonium or water. I also knew that it was usual to incorporate discs of boron to absorb neutrons. I could only find about thirty of these. Nicolas refused point blank to listen and insisted that we loaded a kilo consisting of thirty discs clad in steel in each of his flasks. I made sure they were separated but I knew that if they were flooded with water there could well be a violent explosion, a blue flash and a slow death for those unlucky enough to be nearby. Eventually they were loaded into a truck that had arrived whilst we were working.

"For God's sake tell those clowns that they will kill themselves and half of Poole if that lot gets near water," I shouted.

"You hear that," Nicolas shouted to the driver. "Take it to the Norden Manor where we will meet you. You will go when I give the word. If however you don't hear from me before 20.00 hours, leave for the ship. It is vital we rendezvous with it."

"Now you can show me the flashback kit," he said turning to me.

I told him that it was under lock and key but he insisted on being shown where it was.

"Who needs keys? "He grinned and shot the lock off the cellar door. I hadn't set eyes on the equipment for a few weeks but I knew it was effectively ready for use. I would have to stall for time.

"Right, show me how it works and any documents," he demanded.

"Can't do," I protested, "The control unit is at Norden manor. Rushton holds another one."

It had occurred to me that the panic button Rushton had installed at the manor while Egliston was on the run might still be active. There was also there a tracker device that had been provided in case we were abducted or had to leave without warning. With a bit of luck I might be able to get this if Nicolas could be persuaded to go to the Manor.

"You know that if this is a trick then your two friends will be killed. They don't really serve any purpose apart from keeping your heart and soul on this job," he said menacingly.

I had no choice. I guess that we were doomed anyway if I did nothing and nodded.

His men lifted all the kit from the cellar and I reluctantly handed over the operating manuals Hans had prepared.

A helicopter had arrived while we were in the Hall, and the flashback equipment, Julie and I were put on board with Nicolas keeping us company. In the fading light we took off. Charles was tied up and left alone in the study. Gladys would find him the next morning. Nicolas clearly knew the area and directed the chopper.

We flew in towards the setting sun and over the craggy ruins of Corfe Castle and down to the lawn of the Manor. While Julie was supervised in the chopper Nicolas escorted me indoors. I knew a control unit was in the study as were the panic button and the tracker. All I had to do was to distract Nicolas while I operated it and pocketed the tracker. I'd told Julie to start screaming two minutes after we went into the Manor.

On cue she did well and Nicolas rushed out, leaving me momentarily alone. I pressed the alert and found the tracker device but only had time to lodge it inside the control unit. When he came back in I was carrying the unit.

"I've had enough of you two. I'm taking you back to the Hall; someone might come snooping. Get in the helicopter."

He handed the unit to the men in the lorry and told them to get moving. He said he would join the ship in the Channel as he had business to attend to.

It was clear to me that he was intending to kill us together with Charles and perhaps burn the Hall. The helicopter took off and in the darkness headed towards the Hall over the ruins of Corfe Castle.

I felt it was our last chance and threw myself at Nicolas, who was looking at the Castle while covering us with his Uzi. The gun went off, grazing my head but the pilot obviously was hit and the helicopter blade hit the top of the ruin.

The whole world seemed to spin and with a jarring crunch the machine jammed itself between the remaining walls of the castle some fifty feet above ground. Nicolas had been thrown out of the door that had opened in the crash and was trying to grip the side of the machine but I kicked his hand and he fell to the stony ground below.

Julie had fortunately been strapped in and was upside down in her seat. I dreaded fire breaking out but there was no sign of that and every thing went quiet apart from Julie's sobs. The pilot appeared to be dead, shot by the stray bullets from Nicolas's gun.

It would have been highly dangerous to release Julie because of our precarious position and danger of the whole wreck falling down and there we stayed for twenty minutes. Then people started to appear and within minutes came the sound of an ambulance siren. The paramedics could not reach us but confirmed that Nicolas was dead. We had to wait a further half hour before the fire-engine arrived with equipment to lower us to the ground. It was a miracle that Julie and I had survived apart from minor injuries.

I wanted to get in touch with Rushton's men as soon as possible and had managed to get one of the paramedics to contact the SBS and the leader of the team that had led the attack on the Hall in particular. They came out in double quick time. As we sped towards Poole the call came through that the tracker signal had been picked up coming from a speed boat that had just left Poole harbour.

I warned them about the lethal cargo they had aboard. Rushton, who had by then been told of the events, decided that the boat would have to be intercepted in UK waters, if necessary by lethal means. Once they got out to an Iranian ship that was seen waiting in the English Channel it would be difficult to intervene. A helicopter was ready for us as we got to the SAS unit and we leapt in. Rushton had let it be known that I should be there in case any nuclear expertise was needed.

"You're the best we have at the moment," he replied to my objection that everyone thought wrongly I was an expert..

By this time the boat was well out into Poole Bay and was approaching Old Harry rocks. These were imposing limestone pinnacles at the south of the Purbeck peninsula, about a hundred metres high, and were habitually given a wide berth by shipping.

Our helicopter positioned itself over the boat and caught it in a powerful beam of light. By loudspeaker it was ordered to heave to. This was ignored.

"For God's sake don't sink it or you might trigger a nuclear incident!" I shouted. The SAS man sitting in the door of the helicopter had a sniper rifle and as the helicopter was steadied targeted the helmsman despite a passenger in the boat firing up at us. Our man was successful in bringing him down and the boat spun round out of control. The second man moved to the helm but he was brought down as well. The boat was then unmanned and started heading directly at the Old Harry pinnacle itself.

"We must get someone on board!" I shouted. The helicopter was fitted with a winch and as we followed the boat as it was heading for the rocks one of the men started a descent.

As he jumped aboard the speeding boat it bucked, throwing him overboard. Then with a sickening crash it ran up on the rocks surrounding Old Harry. The SAS captain looked at me, "You and I are going down there. You tell me about the nuclear part and I'll try and get a line aboard to stop it sinking."

It was the worst moment of my life. We hovered above the pinnacle while the two of us were lowered swinging like a gigantic pendulum. After several attempts, during which we crashed against the limestone several times, we managed to get aboard. The boat appeared to be firmly fixed on the rock and I went below to inspect the nuclear packages.

To my horror, water was coming in through a hole in the stern and filling up the front of the boat. It would only be ten minutes before the nuclear capsules were under water. Feverishly we took the cable on which we had been lowered and made it fast round the boat's propeller and stern.

While I was marooned on the edge of the pinnacle the helicopter lifted and towed the boat with the SAS guy holding it as level as he could to the shingle beach a hundred metres away, well above the sea level. The helicopter pilot decided it was safer not to try and winch us back aboard and just hovered to monitor events.

That was it.

We were rescued wet and frozen stiff by the Poole lifeboat while a team of nuclear experts from Winfrith made the plutonium secure before taking it away under armed guard to the Atomic Weapons Establishment eighty miles away.

Chapter 44. Home in the Purbecks

Hopefully there would not be any more unpleasant surprises. The pseudo Eglistons were dead and gone. The weapons-grade uranium and plutonium were gone. Hans Reise was gone. The question for me was whether there was anything left for me in Dorset.

There was a lot of clearing up to do on behalf of Julie and Charles but the two business strings to my bow, the EOR technology and the flashback, didn't have to stay in Dorset. Our recent adventure with Nicolas had drawn Julie back into her shell, bringing back memories of her time locked in the dark and suffocating atmosphere of the underground art gallery.

We had taken again to walking in the Purbecks perhaps for an hour at a time without speaking, each immersed in our own thoughts. Gradually she came back to her old self and we were able to talk through all that had happened in the past year. There was still a mental distance between us and neither of us seemed to want to do anything about it. She had seen sides of me that she had not expected and wanted to work out for herself whether I would fit in to her future.

It wasn't helped by her personal uncertainties. Had she taken the right decision to give up her highflying career in the City? Did she want to live in the backwaters of Dorset for the rest of her life? In the meantime we were both happy just to go from day to day helping Charles sort out his new life as Lord Egliston, landowner and potential industrialist.

It was interesting going up to London to see Charles dressed in ermine and red robes being inducted into the

House of Lords, although it seemed unlikely that he would in the future take an active part in proceedings.

What it did do was to give him contacts in the government and the City. He certainly needed those contacts. The pseudo Egliston, Taylor, as I now called him, had been extremely wealthy. That personal wealth approached a hundred million pounds in property and business and this, being in the name of Lord Egliston, came directly to Charles complete with tax liabilities. Hopefully that would be sorted out by the swarms of lawyers and tax experts and still leave Charles a wealthy man.

Nicolas's fortune, or those parts of it that could be found, went to the government; he had died intestate and without heirs. The Egliston conglomerate of companies was still running either under existing boards and those companies such as Bakuoil that had been engaged in smuggling were being run under a government-appointed trustee.

Charles had no desire to become a captain of industry at his time of life and effectively stood aside. He was able to recruit some very able directors to his holding company to run things in the short term.

What he really wanted to do was to sell off as much as he could and to set up a charitable foundation, leaving enough to run his estate comfortably. He also wanted to throw himself into his hobbies of historical Dorset and, you've guessed, flashback.

Julie found her feet in the idea of a charitable foundation. She had decided that the cutthroat life of the City was not for her. The prospect of running the trust and making an impact on poverty inspired her and we began to see a highly motivated young woman who really now knew what she wanted out of life.

Bakuoil was one of the first companies to be sold. BP had strong interests in the Caspian and wanted to increase its asset base. I had seen all I wanted to see of the region - except perhaps Anna - and was happy to see it go. Summerfield was taken over by the giant Schlumberger service company who set up a division to exploit my EOR invention.

I became a millionaire and had a consultancy retainer that let me travel round the world. I made a point of visiting Baku, but only when Anna was there.

****

My 'Torch'/flashback project was still in limbo. Rushton's civil service friends had slapped a top secret classification on the discovery while committees in the deep recesses of Whitehall still pondered over how to deal with it. I wanted to get a patent on my time 'Torch' design; clearly it wouldn't be possible to patent the scientific discovery itself. It would only be a question of time before other people would discover the principle as astronomers were actively trying to detect gravity waves. I buttonholed Charles on what to do. With his new contacts in the House of Lords he might be able to press the right administrative buttons.

I broached the subject after one of those marvellous Purbeck lamb meals his housekeeper Gladys was famous for.

"Charles, I know you want to get the 'Torch' going again so that you can explore the history of the area. I think you hold the answer in your hands. As a member of the House of Lords you can speak in the House without fear of litigation. I'm sure you could threaten to raise the issue. I know you wouldn't do it if it came to the crunch, but would the authorities call your bluff? Can I persuade you to bring it up with Lord Bolsover, the Minister for Defence?"

"Harry, much as I'd like to help, that's going too far. I'm happy to ask a few private questions but you would get me locked up," he said sadly.

Julie came in at that stage.

"Harry's right, Dad, we can't let it drift. Just think what you'd feel like if the Americans or worse, the French got on to this first." Charles was something of a Francophobe and she knew it would push him towards our point of view.

"I won't promise more than I have, but I'll do my best. Anyway, exactly what do you want me to do, Harry," he said in a more conciliatory tone.

Encouraged, I went on:

"I want them first to allow me to patent the 'Torch'. Then they must make the whole thing public. I would like to put it on the internet. They will need to lean on the Patent Office to couch the thing in general terms first or we will get in a Catch-22 situation where they won't issue a patent without full details and I won't release details without an assurance of a watertight patent. We will need to consult with the Royal Society so that I have help with the scientific development of the concept."

He was as good as his word. Out of the blue came a phone call from Rushton.

"You've got friends in high places" was his opening. "I've been told to allow you to use the flashback 'Torch' at the Hall for the time being, while we get Qinetiq, our military R and D set-up, to work out with you how we go ahead. For the time being - no publicity. We will ask the

Patent Office to get in touch. They are aware of the background."

* * *

Charles and I spared no time getting the equipment working again. I'd been having a few ideas. The principle of the time 'Torch' was that gravity waves of a sharp frequency would mix the time quantum states of the present and a point in time and the radiation fields associated with nearby masses would merge, producing a flash-back image of that past time.

What worried me was that there was no reason why at the past time an image of the future could not be seen. If that was the case there should be reports of such sightings. I discussed it with Charles.

"I'm getting myself into a muddle." I confessed. "If there is a possibility that someone we are viewing in the past might be able to see us – as is possible in principle - then why have we not seen images from people in the future? But, that is not possible because of the paradox: I might see someone in the future, but would be able hypothetically to kill that person now and make sure he didn't appear in the future."

"There is a possibility," said Charles. "One theory that has been put forward, as Hans Reise would have pointed out, is that there is an infinity of futures. As you say it is clearly impossible to see the future if there is only one. If there is an infinity of futures there is no reason why you can't see ahead into one future.

"We should be able to see a future time as well as a past time when we use the 'Torch'," I said "Why don't we?"

"An idea, Harry" said Charles. "Your 'Torch' will produce a polarised beam of gravity waves because of its design, using vertical elements rather than horizontal – gravity waves may be just like ordinary light where we use Polaroid spectacles to cut out glare. My guess is that if you use horizontal polarisation you might get a shot into a future – one of many futures, but one that is the nearest extrapolation from the present."

This was an exciting idea, and one that I could test with a minimum of difficulty. It was simply a case of making mounting brackets so I could turn the whole thing round by a right angle. It was now that I would have valued Hans Reise's advice.

The next day Charles and I started the conversion and by the evening were ready to test. There was absolutely nothing there. We searched for a long time and then suddenly an image appeared on settings that we estimated would give us a twenty-year flash back in time under normal operation.

If Charles's guess were right we would instead be looking about twenty years into a future time. We would presumably know the time, roughly, if either Julie or I appeared, twenty years older. Charles remarked that he personally would be dead and gone by then.

The images of the future we saw were clearly set in the room we were in but the décor was completely different – minimalist office style and the window had been increased in size. Who would appear? When it did, it was a shock. It was me, clearly aged about fifty but I was with a woman who was vaguely familiar. They were using a 'Torch'.

"Who's that, Harry?" came Julie's voice from behind me.

"I don't know," I replied with an uneasy feeling, "perhaps she is a secretary or business acquaintance." The two of us in the flash image had clearly been talking business over a pile of paperwork. Julie knew we were trying to delve into a future that was an extrapolation from today.

"I could be there couldn't I, Harry if you are there doing business?" Julie remarked.

It was at that stage that there was a crackling noise from the 'Torch' and the image disappeared.

"When you get it going again I want to see more," she demanded and walked away.

It was then I realised who the woman was – twenty years later there was Anna in England, obviously part of my life.

"There you have it, Harry," said Charles with a grimace. "You can only see the future when the people in the future are looking at you with a time 'Torch'. Even then that is only one of many alternative futures."

"You had better find one in which Julie is part of the future you want."

When I got the 'Torch' working again Anna and I were reappeared, and she gave me- in the future- a kiss, turned round, and looked straight at me – in the present - across the gap of twenty years. I could also see a coat of arms on the wall. It was that of Egliston.

One of my futures would be one that brought me back into the world I seemed to have escaped from, where at the very least I was double-timing Julie and at most involved with the old Egliston empire.

If Charles were right, as I guess he was, there was infinity of futures. Right then I decided that I wanted a future with Julie.

When the Caspian area or Anna or anything else from the dangerous past started to make inroads on my life, I would make sure that I cut it short.

Time will tell, because there's no hiding...from yesterday.

THE END

About the Author:

Wilfrid N Fox was born
in north Derbyshire in
1934, and after earning
his DPhil at St Edmund
Hall, Oxford, worked at
UKAEA Winfrith on the
Steam Generating Heavy
Water Reactor. Later he
worked on Enhanced Oil Recovery at Winfrith
Technology and latterly as a consultant in the oil
industry, travelling widely in the Caspian region.

Wilfrid has lived in Poole, Dorset with his wife
Janet since 1961, where they have brought up
their three children, Nicola, Caroline and Tony.
He has studied at first hand the landscape and
history of the Purbecks and surrounding areas.

This, his first novel, brings together all his
professional ideas and personal enthusiasms in
one original and gripping tale.